A Slave Boy's

Quest for Freedom

in a Time of

Revolution

HANNIBAL
HOOPS

Best Wishes

Gordon M. Haliburton

Gordon M. Haliburton

HANNIBAL HOOPS

A Slave Boy's Quest for Freedom in a Time of Revolution

ISBN-13: 978-1-926676-72-2

Printed in Canada.

Printed by Word Alive Press
131 Cordite Road, Winnipeg, MB R3W 1S1
www.wordalivepress.ca

WORD ALIVE PRESS
Just Write!

For my grandson,
NICHOLAS

table of contents

PART TWO: Hannibal Hoops in Nova Scotia

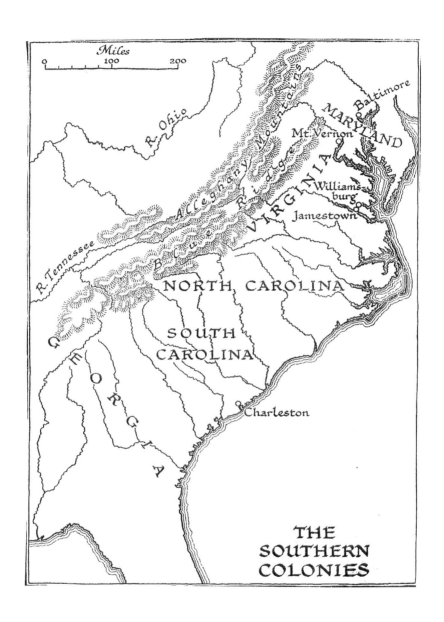

Miles
0   100   200

R. Ohio

R. Tennessee

Allegheny Mountains

Blue Ridge

Baltimore

MARYLAND

Mt. Vernon

VIRGINIA

Williams-
burg

Jamestown

NORTH CAROLINA

SOUTH
CAROLINA

GEORGIA

Charleston

THE
SOUTHERN
COLONIES

WEST AFRICA IN OLDEN TIMES

THE SIERRA LEONE RIVER, FREETOWN, & BANCE ISLAND
(Bance Island was an important headquarters for Slave Traders)

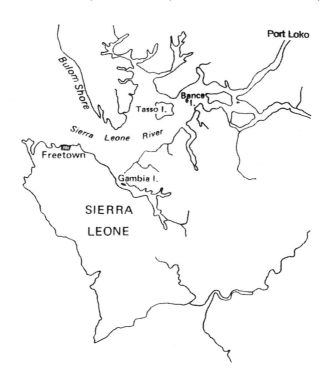

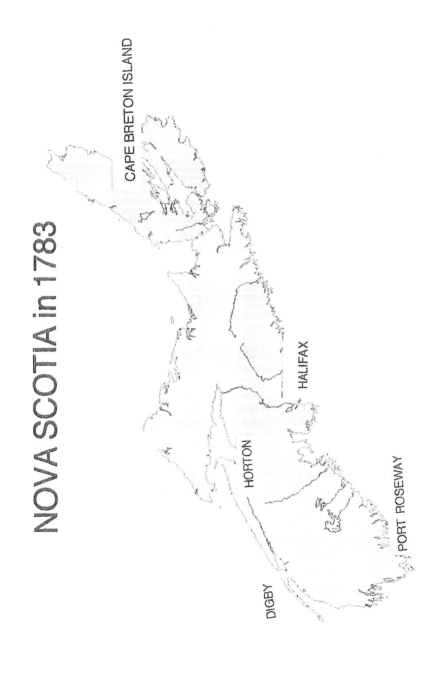

NOVA SCOTIA in 1783

CAPE BRETON ISLAND

HALIFAX

HORTON

DIGBY

PORT ROSEWAY

introduction

Freetown is a city located on the coast of West Africa. It faces the wide estuary of the Sierra Leone River and the ocean. The city was established there more than two centuries ago by African settlers, formerly slaves, who came across the Atlantic Ocean from Nova Scotia.

This is the story of one of these settlers who struggled against great odds to rise from slavery in Carolina to freedom in Africa. It is based on the historical facts of the period from about 1765 to 1792.

PART ONE:

Hannibal Hoops
in the Old South

chapter one
THE BEGINNING

Hannibal Hoops was terrified. He was looking death in the face and had no other thought than to beat it off somehow. A big burly over-mountain man filled with fury and contempt was swinging his musket up by the barrel, and when it swung down, the heavy stock would split his skull and that would be the end of him. The big man intended murder and the boy, barely a teenager, faced a violent end to his brief life. All he had in the way of a weapon was a stout chunk of wood from a dead tree, gathered for firewood; not much of a defence against this hate-filled giant with his heavy gun.

The man's hairy face was so close that his spittle spattered on Hannibal's face as he cursed him through crooked yellow fangs.

"This is the end of you, you black varmint! You'll learn what it is to get in the way of free-born white men who have a job to do! Curse you,

you misbegotten animal! You're finished, you and your fine Tory friend on the ground there!"

Why did he hate this brown-skinned stripling? He hated him because he was brown-skinned, because he was an African, and clearly a slave. He hated him because he was trying to defend the young white man with him, who he was determined to kill. Maybe he hated the boy because he, even as a powerless chattel, was part of the ruling society of wealth and privilege he wanted to overturn. It was a time of political turmoil in South Carolina and rival groups of men fought each other without mercy. Hannibal and his "master" had been unlucky in their chance meeting with this man.

A moment before Hannibal had sprung out of the trees to save his master, Clifford Courtney, who had fallen unconscious on the ground a few paces from the terrible over-mountain man—a man from the frontier region away to the west. From the side of Clifford's head, blood was oozing where this man's bullet had grazed his skull. He had been surprised and helpless when the man levelled his gun to kill him. Hannibal's intervention had saved him from being shot straight through the head, but unless the boy could defend himself from their would-be killer, he and Clifford would probably both be dead anyway in a matter of minutes.

Is this the end of a life scarce begun? he asked himself. *Is it the end of hope? Is it the end of my mother's dreams for me?*

Hannibal had lived for thirteen years before this incident, and was still living four decades later when he wrote an account of it, but in some ways this was a watershed in his life, and before explaining what happened in this crisis, it would be well to tell about the life that came before it.

Hannibal Hoops was born on Ellenboro Plantation, up the Cooper

River in South Carolina, not more than a couple of days' ride from Charles Town, the finest city in the South. The plantation grew rice there, the famous 'Carolina Gold,' and ships came upriver to the plantation dock to carry the harvest to England and beyond to other far places. Though it was not a real port, like Charles Town was, it was vital to the prosperity of the plantation's little world, where the workers loading and unloading its cargo met men from the greater world outside and heard their news. It was a place of great excitement and activity when boats sailed in.

By the time of the incident described above, Hannibal had been to Charles Town, which was very much part of the great world. He had seen the big fortified harbour full of ships. There had been lots of pirate ships, people said, in the old days, but the scariest ships he saw there were the slave ships coming straight from Africa with their sad cargos. They had a special meaning for him, because he knew that his mother had come across the Atlantic from the Sierra Leone River on such a ship a few months before he was born. She had been young and strong, but she was a sad sight when they stood her at the auction block with all the others from the ship. Colonel Courtney of Ellenboro Plantation was there by chance—maybe something about her caught his interest. Anyway, he bid her in and brought her home to be a kitchen maid at Ellenboro. She was treated in kindly fashion by the colonel's wife, who called her "Hester," and being intelligent as well as beautiful she soon learned to speak English and cook meals to the satisfaction of her master and mistress.

Hannibal was born in her small hut near the kitchen on a chilly autumn morning a few months later, and the colonel entered the birth in his ledger, along with other details of business: "Hannibal, boy child, born to Hester ye 27th September, A.D. 1767." Years after, before he left Ellenboro for good, Hannibal was shown the entry by Master Clifford and recorded it in his mind, never to forget it.

The colonel decided on names for new slaves and new slave babies. As it happened, that year he was rereading some of his favourite classics from the later days of the Roman Republic. He found lots of good names from those books—Hannibal, of course, and other boy babies were called Caesar, Scipio, and Juba, while the girl babies included Cleopatra, Julia, and Helena. Of course, all those names got changed in the slave quarters, if they were used at all. The Scipio in the ledger became Skippy in common parlance. The name Hannibal stuck unaltered, but another name was added to it when he was about two. He caught the whooping cough and was coughing in his mother's arms when the colonel happened to come in on his regular weekly inspection of the kitchen. He recognized the child and remembered his name, suddenly deciding that the cough could be the excuse for a good joke.

"Hannibal Hoops!" he shouted, laughing, and, as he shared the joke around, "Hannibal Hoops" the boy became and remained.

Only his mother did not call him by the slave name, no more than she called herself Hester, though she had to answer to it when the white folk spoke to her. Deep down, she was still her African self, Fa'mata, and her son, though all the white and coloured folks called him Hannibal Hoops, knew his real name was Kanday Kontay, like his father before him. But that was a secret known only to his mother and himself.

His first friend was Skippy, who lived in the next cabin and was only a few days younger. They played in the dust around the cabin, an older girl keeping an eye on them. Then, as they grew bigger and able to go further on their own, they invented games in the thickets and swamps along the edges of the fields. The workers' village of two rows of small cabins (most of them made of mud and wattle, like those in Sierra

Leone, and thatched like them, too) lay some distance behind the kitchen of the Big House; it was known as "the Quarters." It was about a ten-minute walk to the kitchen for Hester, and she worked long hours there. When her child was small, she carried him with her, tied to her back in a shawl; even when he was older, she sometimes took him along for a treat, and on such occasions he often had another playmate, Dolph, the white boy who was the youngest of the Courtney children and was just about the same age.

When the three boys were all a little bigger, Dolph would find his way to the quarters and play with the other two. His proper name was Adolphus, and he told the other boys that he was named for a prince, one of King George's sons who lived across the ocean. He told them that his father was a friend of the King, and that one day he would take him on a ship to go and see him in London. Dolph explained that he looked like a prince, too, the same as King George's sons; he was fair-haired, blue-eyed, and chubby, and these were the signs of a prince. Hannibal and Skippy looked at themselves and saw black hair and eyes and dark brown skin. They had not thought about those differences until Dolph pointed them out, telling them that it made him special. He lorded it over the others in their games because these things made him their master.

They didn't let that interfere with their play, but as they got older, the two little slave boys didn't have so much time for play. When they were six years old, they were made to keep an eye on smaller children. By the time they were eight, they were spending their time doing light chores, such as carrying water to the men and women in the fields, or sweeping and tidying the lane and yard around the cabins. Dolph sometimes helped with these chores; it was a game to him, and when he got tired of it he would wander off.

This was Hannibal's life, until one day, without warning, everything changed.

He was hoeing alongside Skippy in a cornfield not far from the Quarters when a little girl came running up and told him his mother wanted him. He put his hoe over his shoulder and ran across to the cabin which was his home.

"Wash up, my son," his mother said. "Put on your good shirt and breeches. The Master wants to see you in the Big House right away."

To his eager and fearful questions she could only answer that she had no idea what was intended, but hoped it would be something good. He washed off his dirt and dust in the little creek and put on clean clothes. Hester led him straightaway up past the kitchen and store-houses and through the back door of the Big House, in which he had never set foot before that day. There the grey-headed butler, chief of the house servants, was waiting for them. He was impressive in his blue tail-coat, with white shirt and breeches, and spoke kindly enough to them.

"You go back to the kitchen now, Hester. I'll look after your boy. Follow me, young Hannibal." He led him through the broad, well-lighted hall from which a beautiful curved stairway rose up as if ascending to Heaven. However, they did not go near it but towards a door midway along. He turned to Hannibal and said, "Stand straight when the Master speaks to you and don't say anything but 'Yes, sir,' no matter what he says. You hear me?"

"Yes, sir," the boy said.

Then he turned and knocked on the door and, without more than a polite pause, led the way into an amazing room. Hannibal's world up to that moment had been the Quarters and the kitchen, and he had never before seen anything like the strange objects surrounding him now. Of course, it was Colonel Courtney's library, and the strange objects were bookcases full of leatherbound books, framed pictures and maps on the walls, shiny armchairs, and a shining desk, and on the desk a set of globes, and writing paper and quill pens beside silver inkwells. Hannibal came to know and recognize all these things later, but on that first introduction he was like a blind man suddenly receiving sight; he just had no idea what he was looking at.

Colonel Courtney, master of the plantation and all who lived on it, sat in a big armchair with his two older sons Clifford and Frederick standing behind him and the youngest, Adolphus, standing at his side. In the shadows behind them were a couple of young servants who Hannibal had seen in the kitchen sometimes. He was frightened and must have been shaking as the butler led him forward and with a firm hand brought him to a stop right in front of the Courtney family, with all eyes focused on him.

He looked timidly toward Dolph, to try reading some message in his face. He could see that Dolph was flushed and excited and apparently happy. He took some comfort from that.

Colonel Courtney examined him closely, as if reading his character from his eyes. He addressed him in a kindly tone. "So, Hannibal Hoops! You've grown up sturdy and strong, I see; the whooping cough didn't do you any permanent harm. You look well fed. Eating well from the kitchen, I'll be bound."

"Yes, sir," Hannibal replied politely, as the butler had ordered.

Colonel Courtney put his hand on Dolph's shoulder and went on. "You know who this is beside me, I think."

He must have been aware that Hannibal knew Dolph very well, even though he had never seen them playing together. Again the reply was only, "Yes, sir."

Dolph, he noticed, was wearing a fine new outfit; it was clear that he was the centre of attention. Hannibal actually wondered for a moment if Dolph was going off to England and if he, Hannibal, had been brought in to say goodbye. But that was not a very good guess.

"Master Adolphus is nine years old today," said the Colonel, "and it is high time that he had a personal attendant to look after him instead of the women. He tells me you are a bright and likely lad, Hannibal Hoops—and he has done you the honour of choosing you to be his personal servant. From now on you belong to him, and will attend to his needs. Jim there, who does for Master Clifford, will show you what you have to do."

"Yes, sir," Hannibal repeated, as the slim young fellow called Jim, about twenty years old by the look of him, detached himself from the spot behind his master of about the same age and came closer.

Colonel Courtenay then looked with a serious face at his son and said, "Adolphus, I am putting a great deal of responsibility in your hands, as I did with your brothers at the same age. Hannibal has his obligations to you, but you also have your responsibilities where he is concerned. You are not to spoil him by indulgence, nor to injure him by abuse. Treat him properly and show that you can carry this responsibility like a man."

"Yes, sir. Thank you, sir," he said to his father and, starting to move, said, "Follow me, Hannibal." Off the two boys went, out of the room, followed by Jim.

Then the slave boy saw even more things never known before. They went up the beautiful staircase and along a hall to Dolph's room, where he showed off his bed and his wardrobe, a large cupboard of fine wood that stood against the wall. He sat on a sofa in front of the open window while Jim opened the doors of the wardrobe and showed off the coats and shirts hanging on one side and drew out the row of drawers on the other, full of handkerchiefs and small articles of wear. He explained that it would be Hannibal's job to know where everything belonged, to bring out the right clothes each day for Dolph to wear, to see that the dirty clothes went into a basket to be taken to the laundress every few days, to make sure that clothes were mended when torn and the buttons made secure (and he would have to learn to do these things), and in general he was to perform every service necessary to make sure Dolph was properly fit to be inspected by his parents every morning at breakfast. Hannibal was relieved when Jim said he would help for the first week or two until he was able to do it properly by himself.

It was all a great adventure for the slave boy, and he liked it, especially as there were no more tedious field chores for him. In the weeks that followed, he was in the Big House and in Dolph's company a great deal more than before, and much more his playmate even if Dolph sometimes gave him orders in an unfriendly way. Now, too, he had to speak to Dolph and his brothers as "Master," with a show of respect. Sometimes there were visitors, including cousins or family friends of their own age. Then Master Dolph might tell him to stay out of sight. On the other hand, Hannibal might be needed to play a part, and would be told to stay close. He also had to stay close behind when Dolph took his horse for a ride; this meant that he had to learn to ride, too, and had a quiet mare assigned him for those occasions.

Being around these white people so much was an education for him. He unconsciously picked up knowledge and ideas he would never have encountered in the Quarters. At mealtimes, he was often set in a corner to pull the big ceiling fan back and forth, thus moving the sultry air over the table, and unnoticed he would listen to the table conversation. At other times, he sat in a corner of the library while Dolph had his lessons, and learned from what he heard as fast as Dolph did. For about five months, Dolph worked at his lessons with a tutor who stayed with the family before moving on to another planter's family on another plantation. After that, his brothers spent an hour or so with him almost every morning, and they were good teachers. Clifford was the best educated of the two; he had spent a couple of years at school in England and seemed to know everything.

By the time the tutor had gone, Hannibal was beginning to learn purposefully through Master Clifford. Clifford was very kind to him, perhaps because he had some thoughts about becoming a clergyman and believed that African people, too, were God's children, even if inferior ones. Anyway, he believed that education was good for everyone, so instead of leaving him alone in the corner he put him at a table with a book and taught him to read and to write while Dolph worked on his preparation. It wasn't easy, but gradually Hannibal could read a bit, write his name and simple sentences, and do simple sums in adding and subtracting numbers. It was not until much later that he realized Clifford might have been taking a big risk in letting him learn these elementary things, for the authorities believed it was dangerous to teach slaves anything but how to work.

Hannibal had some hopes of learning more than that, though it was not clear what use it would be. At least it helped to pass idle hours when he was back at the Quarters with Skippy, when he surprised him by writing names and numbers in the dirt with a sharp stick.

As he understood more, he thought things might not always be as fixed as he had thought. From talk among the white folk as they sat at their meals, he came to know that the times were not as they had been, and that things were happening that had never happened before. There was talk around the table of rebellion and revolution, of governments being overturned and of new men becoming important. There was talk of fighting with the Indians, of the departures of royal governors, and of the campaign being waged by George Washington, who had long ago been with Colonel Courtney fighting the French, somewhere up north. Strangely enough, it was not Frenchmen he was fighting now, but Germans.

It was confusing to him, and to Dolph, too, but it seemed the white folk were worried about many new happenings they had not expected, and there was a lot of coming and going from neighbouring plantations and excited talk.

chapter two

THE HUNT

In the eighteenth century, when Hannibal was a growing boy in South Carolina, the forests fringed the fields where crops grew. Those forests were densely full of birds and animals, and men and boys often went out hunting and brought back wild meat to supplement the pork, poultry, and fish that were the common fare.

Hannibal's journal noted some such forays into the forest, the most memorable of which took place on Dolph's eleventh birthday. Dolph called him just after the family dinner, when Hannibal had taken a few minutes to gobble his dish of mush and fat pork in the kitchen. "Come on, Hannibal," Dolph shouted. "Cliff and Fred are taking us hunting for a treat because it's my birthday."

It had been a lovely hot day and was cooling off a bit when they set out.

The two young men had their own collection of guns; they went out hunting a couple of times a week by themselves, and usually brought back something for the table, even if it was only a couple of squirrels for the stewpot. Thick forests grew inland and here and there around the plantation were groves of trees left when the cropland was cleared. They were full of wild life. They headed for one of these bits of woodland now, along the sunken rice fields and across and beyond a field where Guinea corn was growing. The older boys thought there should be something worth finding there, as it had been a few weeks since they had last visited it.

On the day in question, the young master Adolphus was not so happy. This was supposed to be his birthday treat, and he had not even been allowed one shot. He had been hoping to have a gun of his own as a birthday present, but though he had let his father know of his hopes, there had been no gun. He had promised Hannibal that when he got it, the two of them would go on their own hunting trips, and that he would let him learn to shoot. Hannibal knew, of course, that despite his daydream there was no chance that he would ever have a gun of his own. Even when he grew up, he would still be "a slave" and thus forbidden to own firearms. That was because white people were afraid that if African people had guns they would use them to kill their masters and make themselves free. They were probably right to have that fear.

Hannibal had a good time hunting without a gun, and so did Dolph. They had "catapults," forked sticks with strips of India rubber fastened across the fork. With these weapons they could shoot small stones as fast as bullets to bring down rabbits, squirrels, and unwary birds. Fred had brought the strips of rubber from Charles Town and showed them how to make them into weapons and how to use them. He said a young Spaniard from South America had given them to him as something specially interesting. Hannibal was pleased to think these catapults were hand versions of the big weapons the original Hannibal had used against the Romans, as Clifford suggested to the boys. Of course, he pointed out, Hannibal had used leather, not rubber.

Whatever the resemblance to ancient weapons, these toys were effective enough in bringing little things to the kitchen or to the Quarters, where there was always a stewpot glad to have them.

On this day, the boys had not brought their catapults. Their interest was focused on the guns and what they could do.

The older boys led the way, talking in quiet voices, and once they reached the trees they stopped talking altogether and were very wary, treading cautiously so as not to snap a dry stick underfoot and looking up into the trees for any kind of game.

Suddenly, Fred swung up his arm and signalled "halt!" They stood still as he loaded his gun and held it to his shoulder. They boys could not see anything that would be a target. Then, as they followed the line of the gun barrel, they saw a dark shape on the limb of a huge cotton tree a couple of hundred yards away. It was a huge bird and moved restlessly; perhaps it felt the danger. It seemed to puff up in size, opening and spreading out its great wings for flight. Just as it flapped off, Fred fired, staggering back against them from the recoil. Clifford behind him quickly steadied him as they watched that great feathered mass, already launched into the air, shudder backward and then come tumbling down the tall length of the tree to collapse with a thud in a hollow among its exposed roots.

The little boys shouted in excitement as they struggled through the thick bushes to get to the foot of the tree.

"What is it?" asked Dolph. "What kind of bird was it? I couldn't tell."

"It was a turkey, of course," said Fred, "a natural wild turkey that'll make a good sweet dinner for all the family."

When they reached the spot where the turkey lay, they gasped at its size. It had landed upside down and its wrinkled red head and neck could not be seen under the billowy mass of black and grey feathers out of which its two thin legs and claws of feet stuck up. They served as handles for lifting up the creature, caught as it was in a trap of tangled dead branches, and Clifford and Fred each took a foot and hauled it up and carried it over the tangle of bushes to the open, where they laid it down. For a few minutes they looked it over. Fred's shot had caught it near the neck, almost severing the head from the body, and there was blood on its feathers. Fred took it by the feet and hefted it; he grunted with surprise at the weight.

"This will provide a good dinner for the whole household! Just lift it, Cliff; have you ever seen a turkey this size? Why, it must be twenty-five pounds, at least. It looks as though I'm the lucky hunter today."

"Well," his brother agreed, "I guess there are no other birds like that around here, so there's no chance I can do better than that." He was good-natured about it, and Hannibal noticed then and later that Fred was more anxious to be a better hunter, and a better everything, than his brother, who was not really of a competitive nature. "Now, who's going to carry this prize back to the kitchen?"

"Certainly not I," said Fred. "I did my share when I shot the creature. Hannibal and Dolph can take it along. Let's make it easier for them by putting it on a pole. Luckily I put some thongs in my pocket before we started out, in case we had to carry game. I didn't expect this much luck, though. I'll tie the feet together. You boys get busy and find a good stout branch."

Dolph found a good piece of a branch, about four feet long or a bit more, and Clifford trimmed off some twigs on it and slid it between the legs. He and Fred held it up till it took the whole weight and the bird dangled in the air, and Hannibal and Dolph stood beside them while they lifted the pole ends onto the younger boys' shoulders.

"How's that?" asked Fred as they buckled a bit under the sudden weight. "Can you get that back to the house without dragging it?"

The turkey was not too heavy, but it dangled as long as the boys were tall, and hung so low on the slightly sagging branch that its head and neck still lay lolling on the ground when they stood upright—at least as upright as they could manage. The head caught in every brier and threw them off-balance, making the rough stick scratch their necks where the muscles ached from the unaccustomed burden. Fortunately for Hannibal, Dolph, not used to any kind of work and not ashamed to complain of pain, was not long in telling his brothers he couldn't do it.

"We'll have to take it, Fred," said Clifford. "It's just too awkward for the boys to manage. Anyway, we can call it a day and go home now, too; I don't care if I don't shoot anything."

So the two of them gave their guns to the youngsters to carry and shouldered the branch and the turkey themselves. Even they had a job to keep it above the thorns and brambles until they emerged from the grove and on across the field to the broad raised path, the rice bank, that ran between the swampy rice fields.

It was close to sunset, and the wet rice fields, strung along the river where the plants were heavy-headed and nearly ready for harvest, shone like golden pools slashed here and there by violet shadows. Dolph and Hannibal followed behind the older brothers, who were moving as quickly as their burden would allow, a steady walking pace. Hannibal knew that it was not his place to join in the conversation as these young men discussed the hunting available on the plantation. In fact, he could feel equal friends with Dolph when the adults were not around, but his

mother often cautioned him about being familiar with the older brothers, even when they seemed friendly. Friendship between a slave and
master was not a real friendship, as between equals, and Hester knew
that in her bones. She had grown up in Africa with that knowledge.

However, Hannibal was allowed to listen, along with Dolph, when
Clifford and Fred boasted about their prowess with their guns. They
preferred the serious hunting of the forest country in the uplands in the
West. It was cooler there in the summers, when the plantation was hu-
mid and hot, and the whole Courtney family would pack up wagons
with provisions and bedding and whatever else they needed and spend
the hottest months of the year there. It was a kind of camping, and they
had never taken Hester or her son. From what Dolph said, it seemed
there was much more to shoot at there, both of deer and possums and of
other food animals. And there were also fierce and dangerous animals
like wolves, bears, and mountain lions. Hannibal liked to hear the hunters reminding each other of past triumphs in the hunting line, and
dreamed of one day doing the same.

Once the group left the grove, they had a wide expanse of sky open
to them, broken only in places by clumps of giant cottonwoods with low
trees and bushes clustered around. In the distance was the river, detect-
ible where reflections of sunlight glittered off the waves splashing lazily
against the shore. Along that river the low rice fields stretched out, rice
fields that made Colonel Courtney rich and required the labour of many
slaves, both men and women, to plant, tend and harvest

The sky was absolutely clear, but strangely enough, as they went
along, they began to hear a noise like that of an approaching storm. Masters Clifford and Fred put down the turkey and looked carefully at all
points of the circling horizon. The sound increased; it was like the roar
of wind raging in treetops far away. Carefully listening, the boys had a

sense of its direction. It seemed to be coming from the distant forest to the south. They shaded their eyes and looked hard and seemed to see a dark cloud over it getting bigger and closer as they watched.

"Wild pigeons!" shouted Clifford. "I'm sure of it. That was the way we saw them coming at us in the mountains."

"I remember!" replied Fred. "That was seven or eight years ago, but we've never seen them here before."

"Probably they generally keep inland, away from the coast," said Clifford. "They like to find food in the deep forests, where there are oak trees and acorns. But perhaps they like rice, too, when they find it. Here are our fields ready for harvest; I think we'd better get ready to fight for them."

Meanwhile, the younger boys were watching in wonder. They had never seen anything like this self-directed cloud, still a long way off but clearly moving at great speed in their direction.

"Will they come down on our rice?" Dolph asked.

"If they are hungry they will," Clifford replied, "and they probably are. Run for help, you two. You, Hannibal, run to the Quarters and get out all the men and women there and send for the rest, wherever they are. Tell them to bring brooms and hoes and anything else to hit the birds. Dolph, you run and tell father; he's probably in the house. On the move, both of you, as fast as you can run."

They sped off while Clifford and Fred loaded their guns and prepared to shoot when the birds were within range. The cloud of pigeons were flying at the speed of a mile a minute and would be in range before help could arrive. There was a slim chance that the noise and smoke of the guns would scare them away. However, Hannibal had heard talk of these wild pigeons, passenger pigeons as they were also called, and knew that they made good eating. As he ran to the Quarters, he hoped that some, at least, would fly down and get killed so that his friends living in the Quarters might have a change of diet from the everlasting pork belly they were given.

While Dolph and he ran off to get help. the older boys tried to scare the birds off. Later they estimated that there were between fifteen and twenty thousand of them, and they were deafened by the thunder of their flapping wings as the birds braked their descent and gradually settled to the ground

Fred and Clifford shot at the fowls. When their bullets and powder were spent, they prodded at them with their rifle barrels, but they could barely make a dent in the throng pecking at the heads of rice. New waves were constantly sweeping over and settling down beyond, and the fields were pulsating with their movements.

The two young men picked up their guns and the turkey and, in the belief that their father must now be on his way, went to meet him. In a few minutes, in fact, Colonel Courtney galloped onto the scene with pistols by his side and dogs and house servants at the horse's heels, and at about the same time field hands, both male and female, appeared with whatever tool seemed most useful.

Hannibal ran back to the scene to find Clifford and Fred conferring with their father.

"They will have to go find a roosting place for the night," Clifford was saying. "They won't stay on the ground after sunset. If we can make it hot for them here, they may move on tomorrow morning."

"That seems to be our only hope," replied the Colonel. "We certainly cannot kill them all before they completely destroy the crop."

Hannibal was wondering if there would be any crop left. Everywhere he looked there were birds with gleaming blue backs and orange breasts—the males—and beside them, inconspicuous and blending

with the shadows but with their bills just as busy, were the dowdy fe-
males. Their shining heads bobbed incessantly as they stripped the grain
stalk after stalk. It was only a short time since the two young boys had
run to spread the alarm, but already immense damage had been done.

Now that the workers had arrived, a serious battle against these in-
vaders began. The Colonel fired his pistols in the air to frighten the birds
and distract them from their meal, while everyone else used a broom or
hoe to hit them on the head or neck, and as they laid them low, they
tossed them into heaps. Some of the women and many children followed behind with baskets and bags into which they packed the birds to
carry back to the cabins. The old folk there, not fit for the work in the
field, waited to pluck and clean the pigeons. They had scores of the birds
naked and neatly arranged on clean straw before they were cold, ready
for the spit.

Hundreds of pigeons were killed during the last half-hour of daylight
without making any real impression on the mass of the flock. However,
its members were obviously unsettled by the noise of the firearms, the
yelling of the people, and the barking of the dogs, and everyone hoped
they would look elsewhere for the next day's food. It was a big relief to
them all when the sun at last began to slide from sight and the great flock
began to rise into the air as if a signal had been given. By the time the sky
turned purple and the evening star came out, the last of the pigeons had
flown off to the northwest, and the exhausted men sat or lay down for a
breather.

"Will they come back tomorrow, sir?" asked Fred of his father.

"Who can tell?" answered the Colonel. "But they will travel a few
miles tonight before they find a roosting place, and I'll wager they will
find fields closer at hand for their breakfast tomorrow. The odds are that
some other plantation will have the pleasure of feeding them. Now then,

boys, let's go home and clean ourselves up. You three look like outlaws."

He took Dolph up before him on the saddle and trotted off, his older sons following at a good pace and a couple of house servants carrying the turkey. As for Hannibal, he had to follow as best he could and finish his working day. It began to get dark, but the women brought pine knot torches and by their light the last of the booty was safely brought to the Quarters. They were getting ready for a party, in which they would be feasting on grilled pigeon along with singing and dancing, until stomachs were full, throats sore, and bodies tired and ready for sleep. It was a break that came only once or twice in their year of hard work and monotonous rations.

Hannibal still had his usual evening work to do, so he reluctantly went to the house, hoping Dolph would be in a good mood and thoughtful enough to let him get back early before the feasting and fun had run down.

chapter three
REVOLUTIONARY IDEAS

In later years, Hannibal looked back on the evening the passenger pigeons had come as the day he first heard of events and ideas that were going to change his life forever.

He got back from the Big House in time to join Skippy and his family by a fire that had burned down a bit and was showing plenty of hot red coals. The pigeons, impaled on green sticks over the embers, were already sizzling. They were turning to golden brown and giving off delicious scents, and the fat dripping onto the coals sent up little spurts of flame that revealed the circle of happy faces waiting hungrily.

Along a line of fires, the rest of the little community of workers and children could be picked out by the leaping light, all of them enjoying themselves, for once, in complete harmony.

By the light of the fire where he was settled, Hannibal made out a face new to him, a strange man of unusually large build. He watched him a few minutes and noticed the flashing smile and jovial laugh that made him seem very likeable and trustworthy.

"I've never seen that man before," he said to Skippy. "Do you know who he is?"

"Oh, him," came the answer. "That's Jupiter Brown, the cabinet maker from town."

Hannibal knew that name, though he had never seen the man who bore it. Jupiter Brown was well known for his skill with wood. His master, a well-respected craftsman in Charles Town, hired him out to do fine cabinet work for rich people. One night, only a week or two before, Hannibal had heard his name. He remembered that he had been attending in the dining room when the Colonel had said he was sending for a skilled hand to carry out an idea he had for new panelling in the drawing room. In fact, Hannibal had helped him pass around some sketches to show what he had in mind, sketches his family had said would look very well when turned into polished and carved wood.

The boy guessed at once, and rightly, that Jupiter was the skilled hand come to do the work, and he longed to talk to him and to know him. That was because he looked so much more interesting than the plantation hands, the only other men he knew. Jupiter was so alive and forceful, even only partially seen in the dark, waving his hand as he talked, with a pigeon in it. By this time, the first lot of pigeons were done and each person had one. They were all biting into the crusty outsides of the tender, succulent morsels while a fresh lot were put over the fire for the next round.

What an evening that was with all the high spirits let loose and troubles forgot. Jupiter Brown, with his loud voice and hearty bellows of laughter, was the centre of attention for the men and older boys. He was big and well-muscled, and even though he was obviously good-humoured, something about him would make one hesitate to take liberties; he would probably resent an insult or injury as much as he enjoyed innocent fun. Hannibal, quite unaware of it at the time, was going to know him well in the dangerous years ahead, and found that what he suspected at that first meeting was certainly the kind of man he was. Other men offended him at their own peril.

Jupiter was also one of the best informed men around, because he was sent to practise his craft far and wide, and he kept his ears and eyes open and picked up information like a sponge does water. He was in great demand everywhere he set up his shop for his tales of high-life and low-life, as heard both in the city and the country districts. He was a close observer of the pretensions and follies of the human race, whether black or white, and it was his sharp and amusing remarks on these topics that, on the first evening at Ellenboro, kept the circle around him laughing as they ate their pigeons. The humorous atmosphere in which they feasted was a tasty sauce for the grilled fowl, and made it more exciting than it would otherwise have been.

However, Jupiter's mood changed as they were finishing their food, when there was a quiet interval before beginning their drumming and dancing. He was suddenly more serious, as if he wanted to inform the men of something important.

"Listen to me, I want you to be serious now. Did you know we are waiting for something important, something you should think about, too?"

"What are you talking about?" asked one older man.

"In Charles Town, we're all waiting for *the Day*," he said slowly, and with a solemn emphasis on the word "day."

"The Day! What day?" asked the older people.

"The Day of Jubilee-o," he replied in a rising voice, almost shouting the "O." "The day when freedom sails up the Harbour and black folks will jubilate!"

The men sitting beside and around him were confused and at a loss to know whether he was preaching, talking nonsense, or stating some obvious fact. Some of them had heard tell of fighting away in the North, in which freedom was the cause, so one asked if he was talking about General George Washington. "Is he coming into Charles Town to bring us the Freedom and the Jubilee?"

Jupiter laughed at their ignorance.

"No," he said, "not George Washington, but King George, from across the water. King George's men will bring us the Jubilee! They are coming soon, too."

These names were not unknown to Hannibal, as they were to Skippy and other young ones around the fire, because he had heard the Courtneys around their dining table talking about George Washington. He had heard things said about King George, too. But it had been hard for him to understand where the General and the King stood in relation to each other, or who the other men mentioned were: Thomas Paine, William Pitt, Thomas Jefferson, Benjamin Franklin, and even two other kings, the King of France and the King of Spain. All of them were discussed at one time or another at dinner by Colonel Courtney, his two elder sons, and their guests. Hannibal was the mouse in the corner, hearing everything, sometimes trying to listen and understand, but never saying anything. So far as the Courtneys were concerned, he had no ears for their talk and no comprehension. Still, from what he heard over time while doing his chores in the dining room, he came to understand that the talk was of old struggles and old wars along with new and fresh ones, and that at times there was much passion and disagreement among the company, even between the two older Courtney brothers.

Now, on the night of the pigeon feast, Hannibal thought about the scraps he had picked up. He had never dared ask about these things he heard, for he knew it was none of his business and in fact he would just make trouble for himself if he let the white folk know he was curious about the things that troubled them. But here was someone he could ask, because Jupiter seemed to know about these white folk's matters and thought everybody else should, too. Hannibal moved closer to Jupiter, to catch everything he said. He was too shy to ask questions, but other people were doing that and he didn't have to do anything but listen.

The man closest to Jupiter challenged his last statement.

"I'm only an ignorant field hand," he said, "but I have heard about King George, and I heard he was a cruel tyrant. Isn't he responsible for us all being brought here from Africa? Didn't his soldiers massacre people in Boston a few years back? Isn't he now telling the wild Indians to attack and scalp the people living on the frontier? How can we get anything good from him?"

It was old gray-haired Matthew who put the question precisely.

"We hear that George Washington and the other patriots are fighting the Redcoats for freedom, freedom for everyone in Carolina and the other colonies. If they are fighting King George for freedom for us all, then what need have we to look to the King for our deliverance?"

Matthew and the others were remembering what they had been told not long before. During the previous summer, when the Courtney household was off in the cool mountain country, the African people at Ellenboro had learned about George Washington from Brother Joseph, a Methodist preacher who visited the quarters secretly when he thought he wouldn't be noticed. He was full of faith in Washington and the

"Declaration of Independence," which said all men were created free and equal, and that all deserved liberty and happiness. He even promised them a day of liberation, a "Day of Jubilee," soon. It was pleasant to hear. but the elders among the field hands, and the house servants too, doubted that things would change. Even so, they prayed it would happen as he seemed to promise, that the good white folks would run the country and make everybody, especially the black people, happy.

Jupiter laughed in a tone that expressed bitter amusement.

"Don't believe everything you hear from white folks," he said. "They know their reasons for the things they say. They don't think about freedom for black folks. King George may not be so bad, neither, nor his army, his Redcoats."

There was silence for a moment, as the group around turned over in their minds these new ideas. It was years since good words had gone around about King George and the British Army. They had once been heroes in the wars against the French, when George Washington from Virginia had been one of their most famous fighters, but these were old stories. It seemed that George Washington and King George were no longer friends. Did it matter?

Hannibal knew he was very mixed up, but thought maybe it did matter. In the Big House, he heard one kind of talk, of confident well-informed white people content with their place in life and afraid of a change for the worse. He heard another kind of talk among the people of the Quarters, who heard about many things they could not really understand, but shaped them by the hope that coloured their expectations. A day of great change was coming, they believed, a day in which they would all be free to live as they liked, to eat delicious food and drink sweet drinks and wear fine clothes. That was what they called the Day of Jubilee, and in all the sufferings of their lives they were consoled by the thoughts that it would come one day. They had heard of fighting far away in the North, and they had heard of George Washington who was a leader in the fight for "freedom," and so they hoped he would win the struggle and fulfill their dreams.

Jupiter Brown's different expectation certainly confused the men who thought they knew what was likely to affect them. If the African people of Charles Town were looking forward to the coming of King George's men, then they would have to reconsider and perhaps rearrange their own ideas about who was the friend and who was the enemy.

"What do you mean, Jupiter? Why do people in Charles Town want the British to come? Do they care about us? How will they help us?"

Jupiter was contemptuous of their ignorance.

"Do you think the 'Patriots' care about black folk?" he asked. "Have you heard of George Washington setting his slaves free? Or any of the rest of them? No! They do not want to pay taxes to King George, so they say he is a tyrant and they must be free! Free from taxes, they mean. All these rich men who are making this war are doing it so they can be richer yet. They're not going to do anything for poor white men, and they're not going to do anything for poor black men. They're in this world for themselves."

There was a big gasp around the circle when they heard these strong words, and murmurs of disagreement or shock spread among them. The fact was that none of the African people on Ellenboro Plantation knew enough about the struggle between King George and George Washington either to agree or to disagree with Jupiter Brown. He knew that well enough, and didn't expect any wisdom from them. However, he intended to educate them a bit more before he had to go home, and went on with his answer to the questions.

"What do the British care about us?" he asked. "Well, maybe not a lot, but maybe they need us, and maybe we can profit from that. I'll tell you something they did a few years back. Have you ever heard of Governor Dunmore in Virginia? No, I guess you haven't. Anyway, he was a real British lord, maybe a cousin to King George, I wouldn't be surprised! Just at the time when this rebellion was beginning, Lord Dunmore thought he'd better find men to fight for King George, and he thought, why not take black men for the job? And why not, I say too. Aren't we as strong and tough as white men are? Maybe a lot tougher. Anyway, Lord Dunmore made a promise; he swore that every black man who came to him and joined his army would be a free man ever after. And you know what? A lot of black men came to him and fought battles for him.

"Why didn't you hear about these things here? Likely because Lord Dunmore and his men had to get out of Virginia, on account of the white folks got real angry when their slaves went to him, and they got too strong for him. But he didn't break his promise to the African folks who trusted him. Later on, the British came on ships and tried to land in Charles Town, but they couldn't get a toe-hold; General Charley Lee was sent by Washington to drive them away and so he did, they just weren't strong enough. Since then, all the fighting has been up North. But now things have changed; then was then but now is now. Our white folks in South Carolina are split.

"In Charles Town, some of the important men want the British to come back and turn out the rebel government, as they call it. People who didn't want King George to rule them in '76 are on his side now. This rebellion has gone a lot further than they wanted, and they are ready to be friends with the British army and join it, too, if it will come back. Well, that's what some of us black folks in Charles Town are looking for. We want a chance to join the army and get our freedom as Lord

Dunmore promised. If the Englishmen assure us of our liberty, we'll leave our masters and go over to them. Even if they don't win the war, they'll have to take us somewhere else where we can live as we should."

Jupiter Brown went on to tell the anxious men lots more about the war, though Hannibal was getting sleepy and not able to take it all in. But he did understand that Jupiter was explaining that British forces, "King George's men," held New York and Philadelphia and that an all-out war was beginning between Great Britain and her old enemies France and Spain, which was going to turn everything upside down. Jupiter's information came from the taverns and workshops of Charles Town, which were buzzing with all the latest news from the battlefields and from London, and from the meetings of the "Continental Congress" of the rebels. Hannibal was too sleepy to listen to any more, so he left the fire and went to his cornhusk bed and was instantly asleep.

chapter four
WHO IS HANNIBAL HOOPS?

It was on the next evening that Hannibal had some time alone with his mother in their little cabin, and he told her as best he could what Jupiter Brown had said about the Day of Jubilee. He was disappointed when she did not get very excited.

"Ah, my son," she said, "if it gives you something to dream about for awhile, I won't say it isn't true. Its not for an ignorant woman like me to know what might happen, and whatever does happen will not matter much to me. I can never go back to the life I lived before I was brought to Carolina. I have grown used to this life; it could be much worse for me, and I am as content as I could be anywhere.

"But it is not right for you, son. When you become a man, you should be a strong and free one, like your fathers were. Although you were born a slave, my son Kanday (she refused to call him Hannibal, a name she had not given him), you were conceived in freedom. Your blood is the blood of kings, my son; your grandfathers back through the ages were kings, and if all had gone well, your father would be a king now."

Up to this point in his life, his mother had told him very little about his origins and her own, but now she seemed to have decided that he was old enough to hear more of her story, and to understand and remember it.

"Tell me everything, Ma," he begged. "You have hardly told me anything about how you and I came here. Why are we not in Africa where we belong? Maybe if the British come and free us, they will let us go to our old home again. But where is it? How can we get to it?" Hannibal's knowledge of geography was very vague; he didn't even realize that Africa was on the other side of the Atlantic Ocean, and that the ocean was very wide. He didn't realize that he and his mother couldn't walk to their old home in a matter of a week or two, if they were allowed to attempt it. His mother, though, knew that it was unimaginably far to her old home, and remembered the long days and weeks of the voyage of the Middle Passage, a voyage through Hell, that all Africans had suffered to pass from their own dear homes into the life of captivity in the Americas.

Now, finally, perhaps because he was now more than a baby, she did not put him off with baby stories, but answered him seriously. As always, when they were alone together, she spoke to him in her own language, one he understood perfectly well, though he was not good at speaking it.

"Our old home is not there, in Africa, anymore, Kanday, my son. Our village of Gbatonga, in the land of the Lokos, does not exist outside of memory. It was a beautiful place to live, among groves and rice fields and beautiful green hills. There in Lokoland our people have always lived, inland from the ocean and the country the white men call Sierra

Leone. When I came here, I couldn't speak this English language, but when I could speak and understand, I asked my Master what name the white people gave to the country I came from, and he told me it was Sierra Leone. That is where we would have to go, and it would be a long, hard sea voyage. But I would like to know that you will go there one day, and if you do, you must use your real name, your true Loko name, not the slave name Old Master called you."

She sighed deeply and said, "Yes, you are no longer a baby. It is time for you to understand how we come to be wretched slaves in Carolina instead of happy free people in Africa. I will tell you what I can. My name, my son, was Fa'mata…"

▲   ▲   ▲

The ruddy swollen moon had risen early that evening as the sun was setting on the opposite side of the village, Gbatonga. By the time the villagers had eaten their main meal of the day, it was halfway up the sky, round and silvery, and when a couple of drums began to tap and set the beat, the villagers began to dance. They danced in the cool white open spaces and whirled now and again into the inky shadows thrown by the huts and trees. In and out they went, appearing magically as they passed from the zone of darkness into light, and vanishing again as the rhythms of the drums carried them on.

At last the moon descended in its turn and slipped behind the forest wall. The pools of darkness had been creeping up the sides of the houses; now they rose up and drowned the village in shadow. The drummers, suddenly exhausted, broke off, and the village went happily to bed by the glow of the dying fires. Soon the only sounds were those of the West African forest at night: the sharp music of the crickets, the keening of the frogs in a nearby swamp, or the despairing squeaks of little animals in peril.

Not far from the village, a broad river ran swiftly among heaped up rocks, the muted roar of its many little cataracts sounded a deep-toned vibration which blended in a drowsy song with the shrill noises of animal life. The village slept.

In one of the thatched houses slept Fa'mata. She lay close to her husband of two months, the village champion, Kanday Kontay. They were very happy, asleep or awake. Kanday was the son of the old chief of the village and expected that some day he would be chief in his father's place. Already he was the foremost of the young men in all their activities. In feats of skill and strength and daring, he was their leader. When they hunted in the forest or raided another village for extra food, they followed him. Fa'mata was proud to be loved and chosen by such a man.

As the couple lay dreaming in contentment, the silence of the hour before the dawn was rent by a scream of warning from the main gate. The watchman on duty had unwisely accepted a gift of palm wine early in the evening and at the hour when he should have been alert and watchful, he was fast asleep. He awoke to find a knife at his throat and a mass of figures climbing the palisade and pushing through the gate. He uttered only a single scream before the knife struck.

Then, as silence was no longer useful, the enemy warriors yelled fearsomely and began to run through the village. Some of them set fire to the thatched roofs nearest the gate, while others stood beside the doors with clubs raised, ready to strike down the occupants as they fled.

Kanday Kontay woke at the watchman's scream and in an instant had seized his war club. He pulled the dazed Fa'mata to her feet. "Get into the storage ditch," he ordered. "Stay there until we have driven them off." By this time, the war cries of the attacking force had warned the villagers that this was no petty raid by a rival village of their own people, the Loko, but was a life-and-death struggle with their age-old enemies, the Temnes.

As her husband rushed from his front door towards the main gate, Fa'mata fled out the back towards a concealed opening in the palisade. From it, a narrow track led to the sacred Grove where the all-powerful Secret Society met to govern. It was forbidden ground to women, but Fa'mata was not going to the Grove, but to a hiding place a hundred yards along the trail. Here was the secret entrance to a trench where yams and rice were stored, hidden from prying eyes by a roof of branches and growing vines. It was to this hidden spot that the women and children had been taught to flee with their goats, sheep, and fowls when the village seemed in danger.

The Temnes, anticipating some such reaction, had taken no chances of having their intended victims escape. As Fa'mata squeezed through the palisade, she was seized by a Temne warrior and hustled off into the darkness. Already flames were shooting up at the far side of the village, and the enemy lay in wait around it to catch all who fled.

Fa'mata was pushed roughly along until she and her captor arrived at a rudely walled enclosure where the villagers sometimes penned sheep and goats. Here she was thrust in amongst a crowd of people. It was not long before the flaming roofs of the village threw enough light to show her the familiar faces of friends and neighbours in the crowd around her, all dazed and terrified. Gradually, as the sky lightened with the dawn, the enclosure filled with captives. Their guards, stationed around, made them squat on the ground to prevent any attempt at flight or resistance. Indeed, there was little likelihood of either, because every-one was confused and afraid. Moreover, they were all women and children.

When the sun came up and it was full dawn, it became clear that the Temnes had succeeded in destroying another segment of Loko land. A few of the village men, tightly bound, were brought to the enclosure, but of the majority there was no sign. The chief of the village was not among them, nor was his son Kanday, and Fa'mata's heart seemed to shrivel in her breast as the belief swept over her that they were dead. Although the shock of the capture and destruction of her home had been wearing off a bit, this second shock sent a wave of numbness rushing over her, and she felt herself falling into a pit of darkness.

She may have wished to die there and then, but she was a strong and healthy girl of not more than sixteen years. She soon recovered from her faint and awoke to find the hot sun warming her blood. She sat up and joined with the other women in their shrill cries of grief.

A few hours later the captives, linked in a long rope at the neck, were herded past the burnt-out village, above which the vultures were circling and gradually descending. Fa'mata did not need to see his body to know that Kanday Kontay was dead, but as they were herded away from familiar scenes, she vowed to his spirit that she would remain faithful in her love and, if she could, she would avenge him.

The captives were led into Temne country and divided among the warriors, who now split up to return to several home villages. They had been watching the captives closely on the march and knew which ones they wanted as slaves, wives, and adopted children. The last were the most fortunate; they would soon forget the past and become Temnes. There was a long discussion, with plenty of give and take on all sides, before the captives were divided up and led in different directions. Fa'mata was told that she was to become the wife of the warrior who had captured her and was led towards his village with the others allotted there.

She proved a difficult case for her captor. In the weeks that followed, she made life a misery for that warrior, who got tired of beating her every day and passed her on to his brother. She refused to take either of them for husband. In her heart she nursed a stubborn hatred for the whole band of Temne warriors who had destroyed her happiness. She would not even bend with circumstances and work in the fields with the other women. When they refused to feed her, she did not complain because she almost hoped that she would starve to death. But she was more valuable than that, so her captors decided to sell her to the next slave trader who passed.

After living for a month among people she hated, it was almost a relief to be moving away with a group of other unfortunates, most of them Lokos, and many of them from her own village. They were bound for a distant place called Port Loko, a place with dreaded associations for a captive. For generations, slaves had been taken there to be sold; no one knew what happened to them once they were taken down the river and out to the ocean. Were they bought to be eaten? Were they sacrificed to the ocean gods? Was there some more horrible fate awaiting them? No one knew, but as long as there were white men willing to buy human beings, there were African men willing to sell. Fa'mata herself had known certain youths sold off to Port Loko from her own village, Gbatonga—two because they defied the orders of the Secret Society, and another who was found to be a thief. However, she had never known that to happen to women, and as she moved along in the file of slaves, Fa'mata supposed she would be chosen as a wife or slave by some man there. She did not think that the men from the ocean would want her.

At intervals, the line halted for food, sleep, or rest in the heat of the day. Port Loko was easily reached, and the slave traders were not in a hurry. At such times Fa'mata exchanged a few words with the other prisoners from the village. For the most part, they were half-grown boys who, like herself, had been too stubborn to knuckle under to the Temnes. They tried to cheer each other up, but it was hard because of their terror at what lay ahead.

Day after day, they walked along the well-beaten path to the West. At times Fa'mata's mind wandered a bit and she fancied they were a line of spiders on a web, for their path was constantly crisscrossed by other paths running in all directions, like the strands on which spiders dash to seize their prey.

At other times, she was roused from her dreams by a sudden change in her surroundings. Out of the forest shade they moved into bright sunlight as they crossed a patch of grassland. Sometimes they carefully chose their way through a swamp and over a stream where three logs tied together with vines made a bridge. Most often, though, the trail ran among the great old trees which grew plentifully throughout that region. These trees, of great size and antiquity, protected the tender under-growth from the parching sun of the dry season and the heavy rains that came after it, and they lent the same protection to Fa'mata and her companions

It was the time before the rains when the slaves were driven to the coast, and as they passed near villages they saw the bush being burned off to clear the land for rice planting. During the day, pillars of smoke rose around them and at night there was a glow of fire in a dozen spots. Fa'mata could not help but weep when she thought of the year before, when Kanday and his friends had chopped and burned a patch for a fresh farm and she and the other girls had planted the rice and kept it weeded as the young plants grew. As often in the evenings, she and Kanday had come together to the field to see how well his young brother was keeping the birds away. They had built him a small platform in the middle of the field, with a thatched roof to make it shady, and here he stayed all day casting pebbles at the birds with his sling whenever they came down among the tender plants.

The days with Kanday would not come again, but if she could forget the past and make herself a Temne, she might again work in the fields with laughing friends. Could she take a Temne husband? No! Never! Never could she subdue her hatred for the Temnes. Never could she forgive the people who had killed Kanday. She would rather go into the unknown future, even if it be with the men from the sea into their strange world, than forget her past and become a different person of a different nation!

It was not more than a week all told before the weary line of slaves entered the trading town of Port Loko. Here was a broad creek up which came boats from the ocean, and here was a renegade of the Loko tribe who bought the slaves from the traders. This man, Jack Copper, worked for English masters who lived on Bunce Island down by the ocean. There the slaves would be carried when word was sent and the boats came for them.

When the prisoners were brought to him and he ordered them into his yard, some of them muttered abuse, asking why a brother Loko should keep them captive. Jack Copper heard the muttering, and seizing a whip he lashed some of them across the shoulders. They had no choice but to run into the yard and into the cage he indicated to them.

The cage was a rough pen, walled with stout poles through which the prisoners could see but not force their bodies, thatched over like an ordinary hut. In the few days she was there, Fa'mata was close enough to Jack Copper's several wives and dozen little children to see and come to know them, and indeed to hear their conversation and be heard if she spoke to them; but she and the prisoners were excluded from the life all around them. The life of the compound was the same as village life, but a barrier thicker than the lattice of poles lay between them and it. Somehow it made the prisoners into something less than humans, in the eyes of the women and children and the husky male servants on the other side.

It was clear in the way they were looked at, or spoken to, which was infrequent, and the way in which, most of the time, no attention at all was paid to them. It was, thought Fa'mata, as though they had become dead people, harmless dead people, unworthy of respect. She wished she had a fowl to sacrifice to summon up the spirits of her ancestors to help her to survive this assault upon her own spirit. Even a word of pity from Copper's wives, even a gesture from the children, would help to restore human dignity. There was none to spare. The faces of the women as they passed food or water in through a gap in the fence were hard and uninterested, and the children only noticed their existence to mock them.

It was not only Fa'mata who was thus affected. The prisoners were free now to talk to each other as much as they pleased, but their conversations were short and cheerless. Their worst fears seemed more than realized. They were being drained of the fire of life, of power, of soul. The hostile indifference of those who tended and guarded them was a dark heavy cloud settling on them, driving life and feeling from the extremities and weakening their resolve to live. Surely their ultimate fate was to be sacrificed to the sea gods, or to be eaten at some cannibal feast by the pale-skinned men from the sea whom they had never yet seen. Several of them became mad from tension; one curled herself up in a ball in the corner and could not be roused, while another tried to throttle the man next to him. The experiences which the prisoners from Gbatonga had undergone during the past weeks was too severe. They had endured the destruction of their home village with so many loved ones, and the pressures applied to them by the Temnes. They had undergone the long march to Port Loko, with its uncertainties and prospective terrors. Finally they were experiencing the deliberate degrading of their self-respect in Jack Copper's compound. All these things had reduced them to a state of shock which might easily have led to death or permanent insanity.

It was in those desperate days that Fa'mata discovered her mettle. Strangely enough, she found a reason for hope and strength in the fact that, as she learned from the talk between Jack Copper and his women, she was not to be kept at Port Loko but would be sent on into the unknown world of the white men, along with the boys and youths. She welcomed a clean break from her past. Kanday Kontay and her village lived only in her dreams. It was best to go far away, or die, than to be reminded by every sight and sound of the life that had been.

So when they were marched down to the ramshackle wharf and embarked on the river boats, she was glad. Calm and relaxed, she watched the great trees glide by as though in a dream. When they sailed out into the broad sunlit estuary and got out onto Bunce Island with its great stone walls and, inside, dark and damp cave-like dungeons, structures she had never even heard described before, she accepted what she saw without curiosity. However, there was a limit to what she could accept, and her reaction to the Europeans at Bunce Island was a mixture of disgust and curiosity that intruded sharply on her composure.

Their long, coarse, dirty hair, the colour of sand and clay, half concealing their faces, made her wonder if they were not related to the hairy and mischievous little monkeys of the forest. Their bodies were so hidden by bits of cloth that she could only wonder what deformities they were intent on concealing. Their looks were fearful, their odour unpleasant, and their language uncouth and strange. All the same, she found it hard to accept them as real. They did not afflict her spirit as Jack Copper and his household had done, for he and his people had been part of her own world turned upside down. These strange beings seemed no more real than the flickering shadows cast by people sitting around the evening fire.

In any case, she saw little of them. The slaves were herded into a high-walled courtyard twice a day to be exercised, and sometimes she saw the white men standing on the walls above, watching. She knew her fate was in their hands and since she was helpless to do anything about it, she lived from hour to hour and tried to think no further.

The slaves were at Bunce Island for about ten days when a ship sailed in to take on cargo. Already this slave ship, the *Emmeline*, had about a hundred and fifty poor wretches aboard; she took on another fifty and her cargo was complete.

Among the fifty were the Loko captives, and very timidly they climbed up the rope ladder which twisted and swayed under their weight. Some were howling, or moaning gently to themselves, but Fa'mata went up steadily without a sound. Only when she was on the deck did she pause and stand still, paying no heed to the guard prodding her with a stave toward the open hatch. She looked back up river, saying goodbye with her eyes to the rich green of swamp and tree, and to the mountains, tawny in the clear air, lifting rounded flanks above the thick foliage which climbed wherever it could find a foothold. The sky was blue and the sun hot and bright; the whole scene seemed to glitter in its rays. Fa'mata, brown and still, felt that she was the one shadow in that blaze of day.

She breathed her final farewell to this river and this land, perhaps to this sun, and most of all to the girl who had been Kanday Kontay's wife, the girl who had been Fa'mata. She had finished an old life, and would soon begin a new one. She was nobody yet, as she turned to the open hatch and clambered down into the hot darkness of the hold. The next days, weeks, months would mould her anew, but whatever happened, she was going to fight for life, not for herself alone, but for Kanday Kontay's child whom, when her time was fulfilled, she would bear.

chapter five
BANISHED TO THE FIELDS

When his mother had finished her story, a silence fell in the little room, for both mother and son were under the spell of her recital. She was immersed in her memories. Hannibal was stunned by the realization, for the first time, of the other world to which he so nearly belonged. He realized that even if he did not live in Africa, he was still an African, and so were the people he lived among, all except the family in the Big House. His people were Africans and needed to take pride in that fact, and he resolved that he would always do so. As he drifted off to sleep, aspects of his life arranged themselves in his mind: why his mother was so gentle with him, why he had no father or brothers and sisters, and why his mother seemed so alone.

In a way, the two of them had been lucky to have been in Colonel Courtney's care. It was lucky for them that Madam Courtney had asked for a kitchen girl at around that time, and that the Colonel had been in Charles Town on the right day to find her. Even luckier, that he had been struck by some quality in that particular slave girl, a mother-to-be, when he visited the market to look over the cargo fresh from Sierra Leone being auctioned off. It was not easy for him to acquire her, he had had to bid against several others to get her, and paid more than Madam Courtney would have thought reasonable, considering that the girl was "straight from the African bush." Nonetheless, Colonel Courtney had paid the money and brought the girl home, and when Madam Courtney later learned what he had paid she let it go, having decided that Fa'mata (or Hester, as she now was called) was a solid investment.

Hannibal went to sleep with pictures in his head of life in Lokoland, and the determination that if ever a chance came to return to Africa and look for his own folk there, he would take it. And he would take his mother, too.

In the weeks that followed, he and his mother had many evenings together when he had no desire to go to the slave quarters to find companionship, but wanted to hear more about Africa. Then his mother told stories about his father and his ancestors, warriors all; she crooned the songs, familiar from his babyhood, and told the traditional tales of her people. She fired his imagination with the description of a hundred things he had never seen, until Hannibal felt he would recognize Lokoland when he found it, even without hearing a syllable of the Loko tongue for identification.

But waking in the morning from dreams of Africa and finding himself still a slave in Carolina was a shock, like rolling out of bed and landing with a thud on the floor. Sometimes the reminder was particularly sharp; and once it came most cruelly during an exciting moment while on an outing with Adolphus when he completely forgot that he was a chattel, not a real person.

One morning, after helping his mother get the cooking fires lighted in the kitchen and helping the maidservants carry the various good things to the dining room, he was enjoying a quiet moment to eat his bowl of mush and a bit of bacon by the kitchen door when a summons came.

"Hannibal, Hannibal! Come on, you idle hound. I'm going out to shoot some squirrels."

In the weeks since his eleventh birthday, Adolphus had complained to his father with good effect that he was being treated unjustly in the matter of a gun of his own. His birthday present, a few days late, was a rifle, an ordinary "Pennsylvania" type such as every farmer in the colonies owned and used. Colonel Courtney himself had taken Adolphus out for his first lesson on its proper use, and after an hour had pronounced him capable of learning to use it by lots and lots of practice on his own. Several times since then he had taken Hannibal along on expeditions with his brothers.

"Get the bag of shot and come along," said Dolph from the steps of the Big House, and without waiting he came down and started off. Hannibal ran quickly to the gun room, and took the bag which held the gunpowder, greased shot, and spare flints, kept ready for such outings. Fast as he was, Dolph was some distance away when he got back to the steps, and he had to hitch up his leather breeches and run after him. Hannibal dared not call for him to wait or to follow at his own pace. Sometimes the two boys were equals, and the slave boy could take liberties; but sometimes they were clearly master and servant, and this seemed to be one of those days.

Soon the two reached the western edge of the plantation, and followed a trail which led under the great trees festooned with Spanish moss. The first game they spied was a squirrel chattering impudently at them from a low branch. Hannibal saw him first, but Dolph did the shooting. As the flint was struck, the force of the resulting explosion drove the rifle butt into Dolph's shoulder and, although he was expecting the recoil, it knocked him over on his back. Hannibal couldn't restrain a hearty laugh, but as he laughed they both saw the squirrel bound away, unhurt, while a severed leaf fluttering down showed where the bullet had gone.

As he got up, Dolph laughed lightly too, but he did not really think his fall was very funny. After an hour, he was even less pleased. By more luck than skill, he managed to get one squirrel, but he missed several others, and after that the squirrel population of the area must have gone into hiding.

"Let's have a little shooting practice, Hannibal Hoops!" he suggested, or rather, ordered, for Hannibal knew that his part of the practise was to set up the target (this time, a pale stone balanced on three sticks in a wigwam shape) and supply the bullets as needed. Adolphus shot again and again, sometimes lying down, sometimes standing, and the other boy was kept on the hop replacing the target and supplying bullets. Finally Dolph's shoulder was so sore from being kicked by the gun that he decided he'd had enough. Instead he would give Hannibal a short lesson and show him, incidentally, how much shooting a rifle hurt, and how brave he (Dolph) had been all afternoon not to complain.

Hannibal, the chattel, could hardly believe it was happening, but listened carefully as Dolph showed him how to aim, cock, and fire the gun. At last, he was allowed to hold it himself, go through the steps, and shoot. Of course he missed by a wide margin.

"Let me try again," he begged.

"Once more then," said Adolphus.

This time he was lucky: the target stone flew off the wigwam. Hannibal, not pausing to put down the gun, ran forward, laughing loudly with pleasure and excitement, put the stone back in place, and ran back to where Dolph was waiting. For some reason the latter was annoyed. Perhaps Hannibal had been too lucky, or maybe he didn't like him holding onto the rifle after his shot. At any rate, instead of congratulating him on his shooting, he sharply demanded the gun back from Hannibal.

"Oh, please," the other lad begged, "let me try once more." He held the rifle tightly to his chest, reluctant to give it up.

Adolphus lost his temper. "Give it over!" he screamed, pulling on the barrel. "You had your turn. Anyway, you're a slave, remember? I made a mistake when I let you shoot. You're not even supposed to learn how to use a gun unless Papa permits it."

"Wait!" Hannibal begged. "You told me to have a shot. You showed me how! Why are you taking the gun away from me so soon?"

He held on and they wrestled for possession of the rifle. The slave boy was the stronger and had the better grip, and Adolphus couldn't wrest it away from him.

He stood back with a scowl on his face and said, "Well, sir, I know what'll be good for you," turned on his heel, and walked away.

For a few minutes, Hannibal was in a golden haze, and even loaded the rifle and took another shot before the seriousness of his action burst upon him. He had been conditioned to obey Dolph on all matters, big and small, whatever his own feeling were. He had often been beaten, quite often for things Dolph had done; he had patiently borne the blame for some little mischief. But this time Dolph would testify against him, and it was not a matter of a harmless prank but of refusing to give his master his gun. What sort of beating would he get for that?

He snatched up the shot bag and gun and ran towards the plantation. Adolphus, not anxious to show himself at home without the gun, was not walking fast and he soon caught up with him at the edge of the woods.

Panting and miserably afraid Hannibal said, "Here's your gun, Master Dolph."

In tense silence, Dolph took it and they walked home without exchanging another word. At the steps of the Big House they parted, as Adolphus went in and Hannibal, after returning the shot to the gun-room, left the dead squirrel in the kitchen and went to lie face down on the grass at the door. Something horrible would happen, he was sure; he wept silently into his clenched fists.

He must have lain there some hours before he heard the sound of the dinner gong and knew that old Rufus, the butler and general overseer of the household staff, was standing at the foot of the main staircase. Once a day, at about four o'clock, he struck the great bronze gong which hung there with a padded stick, summoning the family to dinner, the big meal of the day, and Hannibal to his corner to work the ceiling fan.

Hannibal didn't want to do it. He didn't stir. A few moments later, his mother looked out of the kitchen and saw him.

"Son, what are you doing there? Rufus says get to the dining room and hurry. Dinner has started. What's wrong, are you sick?"

"I'm all right, Ma," he said, though he did have a peculiar feeling in the pit of his stomach. "I'll go now."

No one took any notice of him during the meal, but when the family had risen and gone out, with Adolphus the last to go, not saying anything but making an ugly face at him, Hannibal was braced for whatever happened next. Before he could leave the room, Rufus put a hand on his head and said. "Well, pickaninny, you have gone too far this time. I've got a message from Colonel Courtney for you. He sent it by me because he doesn't want to see you. Nobody does. You are going to be a field hand now and know what it's like to do real work. Report with the field hands tomorrow morning, prompt."

Without stopping in the kitchen for his own meal, the boy went back to the cabin and brooded.

His mother came at last. She had heard from Rufus of his punishment, though not its cause, and now she heard his account of his crime. Her eyes filled with tears, and she mourned for their situation in her own language.

"My son, my son, with warrior blood in your veins! Can you forgive me that you were born a slave? I should have killed myself rather than see you grow up thus. I could have done so, time and again, on the broad ocean when they brought us up on deck to dance. They did not want us to lose the use of our limbs, and I did not lose mine. I could have danced to the side and leapt over before they could have stopped me. I was selfish. I thought life was too precious to end it that way. I was wrong."

Now the son had to comfort the mother.

"Mammy, it's not so bad. We have had a happy enough life here. I like it most of the time. But Dolph is changing; he is not the same to me as he used to be. He used to forget that I was his servant, and so did I. We were like friends. But now he remembers that he is the master most of the time."

"You are both growing up. Black slaves and white masters cannot be the same sort of friends as little boys of any colour. Soon he will be a man, and he can take his gun and his horse and travel anywhere and meet with respect, while you can go nowhere and do nothing.

"Aiyee, aiyee," she mourned. "Your father would have wept to know his son would be the lowest of the low in this far country. Where is his spirit tonight, where are all the ancestral spirits of our village? There is no one to remember them and sing of their great deeds, none to make the sacrifices and feed them. Aiyee, aiyee!"

"Mother!" the boy scolded, shocked. "Don't say those things. Don't you believe what the preacher says, Mother? That the souls of the dead are in Heaven? He told us we would find them there one day, wearing white gowns and playing on harps."

My mother was shocked in her turn. "Oh no, my son! The ancestor spirits stay around the village, and watch over the living. For us, who have been taken away, it may be different; perhaps we shall be taken to heaven and wear bright robes. I would rather be with the spirits of your father and his ancestors, but when I die can my spirit find its way back across the ocean?"

On this despondent note, she pinched out the pine sliver that did them for a candle and they settled down in silence to a restless night.

Next day at sunup, Hannibal was in the rice fields where the fields gang was busy with the harvest. His arms were sore and his back felt it was breaking by noon, but he had to keep going. Worse than the threat of the whip, which the foreman, a hard-headed Scotsman, carried tucked into his belt, was the abusive language he lavished on the humble slaves. He had indentured himself for fourteen years to get to America, and was filled with a bitterness he had to take out on someone. The defenseless Africans were at his mercy, to be insulted and struck as he pleased, without right of complaint. Hannibal, who had never been subjected to this kind of ceaseless abuse, fell into a deep depression.

For nearly two weeks, he worked in the fields, stumbling to bed every night half-dead from weariness, until one night his mother delivered a message of hope.

"They say you've been out in the fields long enough. They miss you in the house, and they think you've learned your lesson. So tomorrow it will be just like it was before, and you can forget all about the hard work in the fields."

"Who told you?"

"Rufus gave me the message."

"I won't!" the boy cried. "How can it be like it was before? I will go to the field, even if I die there. They won't win me back so easily! Dolph has got lonely and wants me around for company again. Does he think we can play games together as if this never happened? Who does he think I am?"

"Not *who*, my son, but *what*, and the answer is that he knows you are his servant, and that he holds your fate in his hands. If you do go into the field tomorrow, you will be beaten. Hard!"

Hannibal broke down from tiredness and frustration.

"Oh Ma," he sobbed, "What can I do?"

His mother took him and cuddled him in her arms as if he were a baby again. After a fortnight of having to be hard and tough, he was suddenly soft and helpless, and she rocked him back and forth on the edge of the bed, singing an old Loko lullaby from her own childhood. Gradually he became calm, and she spoke softly abut the hardships in her own life, reminding him that even when her body was in chains, they had not been able to break her spirit.

"We must bend with the wind when it blows strongly enough to break us," she said. "When it passes, we can stand straight again. Do not brood on the evil done to you, and forgive those who treat you badly. Do what Master Adolphus asks; you have no choice. The more willingly you do it, the easier it will be for you. I know."

He realized that she was wise and that her advice was good. For his own sake, and for her's, he had to survive.

"Ma, I swear to you, I won't always be a slave. I am going to be a free man some day, and if I can I'll go to Africa. And if I do, I want to take you with me. I promise it."

His mother started in astonishment. "Kanday-son! Haven't you understood what I've been saying? We can never dream of going back to Africa, because we are slaves and we'll always be slaves! Haven't you learnt that during these last weeks in the fields? Just because you've been a little boy up to now, the Courtney family have made a pet out of you, but as you get older they may very likely get tired of you. Before you are full-grown, it's likely you'll be put out in the fields for good."

"They may do what they like. I will never forget that my father would have been a king in Lokoland. Someday I will go there and maybe I shall be a king, too. Perhaps if I pray, God will help me."

"Right, my son. You pray to the white man's God, and I will take a white rooster and sacrifice it at Old Pompey's secret shrine. Perhaps the spirits here will help us, or send word to the spirits of Lokoland, and one day you may be a free man and a prince in our own country."

A silence ensued, as mother and son really had nothing more to say on the subject, and soon they settled down to sleep. She evidently realized that it was useless to argue her son out of his hope, extreme though it was. The boy himself thought that hope would be as strong a strengthening of his spirit as any of her white roosters, but he did not say it.

chapter six
POLITICAL TALK

Despite his defiant feelings, next morning Hannibal was back at his old routine, waiting on Dolph and attentive to his work of fanning the dining room at meal times, but days passed before his helpless rage was subdued. Often he ground his teeth in silence when he really wanted to scream his anger at Dolph. Never again was he given a chance to use the rifle. He felt unwilling to give Dolph the deference he seemed to want, but he felt that as a consequence Dolph mistrusted him. Perhaps, he thought, Dolph, like all masters, believed he would rebel if ever he got the chance. Hannibal thought maybe he would rebel, if ever a real opportunity came along.

On Ellenboro Plantation, the September harvest was good. By Christmas, it was all threshed and cleaned and ready to be shipped, and Colonel Courtney was happy. As always, ships came up the main creek to be loaded with rice from the storehouses, but they were flying strange flags and not the English flag Hannibal knew. This, as was made clear by Colonel Courtney at the dinner table, was because South Carolina, by decision of its Assembly, was in rebellion against the King, and so trade with the Mother Country was officially at a standstill.

This fact didn't disturb daily life. The only real difference was that most of the sailors who came ashore had difficulty in being understood, since they were not English. Now the ships were coming from the foreign islands of the West Indies under Dutch or Spanish flags, and returned there with the rice. It wasn't eaten there, but loaded onto other ships for passage across the ocean. The same ships brought goods from over the ocean to the rich people of Carolina, goods from France and Italy and Holland, so they had no complaints. As for the poor people, it made little difference for them, too.

Plantation life, which Hannibal was now old enough to notice, revolved around the seasons. As the seasons turned, and especially at the Christmas season or in the hottest part of the summer, he might be away with the Courtney family. But otherwise, particularly in the spring and autumn, he was with them at Ellenboro. He was a big boy now, and was often called on to give a few free hours to help out. Through the spring there was plenty of planting to be done - first the sweet potatoes and the corn that would feed everybody, then in April the rice fields had to be made ready. Most of the men, women, and older children were involved in the effort to get a good crop of rice for the plantation, their welfare, as well as that of the Courtney family depended on it. So they began by wading in the soft mud of the swamp fields. Every weed growing there had to be pulled, then deep furrows were made by the men and the women followed and scattered the rice seed.

As the rice plants shot up and grew, they had to be kept well watered and there were ponds connected to the fields by ditches. When the water was needed, certain trusted men opened a wooden gate into the ditch and the water flowed through freely and filled up the furrows. When the rice had lots of water around it, the men shut the gate again until it was needed again.

There were plenty of weeds growing among the rice plants as the season passed and all hands had to go in and grub them out of the soft mud and work at it knee-deep. It was hard, miserable work and Hannibal was glad he was still too small to be doing it. However, it might be his future, unless some kind of miracle intervened.

As the months trickled by, the Courtneys, like the other rich planter families, followed a well-established pattern of movement, and the household, now at last including Hannibal and his mother, normally went with them. For Christmas and January, they went to Charles Town, where Colonel Courtney owned a fine house. During the fresh months of spring, they were back at Ellenboro, seeing that the rice was properly started, and then for the hot months, till the first frosts of autumn, they moved to the pine-covered hills inland. Lots of other families, many of them kinfolk, came there from Charles Town and tidewater. They all lived a simple healthy life in their cottages. The Courtney's house in the woods was called "Old Pine." Here the nights were cool and dry, and the Courtney family and their guests escaped the swamp-bred sicknesses, malaria and yellow fever, which ravaged the lowlands in the hot weather.

Hannibal had not understood all those yearly movements in his young days. He just knew that the Courtneys were sometimes at Ellenboro and sometimes were not. He found out about these movements when finally he was considered old enough to be admitted to the household and go with them on their annual round. He had always expected to be sick at times during the summers, but found out, to his amazement, that there was no law of nature that decreed it. When he went to the mountains with the family, he didn't suffer the usual sicknesses, which was quite a miracle in his eyes.

There was another type of fever, political fever, that could not be evaded, even there, and that he only came to understand years later when he was much older and thought back to that early part of his life. The fever of political opinions, warmly held and argued, made divisions even in the Courtney household.

Although Colonel Courtney maintained good relations with the colonial government which controlled South Carolina but proclaimed itself independent of Great Britain, he had been educated in England, and had many attachments of principle and sentiment to the monarchical and aristocratic regime there. Probably that was natural for a man who owned slaves and was rich because of their labour. More to the point, he was not in favour of allowing the backwoodsmen of Carolina to be equal in politics to himself and his friends. He and the other gentlemen of the tide-water country were accustomed to ruling their land under the indulgent sway of a governor sent from England.

They feared the rough men of the back country, clannish and intolerant immigrants coming largely from Scotland and Northern Ireland, who showed no respect for their betters in the older settled areas of South Carolina. They were too dangerous to be allowed power, even if the royal governor had to give it up.

Colonel Courtney's eldest son, Clifford, claimed to be a complete Royalist, partly because he believed it was a part of his inheritance. The first Courtney to come to America, in the time of Cromwell, had been an indentured servant; Clifford insisted that he was one of the Cavaliers, taken prisoner while fighting for King Charles, the martyr whose head had been chopped off. The younger son, Fred, on the other hand, was proud of this same ancestor for a different reason, because from the humblest beginnings of temporary slavery, he had become a rich and respected planter. In his mind, the Courtneys owed King George nothing; they were a self-made family and should support an independent Carolina and America.

Although the two older Courtney boys had been in England for part of their education, they had been mainly taught at home by a young Anglican clergyman. He had recently returned to Europe on a Dutch ship, taking his pay in the form of tobacco which he hoped to smuggle into England. If he succeeded, he would be well paid for his years in Carolina.

He had given the boys a good and liberal education, with a love for reading and argument. They used these faculties in their frequent discussions, to which Hannibal listened carefully in an effort to understand what was happening in the world and why. Some things were said over and over again in their arguments, as when Clifford said that King George had ceased to be an ordinary man when he was anointed with the sacred oil at his coronation. A certain divinity had descended from Heaven upon him at that moment which demanded respect and obedience from his subjects. Fred ridiculed such a belief.

"If you would read what Tom Paine wrote," he said, "you would soon drop such fantastic ideas. If George III had not been born where he was, he would be an ordinary farmer or tradesman, and perhaps not a successful one at that. Read *Common Sense* and you will learn how ridiculous it is for intelligent men to be ruled by kings."

"There have always been kings," retorted Clifford, "and if this rebellion succeeds, then there will be a king here. Without a king, we are in the position of the ancient Israelites, who were in a state of confusion and weakness until Samuel anointed Saul and set him up over them. So it will be here. If they succeed in throwing off King George, they will find another king; perhaps one of the royal dukes will come over."

"Paine says that what we want is a republic, like the Athenians had—have you forgotten them?—or the ancient Romans."

"I remember, and Oliver Cromwell gave England one of the same. And all these republics turned into tyrannies, sooner or later, and reduced the citizens to slavery."

Fred, getting angry, began to resort to violent words rather than calm argument. "Better that kind of tyranny, where a good man makes his own way to the top as Oliver Cromwell did, than the tyranny we have now where a fat double-chinned nobody sits on the throne and lords it over men better than he, just because his grandfather was king before him."

"King George is not a tyrant. He is a constitutional monarch who works with parliament, which represents the interests of the whole Empire," protested Clifford. "I am not arguing that George III is a better tyrant than George Washington or Thomas Jefferson would be. I am saying that every man's freedom is safer under a system of laws and a constitution in which a man of ordinary capacity, which King George might be, is monarch, than under a free-for-all situation where men are cutting each other's throats to get to the top of the heap, and when they are there rule with a rod of iron so cunningly that they cannot be shaken off."

Many such arguments the brothers had without coming to an agreement, and Hannibal, often in their company in the woods, or waiting to be useful in the house, pondered over them without being able to make up his mind over which he favoured. Certainly as the son of a line of kings, he liked the idea of kings, but in his present state of servitude he liked the idea of freedom and equality. Because Clifford treated him more kindly than Fred, and because he still pinned his hopes of freedom on the theory expounded by Jupiter Brown, that the British would offer it, he hoped, on the whole, for a British victory and the quelling of the rebellion. But not too soon. Not until he was a little older.

Often in his dreams he found himself in an African home, where he was no more called Hannibal Hoops, but was Kanday Kontay. In that land, everyone was a dark and chocolate colour, as he was, and white men looked like pale and insubstantial ghosts. There it was not the African man who was laughed at because of his colour; it was the white man for whom the people had offensive nicknames. He liked those dreams.

He had other dreams, too, in which he was fighting, with a musket at his shoulder, and other men, all in uniform, standing beside him. In those dreams he was a fighter for freedom. Not "freedom" in a political way, as Master Frederick used the word, but freedom from masters who owned African men's body and (they believed) soul.

That was the year 1778 running its course. The elder Courtney brothers saw many young men of their own age, relatives and friends, take off to the north to join one or another of the opposing forces. They, however, obeyed their father's wishes to stay out of it, and busied themselves at home. Clifford, who was good at mathematics, worked for some months with a local surveyor and then, in the company of his personal servant, Jim, went around the country finding plenty of opportunity to exercise his skill. He found it very interesting to travel through new districts and to get to know the whole province better, but, as a convinced "Loyalist" (or Tory, as some termed it), he sometimes found it hard to keep on amiable terms with the outspoken "rebels" he met. Fred did not travel; he was interested in plantation work, and his father gave him responsibilities enough to keep him busy. As for Adolphus, he enjoyed an idle life with no lessons, and when the family was at Ellenboro Plantation, he depended very much on Hannibal for companionship.

The quiet nature of existence in the Carolinas began to change with an event which took place at the end of December 1778, though it was several weeks before the news of it reached Charles Town, where the family was spending the Christmas season. News came that the British fleet had appeared before Savannah, in Georgia, and had driven the American General Howe out of the town. Great was the jubilation of certain young-bloods of pro-British sentiment, and many a pair of them took horse and gun and rode south to offer their services to Colonel Campbell, the British commander there. He gave them a hearty welcome, as it turned out, and found them useful as scouts.

"At last," Clifford told his family, "the British army is beginning to set a proper value on loyal American manpower."

Unhappily, not all the young Loyalists heading south reached Savannah. Some accounts were being heard in Charles Town of groups of them meeting hostility on the road, being attacked, captured, and tried for high treason by bands of rebels. It was the beginning of civil war in both the Carolinas.

Again Hannibal had gone to Charles Town with the Courtneys for Christmas, and was wildly excited when he heard that the British army, now under General Prevost, might come that way very soon. He desperately wanted to know whether they were bringing "the Jubilee" with them or not, and one day, a few weeks after the taking of Savannah, he stole out of the yard and went straight to the workshop of Jupiter Brown's master. He was in luck, for Jupiter was there at work and his master was away. Timidly, he reminded Jupiter of what he had said at Ellenboro on the night of the feast.

"Is it coming true?" he asked.

Jupiter laid down his chisel and a wide smile opened up on his face.

"It is, son, it is. Black folks are looking for something good to happen soon. Those closest to Savannah are running away from their masters and going to General Prevost. Those far off, like ourselves, will wait until the British army gets here. We wouldn't get far if we tried to run away to Savannah just now, when even white men get stopped. But just wait! Another few months and we'll have our chance at liberty, too."

"But are the British really good to slaves like us?" the boy asked, wondering whether African people were not in danger of jumping out of a frying pan and into a fire. In recent weeks, he had heard much in the streets about British tyranny and treachery, as the South Carolina government tried to whip up support in the face of the British advance, that he found it hard to preserve a particle of hope.

"We have our ways of knowing what is going on at the British camp," said Jupiter, "and the word is that any slave who goes there is not turned away. It is true that General Prevost has not formed our people into a corps of "Black Pioneers," like Lord Dunmore did at Norfolk in '75, but it will come if we keep our faith strong."

That news cheered Hannibal and he went home happy, resolved to keep his faith strong. When he got the chance, he visited Jupiter again, to discuss the rumours that came his way and to feed his hopes. Within a few weeks, the skinny boy and the big man had become good friends, and the boy had an open invitation to come in the evenings to visit him and his family in their quarters.

chapter seven
THE END OF AN ERA

Naturally the Courtney family were as much interested in the possibility of a British advance as their enslaved workers, and there were loud quarrels between the two older sons, Clifford and Frederick, as British forces advanced and retreated. They exchanged hot-headed words again and again over the several weeks of Christmas, and both hoped that the new year, 1779, would settle things one way or the other.

"I wish General Prevost would march this way without losing a moment," declared Clifford. "He would find recruits everywhere; his army would triple in size in no time and drive every rebel out."

"What nonsense! That is simply not so," objected his brother. "The people are for change and it will come."

"How would you know?" queried the other. "You haven't been out of your own little territory. My work has taken me to all parts of the two Carolinas this past year, and I would judge from everything I heard that only the small minority are for the rebellion."

"Perhaps that is true, but are the majority willing to fight about it? Won't they just stay quietly at home until the matter is all settled? Or if the British come through and steal some chickens, entice all the slaves away and insult wives, won't they change their minds? Or what if a full-scale slave mutiny breaks out? That's what the British are encouraging."

"I don't believe that," said his brother. "What evidence have you for saying that?"

"No evidence yet, but I'm suspicious."

Very soon, the comparatively peaceful life of South Carolina was shattered, if only briefly. The Courtney household was back on the Plantation when, a few weeks into the New Year, General Prevost did appear before Charles Town. Although he had many sympathizers in the city, there were also numerous troops of the Continental Army (rebels) and militia there, and the fortifications were stronger than he'd expected. He therefore drew back slowly to St. John's Island and later by sea to Savannah, taking back with him many recruits.

There was no way for anyone at the plantation to join his force. Colonel Courtney kept a close watch on all his household, for he did not want anyone belonging to him to be committed to either side, so long as it could be avoided.

Months passed and Hannibal's life did not change. Then, in early September, while he and the whole Courtney family were coming to the end of their happy days at Old Pine, his life was painfully put on a new track.

It began innocently enough as a rather perfect morning, slightly autumnal because of a vague sensation of golden ripeness in the air. Hannibal was finishing breakfast with a bit of hoe-cake when Adophus whistled for him and, before he could respond, came around the corner and caught him unawares.

"Hannibal, get your knife and things, get a move on, we're going fishing." It was a command, not an invitation, and Hannibal, pausing only to shout "Yessir," ran to the hollow tree where the two boys stashed their valuables. From it, he took a knife, twine, and a couple of copper hooks, and popped them into a little satchel.

Back at the kitchen, he picked up a small spade he had whittled from a piece of hardwood, and going over to the edge of the woodpile where the bare ground was exposed, he turned over the soft moist soil. In a minute, he had exposed a dozen or so plump worms, which he folded in a burdock leaf and tucked into a woven basket. Then he put the spade back in its hiding place, picked up the kitchen hatchet, and was ready to follow the impatient Master Adolphus for a day of sport.

With a confident stride, Dolph led the way through the woods, along a path hugging a ridge shaded and cooled by lofty pines. For most of the way, the boys walked on a soft carpet of pine needles. Then the path left the ridge and they followed it down a bank of splintered blue shale. Their destination was down below, where a clear mountain stream boiled its way forward, leaping from pool to pool and over shallow banks of sand until it vanished out of sight among the bushes. Somehow, over time, it found its way around every obstacle until it leapt for a last fling into the mighty Santee River, and along the lowlands of Carolina into the timeless ocean.

Today, Adolphus and Hannibal were not interested in where the river went or how it did it. They had their minds on tempting the greedy catfish, lurking in cool pools, to stir themselves into taking the juicy bait on their hooks. How everyone would appreciate it if they caught some fat ones for the cooks to broil or fry and serve up as the delicacy of the day! Every now and then, Dolph or one of his brothers, or all of them together and Hannibal with them, would go to a favourite stream and bring home a mess of catfish.

When they reached the pool, Dolph took his hatchet and cut down a pair of suitable poles, while Hannibal spread out the twine, cut two lines, fastened the hooks to them, and then, as each pole was ready, trimmed it and tied a line on. All that remained was to bait the hooks, and each did his own, selecting from the spread-out burdock leaf the most delectable looking worms.

They fished for a while in the first pool, and had no luck.

"Stay here, Hannibal," ordered Dolph. "I'm going to try up at number three pool."

For another hour, Hannibal stayed where he was. He caught two small catfish, which he kept, and a number of tiny minnows, which he tossed back. Suddenly he heard a noise that alerted him to something wrong. He tensed, his pulse raced—there had been a small sharp cry from above, beyond number three pool! He put down his rod and bounded up the rocks along the watercourse.

Beyond the next pool, he found his young master. Adolphus must have screamed from surprise and fear when he felt himself slipping from the moss-covered rocks somewhere up the eighteen foot fall from number four pool. He lay crumpled at the bottom, with the veil of water falling softly over him. Hannibal went to him and gently touched him. He was dead.

Years later, he saw that this moment marked the end of his childhood, in a way his mother had not foreseen. When he carried the news to the family, he encountered all the blame that messengers of bad news seem to incur. Madam Courtney would not even look at him, not then and not later. It was not simply that he had brought the bad news, but also because he had been Dolph's companion and should have protected him. She seemed to blame him directly for the death of her youngest child.

The Colonel himself told Hester that on no account was Hannibal to show himself to the mistress; he feared that to his wife the bitterness of seeing him safe and sound would bring on hysterics or a fit.

Adolphus was buried beneath the pines, and Hannibal was immediately sent back to Ellenboro with Frederick when he returned there for a scheduled inspection. Once back on the plantation, he was put to work as a field hand and there he really learned to do the hard work of harvesting, cutting the rice stalks as tall as himself with sickles, and laying them out to dry. Then he and the others made them up into bundles, which they carried on their heads to where the oxcarts and oxen were patiently waiting. When the carts were piled high, the oxen dragged them to the threshing yard near the Big House.

Hannibal wasn't put to the work of threshing; he wasn't big and strong enough. It took full-grown men to beat the rice off the stalks with their flails. A flail was a three-foot leather strap fastened to a three-foot length of wooden handle. A couple of threshers would lash the stalks in turn with these whips, at a fast regular beat, until the grain lay on the ground and the empty stalks were forked away.

That was not the end of it. There were husks to get off, two of them on each kernel of rice. The first was got off by a kind of mill, which was fairly easy, but the other was stubborn and could only be cleaned off by using a big mortar (as high as a man's waist) and a heavy pestle, a shaped piece of wood a yard long.

Hannibal's mother and the others who came from Sierra Leone were very familiar with the cleaning of the rice, because they had grown up doing this work in their homeland. It wasn't such a chore there, because they only cleaned enough for a meal at a time, and didn't wear themselves out. But Colonel Courtney and the other planters in South Carolina wanted to see fifty pounds of cleaned rice from every worker every day. Usually it was men they put to work with the mortar and pestle, though the women would have done a better job. The men could work longer and harder, but they broke a lot of the rice grains with their pounding and then there was a lot of anger and even whippings because those broken grains couldn't be sold. However that broken rice was given out to the hands and people were glad to eat rice for a change.

Even after that stage was over, the job wasn't done. The chaff had to be got rid of by the use of a fanner. This was not a kind of fan despite the name; at least, it didn't make a breeze, though it took advantage of one. A fanner was a very shallow basket, saucer shaped, woven by the women. They dipped a couple of handfuls of the mixed rice and chaff out of the big pestles and into the fanner, and tossed the heap gently into the air. They tossed the rice into the breeze again and again until the chaff all blew away and all that was left in the basket was the golden rice. Very likely, this method was brought from Sierra Leone also. For a rice plantation owner, it was a great objective to obtain slaves from Sierra Leone, where rice was a staple and its cultivation and preparation well understood. Colonel Courtney had been lucky in his early years to get a dozen adult workers from up-country Sierra Leone, and they had shared their knowledge and techniques with the other hands.

Hannibal remained at the Quarters week after week while the family came home and went again following their established custom. He had no reason to be around the Big House and took care not to be for fear Madam Courtney would catch a glimpse of him. At Christmastime, they were all off as usual to Charles Town, and for the first time in some years he did not accompany them. He scarcely knew that they had gone, for he was kept busy by the foreman in all sorts of jobs. Perhaps the foreman wanted him to make up for the easy years he had enjoyed; at any rate, he found work for the boy, now twelve years old, from morning to night, and whenever he thought Hannibal deserved a beating, it was laid on well. His mother had gone with the family, of course, and while she was away, he lived all alone in her cabin.

These were hard times, but there were some lighter moments. Christmas and New Year's were celebrated in the slaves' quarters with bonfires, dancing, and a special allowance of food. This was exciting, different at least from the festive times in Charles Town, but the novelty was not enough to make Hannibal happy.

One night, late in January (of 1780), Hannibal was trying to sleep, while brooding over the beatings he had received and thinking of how much he hated the foreman. He missed his mother, who would have listened to him and given him the comfort only a mother could give. He got out of bed and wandered towards the kitchen, as if he might find her or something of her presence there. As he got close to the Big House, he saw that there was a light on upstairs—but why? If the family had returned, there would have been a great deal of noise and a big turn-out of the hands, with yelling and shouting. Perhaps the watchmen were in the house, doing things they shouldn't. Hoping to catch them in the act, Hannibal went around to the front of the house. The great front door was open. He quietly crept up the front steps and looked through the open door into the great front hall.

Clomp! Clomp! Down the stairs came the slim figure of a white man.

"Who's there?" he cried as his candle showed Hannibal wide-eyed at the door. It was Master Clifford. He came over, relieved as he recognized the boy. "Oh, it's you, Hannibal. I was just about to come looking for you. I'm leaving, boy, going to war. How would you like to come with me? I don't suppose you are of much use here, and I need someone."

Hannibal was dumbfounded for a moment, then asked, "But, sir, what about Jim?" referring to Clifford's own bodyservant and houseboy.

"Sick in Charles Town; fever," said Clifford. "Very bad, I had to leave him."

"I'll come with you, sir," said the boy, as if he had been waiting for this chance. He thought quickly. He had nothing to lose by leaving the plantation, and perhaps much to gain by getting away. He had no knowledge of Clifford's intentions, but he felt that an adventure lay ahead, and was so excited by it that he forgot about sleep and put his troubles from his mind. He hoped he would not need to think about them again.

That night, he helped Clifford pack several saddlebags of what he considered necessities and put his remaining things in order. Then he packed his own meagre belongings. Early the next morning, the two started out on three horses, Clifford on his favourite, Hannibal on his second animal, and a third, tied to the second, carrying their baggage. The servants who saw them off supposed that they were going to Charles Town, and although they may have suspected that something unusual was happening, it was not their place to question their master's eldest son or to refuse to obey his orders.

As they rode along inland, Clifford, carried away by tension and excitement, talked to Hannibal occasionally as if he had to confide in someone. He explained what lay behind his decision to defy his father and go to war. "I'm over twenty-one, Hannibal, and responsible for my own actions. I'm not content to sit aside and let other people decide the fate of my country. These foreign Englishmen and more foreign Germans in the British army have no real interest in what happens to America, so it is really up to Americans to fight for the government they want. I can't hold up my head any longer unless I show my true colours and fight openly for my beliefs." The boy listened, only partly understanding his motives, but made no comment. It was not his affair at that point to do anything but obey his orders and stay out of trouble; mainly Hannibal was intent on reaching the British army to see if it really would bring the Jubilee, the day of freedom. He was not concerned, just then, with Clifford's politics and philosophy.

"We will ride toward Savannah slowly," Clifford said, "and I will say I'm a surveyor looking for work. If I am offered any jobs, I'll have to take 'em on. Let's hope there's no great need for surveyors in Georgia. Whatever happens, it is important that you back up my story. We don't need to change our names, but we'd better say we're from the hill country, and that we haven't much money."

Thus it was that, as January 1780 drew to a close, Hannibal Hoops was drawn into the thick of the war which, from small beginnings five years before, had grown into a mighty international conflict. As he and his master were to learn, it grew still greater until it seemed that Great Britain and all of Europe were at war. It became a war affecting the every continent, and the fighting in the American colonies was only a small part of the struggle. It was a war that changed the world and many lives with it.

chapter eight
WITH THE ARMY

As it turned out, Clifford did not have to ride all the way to Savannah to find the British forces. When the two riders were about three days on their way, having kept well inland to bypass Charles Town, and then having turned east again to the coast, they encountered a despatch rider of the Continental Army going north at a furious speed. He had no time to stop and gossip, but as he passed on the narrow road, he called out "Watch out for the British!"

At the next posting house they reached, in the centre of a small hamlet, they found great excitement. The messenger had changed horses and snatched a bite there, and between mouthfuls had shared the startling news he was carrying to General Lincoln at Charles Town. A powerful British force, both cavalry and infantry, was now disembarking not far away, on the coast of Georgia.

Clifford was relieved to realize that he would see a friendly army sooner than expected. He led Hannibal and the horses southward without any waste of time, and on February 7, at Tybee, in Georgia, came on the British encampment. The harbour there was full of anchored transports, which were being unloaded without cessation by an endless series of small boats.

Clifford made his business known to the sentry and was directed to General Clinton's headquarters. He left Hannibal to guard the horses just outside. When he introduced himself as Colonel Courtney's son, and as a trained surveyor who had been all over the Carolinas and moreover knew Charles Town well, the General himself made him welcome. Clifford took an instant liking to the pudgy-nosed little man who familiarly put a hand on his shoulder and steered him into his planning room, where across a large table were pinned maps of Georgia, South and North Carolina, and of the city upon which he was about to advance.

"From Charles Town, eh Mr. Courtney? Well, you'll soon be back there again. This time Charles Town has to be taken; then we will see large parts of the South come over to us. Now let's have a good look at the map. What do we face here, and there?" For half an hour, Clifford discussed the state of defence of the town and the amount of opposition to be expected from the Continental soldiers within its walls.

When he had finished the briefing, General Clinton said, "Now, sir, that I've made a start at picking your brains, what would you like from me?"

"A commission, sir, in one of your American regiments."

"Ha—a commission, eh? Any experience in war?"

"No, sir, but I've been shooting and riding since childhood."

"Haven't we all, Mr. Courtney? That, we take for granted in an officer. But you seem to have experience in the terrain, which few of us have; I think you might be very useful to Ferguson's Rangers or to Tarleton's Legion. Any preference?"

"No, sir."

"I tell you what, until we take Charles Town you shall have a roving commission to observe and recruit, reporting directly to me." Calling to his *aide-de-camp*, he said, "Oliver, enroll Ensign Courtney on my personal staff, temporary status, and see that he is outfitted decently. You do have your own horse, I hope, Mr. Courtney?"

"Yes, sir, three."

"Capital! Horses are our big problem right now, we lost so many during the terrible storms we came through on the way down from New York."

This was the gist of their conversation, and while they were talking Hannibal was waiting with the three horses and looking around for signs of runaway slaves. He couldn't see any. All the colourful uniforms were worn by white men, not black or even of a dusky shade, and as they rushed by him about their business they showed no signs of being interested in his condition or fate. By the time Clifford came back to him, Hannibal had decided that he had better keep his eyes and ears open and his mouth shut and should forget about being his own master for the time being.

Within a few days, he looked more as if he were part of the army; not exactly a uniformed soldier, but the next best thing. Clifford had him outfitted with a plain jacket of the same shade as the fine dark green uniform with silver buttons of the Provincial Corps. That was the uniform Clifford put on, and Hannibal had to keep the uniform clean and the buttons polished. Soon he felt quite at home in the army, and began to recognize the insignia of rank, the identifying badges and accessories of the various units, and could guess who was who.

When reinforcements arrived from Savannah, he was cheered to see that there were many African men in the army after all, and the longer they waited at Tybee, the more the runaways who flocked to it. Clifford, thinking perhaps that his family's wealth was based on the labour of slaves, was not pleased with the friendly reception they were given and spoke his mind without regard to who might hear.

In fact, Hannibal heard him say to a brother officer: "Surely the general isn't going to hand out guns to all these Negroes. They could desert and form an independent army on their own, terrorizing the countryside. If that happens, people certainly will lose interest in helping the King's forces."

"No, no," said his friend. "We won't give them guns, though that's what the rebels have been doing up North. We've got plenty of picks and shovels, saws and hammers to keep them busy. That gives our soldiers a chance to learn to use their guns to best advantage."

"But what's in it for the slaves?" asked Clifford, still puzzled. "What do they hope to gain by running away from their homes and coming here?"

"Where have you been these past months, Courtney? Didn't you know that General Clinton issued a proclamation that since the rebels were enlisting Negroes we would have to do the same, and that all slaves who ran away from rebel masters would be treated like free men once they reached our lines?"

"'Treated like free men'? What does that mean? Are they or aren't they free?"

"Well, while this war is on they certainly are free, as much as any enlisted man of any race can be said to be free in the army."

"And after?"

"They think we won't send them back into slavery when it's all over, and I hope they're right."

Clifford had mixed feelings about this information, but Hannibal was happy, because it tended to feed his hope that someday there would be a freedom for he himself to claim.

In the months that followed, he found it easy to forget that he was a slave. Every army officer had a personal servant, white or black, but they were not regarded as slaves. If it had not been for the fact that Hannibal was a Courtney slave by law, and bound to Clifford by shared memories and the place of his mother with the Courtney family, he could almost have thought he was his own master. He might have tried to run away to Savannah with some fanciful story of a brutal rebel master, but for the feeling it would have been dishonourable to begin life as a free man that way. Gradually, as he saw more of Clifford than ever he had on the plantation, he developed a real affection for him and was no longer tempted to leave him. Clifford never lost his temper or beat him, as some of the other officers did to their servants, but rather always treated him with consideration and kindness. Hannibal had no complaints about his master or about life in the army.

Hannibal was behind Clifford when, with the rest of the army, they stood on the bank of the Ashley River, looking over to Charles Town and saw the defenders make the mistake of withdrawing their vessels upstream, thus allowing a flotilla of British frigates to cut the city off on two sides. When Clifford rode in a joint action by Ferguson's Rangers and Tarleton's Legion to Biggin's Bridge on the Cooper, where rebel cavalry guarded Charles Town's communication to the north, he left his boy behind, but when the troops came back he told him about the capture of the rebel stores, horses and prisoners, and praised Ferguson who treated prisoners and civilians gently, unlike the men of the Legion who used brutal methods to wring out information, and greedily plundered the property of both friend and foe.

The rebel forces in Charles Town desperately resisted their fate, putting every slave they could find to work on the defences. The British trenches and guns came closer and closer, pushed by thousands of other shovel-wielding slaves hired from loyal planters of the country around. On the May 9, the city surrendered, and Hannibal rode behind Clifford in the midst of the Rangers as they paraded with the rest of the army through the silent streets. Clifford took charge of his father's house, empty save for a couple of frightened servants, and offered his hospitality to Major Ferguson. This was, if nothing else, one way of making sure that drunken soldiers didn't break in and wreck the place.

From the governor's mansion, the British commander, General Clinton, made a proclamation warning the rich men of the Carolinas that their estates would be taken away from them if they did not return to their allegiance to the king forthwith. He also called on all loyal citizens to form a militia which would preserve order as the army moved on. This prompted people to show their true colours, and a few days later Clifford was sad to hear that his brother Fred had gone to join the Continental Army of the rebel cause.

"Just think," he said to Hannibal, "Fred and I may find ourselves face to face one day, trying to kill each other even though we've always been the closest of friends. War is a terrible thing at best, but most of all when it pits brother against brother, as this one does."

Many people took advantage of Clinton's invitation to declare themselves Loyalists, and although the General realized that some of them were probably "fair weather friends," he hoped that the British successes in the field would keep them firmly on the right side.

Hannibal was jubilant as he shared in the triumph of the British forces, and as he walked about in his neat outfit he was thrilled by the respect paid him by the hundreds of ragged Africans who appeared in the streets. Many asked for help in finding General Clinton, and it transpired that they had run away from their masters on hearing the news that Charles Town had surrendered. Hannibal even saw a familiar face from Ellenboro, an older youth who said that a number of young and active slaves had run away. Hannibal was concerned for him and his friends. He felt he had to warn him of possible trouble.

"The British Army won't take you. Master Clifford is here, and very friendly with the general. They are not going to rob his father of property by setting you all free."

"Then we'll keep out of Master Clifford's sight. We'll say we ran away from someone else," replied the runaway.

But Clifford soon heard, though not from his own boy, that some of the family slaves had arrived in Charles Town and had been received by the army. He went to the officers in charge of this duty and registered a complaint. "My father is not a rebel," he told them, "and furthermore I am his heir, being his eldest son, and the estate being entailed, and if these runaway slaves are not made to go home I, a Loyalist, shall have been robbed."

His complaint was brought to General Clinton's attention and he issued a public statement calculated to encourage rich planters to declare for the king. He said that all slaves who had run away from Loyalist owners would be returned, so long as they were not to be punished. Or if the owners preferred, they could rent the slaves to the army and receive compensation if they happened to be killed. As for slaves running away from rebel masters, they would be neither sent back nor leased, but would be given food, clothing, and pay for their services while the war lasted, and their freedom when it ended.

"I don't like this at all," said Clifford aloud when he read the broadsheet relaying the General's decision to the public. "I am completely against having slaves as part of our army. You don't know," he said to an English friend standing nearby, "how dangerous these slaves can be when they get stirred up. And we never allow them to have weapons." That remark hit home on Hannibal, standing nearby, remembering how a gun had led to his disgrace and suffering. To himself he muttered of his pain that Clifford had never even thought of him when he made that remark. An African boy, even though he was standing nearby, was quite disregarded by the white men. He was a mere piece of furniture in their eyes. Well, that was life for African people, he thought. He already knew it and would learn it better in the years to come.

"What are you afraid of them doing?" asked Major Ferguson, who was in the vicinity and joined him. "I guarantee that with British officers in charge of them, they'll be better disciplined and less destructive to property than the ragtag Continental Army of the rebels."

"But what if they encourage a slave rising?" asked Clifford. "They would kill people treacherously without asking whether they had been kind or cruel to them; they would get drunk and commit atrocious deeds on innocent people. Remember that they are Africans really, even if born here, and they know how to torment and torture people in ways we can't even guess at."

"My dear fellow! What do you know about this war that's been raging in these colonies for the past few years? White men torturing and killing white men, white men massacring red skins and red skins massacring settlers… I think if you had been on campaigns with me, you would agree that nothing more horrible could come out of Africa than what we white people, we British and you colonials, have created and moulded right here in America. Moreover, the rebels are enlisting blacks in their regiments now, and have been doing so for some time, I understand."

Clifford did know about it, and had clear ideas on that, too.

"Yes, the rebels do have blacks in their regiments, but that's a way up north where things are entirely different from our Southern ways. Our rebel governments here have had sense enough to refuse to do it. Only last year John Laurens, who should know better, being from a planter family, came down to try to talk people into it. His father is the president of the Congress, you know... in other words, he heads up the rebel government, insofar as there is one. Anyway, he brought the message from Congress that South Carolina should raise a force of three thousand slave soldiers. Our legislature, even if it is a rebel one, knew better than to agree to that, and refused absolutely to think of it. The legislature in Georgia said the same thing. We in these southern colonies agree that this war concerns white men only, and our servants should be left out of it."

"I say" he concluded, "that the General is wrong in this matter. He is giving black people the idea that they matter, that they have a value to the cause, that they can exist masterless in this country. If the idea spreads, if, God forbid, the British government undercuts the institution of slavery, then what use to defeat rebels and establish the King's authority again? The country may be pacified, but it will be worthless, for without slave labour we have no way of planting and harvesting our crops. Without that labour, we are nothing!"

Despite his strong feelings, Clifford did not think he dared argue with General Clinton, and the latter did not hesitate to welcome useful African men into his army. While at first they were used strictly for "pioneer" work, armed mainly with axes, picks, and shovels to make an easier line of march across rough country for the army, in a short time many of them were issued with guns also, and in many a battle the African troops in British service found themselves shooting on African troops in the rebel forces, the same carrot, the promise of liberty, being held out before all of them.

chapter nine
THE DANGERS OF WAR

For a few months, Hannibal was happy, for Charles Town was a very exciting place when the tide seemed to be flowing in favour of the King's supporters. The African people of the city were hopeful for change in their condition, while those in the army were convinced that their Jubilee had come.

His happiness reached a peak when Jupiter Brown appeared to ask to be released from his master (who had run off to join the rebel Morgan, a guerrilla leader) and was accepted as a pioneer with a British unit. Jupiter was more optimistic than ever in the belief that a good life lay before him, and with all other Africans who could qualify to accept the British offer. His winning tongue was the instrument which added many more African men to British ranks, and he was soon made a sergeant.

From the British Army headquarters at Charles Town, Hannibal was able to follow the general shape of the war in the South. Partly this was because Clifford often spoke his thoughts aloud to him, perhaps for his own benefit in trying to make sense of what was happening, and otherwise because of his frequent discussions with Jupiter Brown, who helped interpret events from the Black Pioneers' own point of view. From the city, the British and Loyalist forces (such groups as the King's American Regiment, the New Jersey Volunteers, DeLancey's Provincial Battalion, and most admired in the city, the South Carolina Royalists) in their fresh bright uniforms, and enveloped in the martial music of several regimental bands, advanced in different directions, gathering many recruits, both white and black, from the countryside.

General Cornwallis came to take command and General Clinton went back to New York, and the army enjoyed the social life of the city while waiting for the crops to ripen and provide supplies for man and beast for the march to the North.

The hopes of the Loyalist forces, buoyed high in early June, soon dropped as news was received of a Loyalist rising in North Carolina savagely repressed before anyone in Charles Town was aware of its existence, and this was followed by a drive southward by a strong Continental Army.

Clifford raged at Hannibal, as he dared not to some of his brother officers, when he heard that whole militia regiments who had pledged allegiance to King George were taking to the woods and making surprise attacks on British regular troops. He even complained that a coolness was developing between the British and Loyalist troops, as the British began to murmur aloud that no American was to be trusted, and that they were all rebels at heart. Either that, or that they were cowards, as they showed at Musgroves' Mill when they turned tail and ran when they should have won a victory. They did not think it necessary to take into account that all the Loyalist officers had been picked off by hidden sharpshooters when the Loyalist regiments had walked into an ambush.

Clifford seethed at the aspersions cast on Loyalist courage and honour. After discussing the trend with Jupiter Brown, Hannibal himself was disturbed by the possibility that he was not on the winning side and hence might lose that distant hope that lightened his life.

Soon luck was changing for the British and Loyalist forces, as General Gates was met full tilt on the field and fled from it on a fast horse, leaving his reputation behind and the honours of the day with Cornwallis.

Clifford and Hannibal at about this time were with Ferguson's Rangers in the hill country in the west, the Frontier area. The Rangers, about a thousand in number, followed a course parallel to General Cornwallis as he advanced northward. As they went along, Ferguson called on the farmers of the Blue Ridge uplands to take the Oath of Allegiance to the King, and was pleased by the universal turnout and support he received.

However, at Gilbert Town, in cattle country, where the Rangers stopped a few days to administer the oath, Hannibal happened to meet a couple of African youths fishing. He was hoping to get some advice on fishing from them, but as soon as they took a liking to him, he got a good deal more out of them. They told the boy to take great care in moving around the hamlet. They said that the thousands of men taking the oath were doing so with their fingers crossed, they only wanted to save their cattle from being taken and eaten by the soldiers. As soon as they dared, they would become open enemies of the King's forces.

Hannibal caught a fish or two while he thought about this information. It seemed obvious to him that Major Ferguson would suspect that many who took the oath so boldly were not sincere, and would be guarding against them. Still, it would be best to report it to Master Clifford, and this he did when he carried the fish to their quarters to fry for supper.

Clifford thought about it more seriously than expected. He didn't usually pay much attention to information Hannibal brought him, but perhaps he had already had doubts about the rough men of the neighbourhood. "Your friends are probably quite right," he said, "but there's not much we can do about it save to be on guard. We won't know who our real friends are until a troop of rebels appears and starts nipping at our heels. Anyway, it's something I'll pass on to the Major."

Major Ferguson had no special way of knowing who took the oath seriously and who was committing perjury, but he did tell his men that any cattle belonging to rebels were fair game for the camp kitchen. So they were overjoyed one day to catch a rebel hidden near a fine herd of cattle and, though he denied all knowledge of the animals and said they were not his, they began to slaughter and butcher them to take back to camp.

As soon as they had enough meat for their immediate needs, the rebel suddenly recovered his memory and said, "Oh Jehosephat! I believe I do know those cattle after all. They belong to Sam Pollard and some other Tories down in Gilbert Town." They did, too, and Major Ferguson had some trouble pacifying the furious Loyalists when they saw their fat beeves going to his kitchen. However, they simmered down when they got a good market price for them.

The British officers were not as easy to fool as the rebels may have supposed. They knew when they moved on the settlers would remain loyal only if they could be protected against the guerrillas from the West, the "over-mountain" men. The Cherokee, who were allies of the British, were on the warpath against the back-country rebels but were not able to keep them all pinned down, so Ferguson decide to send a serious warning to the people there. He sent a junior officer with a couple of soldiers to tell them that if they continued to resist the King's authority, he would march over the mountains, hang their leaders, and devastate the country with fire and sword.

Several weeks passed with no reply from beyond the Blue Ridge Mountains until on September 30, two tired young men appeared at the camp. "Take us to Major Ferguson quickly," they said. "The over-mountain men are coming behind us... fast!"

Ferguson came out to find them surrounded by an excited group of his men and they quickly introduced themselves. "Our names are James Crawford and Samuel Chambers," they said. "We come from over there"—gesturing to the West—"but we are loyal to the King, though we dared not show it. Here's what happened when the Campbells and the other leaders got your threat."

"Not a threat," interjected Ferguson, "a warning."

"They shot the messenger and made plans to do likewise to you. They couldn't come straightaway; some had to be detailed to keep the Cherokee off, but even so, some hundreds got together."

"They're calling themselves Gideons, because when our minister blessed us when we gathered—yes, of course, we were there—he gave his blessing to us as 'the sword of the Lord and of Gideon,' so that's the war cry."

"It was four days ago that they gathered and started off," said his companion, "and the Colonel told us he'd send messengers from all over this side, saying that when we came over here there'd be lots of patriot friends joining up with us."

"How did you get away?" asked Ferguson.

"Why, it was like this," said the first, "They never thought there might be Loyalist among them and the night before last, when we were camped at the very top of the mountain, we lit out when everyone else was asleep."

"How did you know I was still here?"

"Oh, there are spies everywhere keeping an eye on you. They'll soon send word we're here, too."

"That doesn't matter now. Thanks to you, we'll be ready for them."

"Yes, Major, they won't take you by surprise, but you've got to get away from here fast. They can't be more than half a day behind us, if they're coming straight."

"Right. No need to worry about that. Go and get some food and rest now," and with a friendly slap on the back, Ferguson ordered a sergeant to look after them. A number of young officers, including Clifford, went along to ask more about the enemy.

The two men showed their weapons: Deckard rifles, made at Lancaster in Pennsylvania, with a thirty-inch barrel which shot with more precision than Ferguson's prized invention. They showed their other bits of equipment: powder and shot, of course, one blanket, a cup, and for food, only a wallet of parched cornmeal mixed with maple sugar. This was standard issue for the over-mountain men, and the Loyalist officers felt a twinge of respectful fear for an enemy who travelled and fought with so little comfort.

Ferguson decided to march to join Cornwallis, who was at Charlotte, in the midst of an area bare of Loyalists. In order to confuse his enemies, he told the citizens of Gilbert Town that he was returning to the back-country settlement called Ninety Six, but as he marched through the forest his scouts reported that the keen-eyed trackers from over the mountain were not deceived. From half a dozen directions, they were leading bands to converge on the Loyalist forces at the place they chose.

At noon one day, while the column was halted for a quick lunch within sight of a massive flat-topped ridge called Kings's Mountain which dominated the forest landscape, Clifford was called to the Commander. Ferguson spoke to him briefly and to the point.

"There are three thousand of the enemy closing in on us, Courtney, and I must have reinforcements from Lord Cornwallis. Take this letter to him; tell him we have been straining to join up with him along this road to Cherokee Ford. We have to break off the march, for our scouts say we will be intercepted within half a day, so we will occupy King's Mountain there—and we can hold out for two weeks if need be. If you hurry, you should be able to slip though."

Following Ferguson's instructions, Clifford took off his uniform, and dressed in the clothes he had worn when he worked as a surveyor, while Hannibal put on some rather ragged garments as his servant. In less than half an hour, they were on their way, putting some distance between themselves and the army, yet not galloping so fast as to arouse suspicion if the enemy scouts sighted them.

When they came to a trail turning east off the main road to Charlotte, they followed it, because Clifford was hoping to get out of the area of guerrilla activity before heading directly to Cornwallis's camp. That night, they stopped by a small stream to make camp and sleep for a few hours, planning to start again with the first light of morning. Clifford started a small fire and sent Hannibal for some good dry wood while he set out their meagre supper. The boy took the hatchet, and had not gone far when he found and cut up some good chunks. He was heading back and almost to the campsite when he heard the sound of one or more horsemen approaching. Scenting possible danger and staying concealed in the bushes, he crept close to where Clifford waited, preparing himself for some kind of action if the newcomer turned out to be a threat. He hoped he would not be, since he had no idea what he could do if his help was needed.

It was only one horseman, a tall loosely knit stranger on a mangy horse. He drew up when he spied Clifford and the fire and, throwing the reins over the horse's head, he slid to the ground. His buckskin clothing and untrimmed whiskers showed that he was a backwoodsman, and so did his way of speaking when he said, "Howdy, stranger. Name's Stewart, Abe Stewart, from over the mountains."

Clifford hesitated, not sure whether he could afford to tell the truth or not. He decided to take the chance. "I'm Courtney, from tide-water country," he said.

"What's your business in these parts?" inquired Abe Stewart as he squatted down close to the fire and took a pinch of snuff from the leather wallet tied to his belt. He went on to explain who he was while Clifford wondered what he dared to say. "I've been with Marion this past two months. Now I've got to get home and see to the harvest, though I hate to miss the fun that's brewing up here. So—you hail from tide-water, eh? I guess that's a pretty soft bunch there—more than half Tories in those parts, ain't they? Or would be, if they dared."

Clifford felt a bit sick at the shock of being face to face all alone with one of the followers of "the swamp fox," for Francis Marion was one of the wildest of the guerrilla leaders, and his men the most cruel and dangerous of all the gangs that ravaged the Loyalist population. He prodded the fire with a stick while he thought about what he could say; whatever happened, he had to get Ferguson's message to Lord Cornwallis, but how many lies would he have to tell to keep on friendly terms with Stewart? He wished he still had his uniform on.

"What about you?" asked Stewart.

"I'm a surveyor," said Clifford. "I've been doing a job of surveying for some people in Georgia, family by the name of Armstrong. They live near Augusta. Now I'm on my way to Hillsborough where I've got some work to do."

"There's quite a lot of lobster-backs where you've been, ain't there?"

"Yes, quite a few redcoats in Augusta, but of course I was out in the country, so I didn't see much of them."

He saw at once that Abe Stewart didn't like what he had heard, for his face began to get red and his eyes narrowed to cruel slits.

"So, you didn't see much of the lobster-backs, eh? How in tarnation can a strong healthy young man like you see any lobster-backs in the country and not take your rifle to them? These are no times to be looking at posts through surveying instruments. These are times to be catching the head of an Englishman or a Tory in your sights and blowing it off when you pull the trigger. Why, I wonder if you really are a patriot."

Clifford's temper was rising too and in the stiff necked way he always had, he was ready to stand on his dignity and say what he thought, no matter what the consequences. So in the same way in which he had so often irritated his brother Fred, he said, "If a patriot is one who loves his native land, then of course I am one."

"So you do love America, do you? I was just commencing to doubt it. Then why ain't you out in the field fighting for her?"

Clifford was finding it hard to breathe and stood up. "I don't think the best way to show my love for America is to destroy everything that's good and honourable and solid," he said. "I don't think we will find the answer to our problems in rebellion and war."

"Thunderation," growled Stewart. "I believe I really have treed a varmint that's in season. Admit it! You're a danged Tory, ain't you?"

"If you are asking me if I'm loyal to my king and the British constitution, then I willingly proclaim that I am. I am a Loyalist, and I'm proud of it."

In one swift movement, Abe Stewart seemed to rise to his feet with his gun at his shoulder levelled to bore Clifford through the eye.

"If that's the case, you're better dead!" shouted the over-mountain man, and began to pull back the trigger. Paralyzed, Clifford saw the rifle barrel jerk up and felt death very close as the bullet, thrown off course, grazed a trail of pain on the left side of his skull. Hannibal, watching closely, had come leaping out of the bushes and just in time had knocked the rebel off-balance with a chunk of well-seasoned hickory in the small of the back.

Then Clifford lay senseless on the ground with blood running from above his ear, and Abe Stewart, still holding onto his rifle, was swinging to deal with Hannibal in a display of super-human presence of mind and physical strength.

chapter ten

THE FINAL STAGES OF WAR

As soon as Hannibal had thrown his first chunk of wood at Abe Stewart, he darted back for another, ready to try again for a knockout blow. Barely had he armed himself and faced the big man again than he found himself on the defensive. Heavy as he was, Abe Stewart was light on his feet and quick in movement. His heavy weapon was descending in an arc which would connect with the boy's skull. In a flash, the boy saw the danger, and for a second time stood still as his brain weighed his options.

He felt a moment of unreasoning terror; then the instinct of self-preservation galvanized him into a desperate act. He leapt towards the big man, getting inside the arc of the swinging rifle butt, and smashed the hickory chunk on Stewart's chin. The man's head flew back and then he crumpled to the ground, while his gun thumped the boy harmlessly on the back and fell to the ground behind him.

Abe Stewart lay apparently lifeless as Hannibal ran over to Clifford and examined his head. There was a nasty wound, which he washed with water from the stream, and even sprinkled some on his the face in hopes of restoring consciousness. It soon brought Clifford around, and he finally sat up with a groan and began to take in what had happened.

When he saw Abe Stewart lying apparently lifeless, he cried out in astonishment. "What happened? Is he knocked out? Dead? Who did it? Where is he?"

When he heard the boy's account, he gripped his hand and said, "Hannibal, but for you I wouldn't be alive now. I won't forget it and you will never regret it. Now let's be away from here before anyone else finds us."

"Do you think I've killed him?" Hannibal wondered, looking down at the sprawling figure of Abe Stewart with a mixture of apprehension and pride.

"I don't know and I don't care. Don't worry about him. If he's dead, you've done a soldier's work. If not, he can look after himself. Let's go."

The two remounted and travelled all that night and fortunately met nobody else on the road. It seemed they had evaded the noose being tightened around Major Ferguson's little army, but the next task was to break through several more lines of the enemy to reach Cornwallis with his vital message. Luckily for them, they overtook a British military convoy next morning, and were headed for Charlotte again, and it seemed safest to travel with them. To do so, they sacrificed speed, since the convoy moved at the slow pace of the baggage carts and they were another two days on the road before they reached Charlotte. However, they were well within the time limit Major Ferguson had given, and Clifford felt confident that all would be well.

The town was in confusion, with soldiers gathered in noisy little groups and mounted officers dashing to and from headquarters. As they rode along, Clifford hailed an officer that he recognized. "Walker, what's going on? Why the confusion?"

"Courtney!" greeted the other. "Where did you come from? Haven't you heard the news? Haven't you heard about King's Mountain?"

"King's Mountain? What about it? I'm just bringing a message to General Cornwallis from Ferguson, who's holding it until reinforcements can get there. But how did you hear about it? Did someone get here before me?"

"Someone has indeed, and with a very different message from yours. When did Ferguson give it to you?"

"It's about three days now, but I could lead a relief party back with good horses to him by tonight, if we took the straight road."

"Too late, my friend. We can never relieve Ferguson now. He's dead, along with a couple hundred of his men, and most of the rest are prisoners. Your guardian angel must have been looking after you to get you away from that massacre."

It was true, as Clifford discovered when he delivered his useless message to the commander. A couple of Ferguson's men had avoided being taken prisoner and when the road was clear brought the news direct.

The story was a tragic one; the over-mountain men had surrounded the plateau the day after Clifford and Hannibal had left from it. They had climbed to the top in a dozen places, concealed by the forest growing along its flanks, and as fast as Ferguson led a bayonet charge on one group, another appeared in the opposite direction. Ferguson himself had died while trying to lead a breakthrough, felled by a hail of concentrated fire. His men surrendered, though for a time their white flags (their handkerchiefs) were ignored by the rebel marksmen who were enjoying the slaughter.

Clifford was deeply shaken by the sudden loss of the commander whom he admired and friends to whom he had grown very close. He confided some of his thoughts and feelings to Hannibal as he had never done before. A kind of crust over them had been broken by the encounter with Abe Stewart, by the debt he now owed his slave boy for his very life, and the shock of thinking about the massacre at King's Mountain which, had he managed to reach Charlotte in time, might have been averted.

From this time forward, Clifford looked on his teenaged servant in a new light, as one who had saved his life, and often shared his thoughts when they were alone together. It was quite possible for there to be affection between master and slave, and there had been that, but now there was respect on the master's part, a rare commodity in such a relationship. Clifford was the sort of person who did not suppress his feelings of right and wrong, and henceforth he felt it was right to view Hannibal as a friend and as a kind of younger brother.

Although Clifford felt some guilt for not having either stood beside Ferguson on King's Mountain, or of bringing him the rescue he had asked for, he found that no one blamed him for the outcome. General opinion was that Ferguson should not have let himself be penned in, that a forced march would have brought him safely to Charlotte before the attack, that he had crippled the whole British campaign by his suicidal strategy.

Pondering his fate, Clifford was inclined to tell his friends that if anyone was to be blamed for Ferguson's demise, it was General Howe. "General Howe?" they would ask in amazement, "Why General Howe? The man is long gone and was never around here."

"Don't you realize that a few years ago Major Ferguson invented a superior rifle that could fire four shots a minute... and he equipped his men with it and they used it at the Battle of Brandywine, up north, when General Howe was Commander-in-Chief in this war. It shot twice as fast as our muzzle-loaders and twice as far, and we would have had it on King's Mountain and won a victory there if General Howe, for some reason known only to himself, had not made him give them up. I guess he was afraid he would make too much of a name for himself."

General Cornwallis knew how to value Major Ferguson, and had depended on him in his campaign plans for the South. When he heard the news, not a pleasant task for the messenger, he was at a loss. In fact, as the bad news sank in, he seemed to become confused and panicky, and in a few days withdrew the army back into South Carolina. This retreat was not good news for Clifford and his Loyalist friends.

At the Christmas season, Clifford received leave to go to Charles Town, where his parents were again in their town house, refusing to let the habits of a lifetime be changed by war. Hannibal was overjoyed to see his mother there. Colonel Courtney had heard from Clifford of his part in saving him from death, and spoke to him kindly. As for Clifford's mother, Hannibal kept out of her sight, knowing she would never see him without feeling pain.

During the New Year, Cornwallis was once more on the move, for he received strong reinforcements from New York and competent commanders to assist him. Yet he suffered a severe loss when Tarleton foolishly threw away his men at a place called Hannah's Cowpens, and when Cornwallis drove out the Continental Army under General Greene, he found that it had led him a chase which came to a climax in the bloody battle of Guilford Courthouse. He claimed it as a victory, although it inflicted severe losses on his ill-fed and tiring army. Soon he decided to withdraw southeast to Wilmington on the coast and General Greene was able to come south again with renewed strength.

Cornwallis's next moves were awaited anxiously by friend and foe and it was assumed that he would link up with his subordinates in South Carolina and protect the province effectively against rebel infiltration. Instead, to general disbelief, he decided to march north in an effort to conquer Virginia. Behind him, in South Carolina, the hard-won strongholds of the British and Loyalist troops were lost one by one.

Clifford and Hannibal were not with Cornwallis during this time. Clifford had been posted to Camden where Lord Rawdon, a brilliant young officer scarcely older than himself, was the commander. Here there was action, for General Greene, having bypassed Cornwallis, appeared in strength and was smartly defeated. However, Continental troops and guerrilla bands increasingly dominated the western areas, and Lord Rawdon and the other commanders evacuated their positions and fell back to Charles Town. Eventually, only the fortified post of Ninety Six, ignorant of the general withdrawal, remained in possession of the British forces. The commander there was Colonel Cruger, who led five hundred Loyalists from New York and New Jersey. They were tightly besieged when, providentially, three fresh regiments arrived in Charles Town and Lord Rawdon led them inland to their relief.

Clifford saw plenty of fighting during the summer of 1781, and it was a relief to be back in Charles Town in the early fall. However, there were rumours from Virginia that all had not gone well with Cornwallis's plans. For some reason, he had dug himself in at a place called Yorktown on the York River, while his enemies gathered around him by land and by sea. Inside his lines, as the weeks passed in idleness, the food was consumed, the cavalry horses had to be shot, and smallpox broke out. At Charles Town, as at New York, men wondered why Cornwallis had settled into such suicidal inactivity, for after a sea battle between the French and British ships in Chesapeake Bay at the beginning of September, which the French won, it was obvious that he could not be relieved by sea. In October, word came that armies under Washington and Lafayette were squeezing the besieged very hard, and it was no surprise when the news finally came that Cornwallis had surrendered on October 19, 1781...

There was gloom and despondency in Charles Town, especially as it turned out that in surrendering, Cornwallis had virtually betrayed his Loyalist troops into the enemies' hands. Cornwallis had originally stipulated that these men were not to be punished for having joined the British Army, but Washington refused to accept the condition and the British general had made no further effort on behalf of those who had so bravely fought for him. He sailed home to England, leaving a tarnished reputation for loyalty behind him.

There was gloom, too, among the African leaders of Charles Town as they heard from various sources of the fate of Negroes who had been found with the British at Yorktown. The terms of surrender agreed that any American property in the British hands was to be given up to the victors, and unfortunately for themselves a good part of such property was in the form of runaway slaves with the British army. The Continental Army had immediately on surrender been ordered to guard the beaches to prevent Negroes from getting across the water to the ships of the Royal Navy waiting there. The rebel Governor of Virginia wrote to Cornwallis, asking him to have ships searched for runaway slaves. At the same time, French and American officers of the victorious armies were rounding up as many of the Africans as they could for their personal gain, though General Washington tried to put a stop to it by ordering all such men be delivered up to a special contingent which would return the escaped slaves to their masters.

As usual, Sergeant Jupiter Brown, still in Charles Town, was Hannibal's best source of information.

"It looks as though it going to be a tougher business than we reckoned on," he was telling one group of worried runaways and others one evening, as they gathered in a corner of the Battery, "and we're not going to get away from slavery without a struggle. The British will do what they can for us, I'm as sure of that now as ever I was, but it's clear that the rebels are going to make it as awkward as all get-out for them. Men, we've got to be ready to help ourselves when the desperate time comes, as I fear it will."

Soon everyone realized that the surrender at Yorktown marked the end of the British effort to regain the allegiance of the Thirteen Colonies. This was despite the fact that British strength was increasing. The Royal Navy was improving, the British Army in America was still powerful, and King George was determined to fight on. Yet the men who formed the British Government saw the impossibility of holding down such a large part of the American population as were ready to resist the King's will, as well as the danger to Britain's own safety in the face of antagonism on the continent of Europe. These facts made a conclusion of hostilities inevitable.

So, in Charles Town, Clifford soon had to face up to the fact that he had chosen the losing side. He was going to have to decide whether to stay in South Carolina and take his chances as a known Loyalist who had taken up arms on the losing side, or to go to some other part of the British Empire where he would be respected and could prosper. As the New Year of 1782 dawned, he and his father were watching events closely, trying to decide what would be best for him and the future of the Courtney family.

PART TWO:

Hannibal Hoops
in Nova Scotia

chapter one
OFF TO PORT ROSEWAY

It was in the year l782 that Clifford Courtney made the decision that brought himself and Hannibal Hoops to the easternmost of the old Fifteen Colonies of the British Empire in North America, and in so doing made it possible for the slave boy to fulfill his mother's dream of returning to the home of his ancestors, to Sierra Leone. However, that was not even guessed at when Clifford made the hard choice about what course of action he might take. He did not ask for Hannibal's opinion, but since the day the boy had been lucky enough to save his life, he treated him more like a respected younger brother than a slave, and the boy reciprocated his warm feelings.

In the summer of l782, Hannibal was almost fifteen years old, and was tall and muscular, nearly full grown. However, he was still a boy inside, and he knew it would be a few years yet before he could feel that he was a man the equal of the soldiers he had been living among the past few years. At any rate, the clothes he wore were rather like a soldier's uniform, and those who didn't know him respected him as if he were.

His master, as he regarded him, Clifford, naturally had discussions with him about the way the war was going, and the changes it was bringing. Perhaps he was talking more to himself than to the boy, trying by putting into words to understand the reality he perceived. On one occasion he said, "You know, Hannibal, that the war appears to be all over save for the shouting. Since Cornwallis surrendered, it doesn't appear that the King's government is going to even try any further to put a stop to the rebellion. I am sure that the rebel armies have crumbled away in the past six months, and if they were called on to fight again, most of those left in uniform would mutiny. But it does not seem that the will exists to take advantage of it.

"I'm afraid we Loyalists have been betrayed at the top. Without leadership and help from London, we can do nothing to change the situation. In fact, they have put men in the government over there who wanted to cast off these colonies from the beginning. Lord Shelburne, Mr. Fox—these men have doubted and despised us, we who have been loyal Americans from the beginning of the struggle; now they will have their way and abandon this rich country, this empire, to the rebels."

One day, he heard that there was a new commander-in-chief.

"His name is Sir Guy Carleton," he told the boy, "and I think his job is to make terms with Washington and withdraw the British army from this continent. We Loyalists will have to look after ourselves if that is the case."

It became clear that this was the general view. As the months of summer went by, the Loyalists in Charles Town went down to the wharfs several times each week to say goodbye to friends who were sailing away to places that would be secure for them once the protection of the army was removed. There were friends of the Courtney family, plantation owners whose plantations were under threat of confiscation by the rebel government; men, women, children and servants were sailing down the coast to East Florida, which they supposed would continue under British rule.

Clifford Courtney was old Colonel Courtney's eldest son and therefore heir to his plantation, but his father discouraged him from staying in the South. He talked to Hannibal about the problem.

"Hannibal," he said, "I've had some long talks with my father and it is clear that it will not be safe for me to try to live here under the republican government, even if I could stomach it myself. I think I'm going to have to leave, and I don't think that even East Florida is far enough. My father has heard from friends in New York that the whole population of that great city is going to move to Nova Scotia."

Hannibal, of course, had never even heard of Nova Scotia; few people in the Carolinas had ever heard of it or ever needed to hear of it. But if Nova Scotia was to be his new home, Hannibal thought he had a right to know something about it, and why people wanted to go there.

"Nova Scotia is another large colony north and east of the lower thirteen, Hannibal. It borders on Canada, which we took from the French only a few years ago, just before our own war started. It is a land surrounded by waters full of fish; the land itself is full of good timber. Also I understand there is good farmland there and that all it needs is a population to make it into the finest country in America. Loyalists will flock together there from all the old colonies. New cities will be built, and there will be plantations growing food to feed them. It's the land of the future, and why shouldn't I, and you too, be a part of it?"

The boy was impressed by the warmth of his master's words and could not think of any good reason why they should not go to a land of such promise. He could probably not be worse off there than here in South Carolina. Although Master Clifford had told him that he should no longer think of himself as a slave, he did not think that such an African boy as he was could survive without a man to call "Master," whether in Carolina or in Nova Scotia or anywhere in the world—unless, by some miracle, he could find his way to the land of his ancestors in Africa.

Clifford and his father talked about his plan in the autumn, when the Courtney family came in from the plantation to enjoy the town in the cooler weather. It was known that the New York people were considering several spots in Nova Scotia to build new cities, and the one that sounded most promising was Port Roseway. It was a coastal location, with a spacious harbour, close to good fishing grounds. Its excellent harbour almost guaranteed that it would become the capital of the colony, since it was bound to become more important than the present shabby seat of government that was Halifax.

Colonel Courtney thought that Clifford might find the cod fishery a good business venture, especially as the British Government was going to shut off the trade between the Thirteen Colonies and the West Indies, most of which (as Clifford was informed) consisted of dried and salted cod which was the chief food of the plantation workers there. It appeared that the traders of Nova Scotia would have that trade all to themselves and with it the sugar and rum trade, and would soon be rich. Although Clifford had never been in that kind of business, he had helped his father write letters concerning the sale of rice and other things from the plantation, and he thought he could soon learn how the codfish business worked.

Clifford Courtney and Hannibal sailed from Charles Town on a winter morning, having spent their last Christmas on the plantation where they had both been born. The boy said his goodbyes to the kindly folk in the cabins, the folk he had known from babyhood. His parting from his mother was tearful, but full of faith that their parting would not be for long. His master did the same in devoting his last few days with his parents and kinfolk, with the hope that in a few years they would be together again. So on that winter morning, the two wanderers stood on the deck together, looking back at the town as their vessel steadily drew away; the sun was fleetingly visible through the mist and threw flashing gleams of gold on the silvery-blue water, but the town was lost in the fog. Their last glimpses of land were the grey granite walls of the Fort and the Battery, then they were out of the harbour and sailing in sunshine for Saint Augustine in Florida. Their spirits lifted as they looked forward to new adventures awaiting them.

Saint Augustine was a warm and pleasant town to winter in, and it was full of people like themselves.

These were men who had fought for the King or men whose neighbours had driven them from their homes. They called themselves not refugees, but Loyalists. And with them were their wives and children, and servants, slaves too, if they had them.

In the spring, these Loyalists boarded a small vessel called the *Sceptre*. Her full load of passengers, both black and white, waved goodbye to the old Spanish town with its waving palm trees, and the south country they had always known, and headed away out from the coast and ever northward.

There was one very bad storm, somewhere off Cape Hatteras, that blew the ship off-course and set them back a week or two, and just as scary as the storm was the thick belt of fog that they met somewhere off the coast of Nova Scotia. There were lookouts at the bow and on the masts, but they couldn't see a thing in the thick mist; there was not enough wind blowing to move it aside, and as it turned out, not enough to drive the ship, either. However, the captain knew he might be near shore, and made everybody be very quiet so the lookouts could hear sounds from the land—if there were any.

Then there was no sound, save for the drip, drip, drip of the congealed mist falling to the deck from the limp sails and the ropes. After a couple of hours of this inactivity, a slight current of air blew the fog away. The passengers saw beyond the bow a rocky shore, with great gobs of granite piled up in irregular masses here and there. If the wind had risen then and driven the boat onto those rocks, the hull would have been stove in immediately. As it was, the refugees were frightened at the sight and some of the timid passengers moaned. The captain quickly ordered a couple of boats out with lines to hold the craft against the lazy current which seemed to be driving her straight in. At the same time, anchors were dropped at bow and stern and after several tries took hold and held the boat steady. When the captain was confident that they would do the trick, he called the boats in. There was nothing more to do until the fog lifted off the water, and the vessel lay at anchor all that night waiting for a change.

With the sunrise came a freshening breeze that blew away the fog, and the captain set some sail and moved cautiously among many small rocky islands. Most of the men and boys were on deck or hanging on the sheets hoping to see something other than hard rock and scrubby evergreen trees.

"Nova Scarcity, some call it, " said one old gentleman, "and by George, if it's all like this, it's well and truly named."

Hannibal was standing by a new friend, Pete, a drummer boy his own age. He and all the rest of the band of the Loyal American Fencibles were on board; they had been slaves, but they became free men when they joined the army, and their dream was to have their own farms in Nova Scotia.

"It sure doesn't look like Carolina," Hannibal said to Pete. "What do you think we can grow here?"

He just looked sick, and so did the rest of the band. They knew about growing rice and corn, tobacco and cotton, but this country didn't look fit for anything.

After dinner, people were mostly lying around having a midday nap when they were jolted awake by the thundering of the ship's cannon. They got to their feet and were jumping up all over the deck, thinking that a French ship must be attacking, when the first mate called down from the forecastle to keep calm. "We're signalling for the pilot," he called out, "Port Roseway is somewhere up harbour; we have to be piloted in. We are just going to anchor here until he comes."

Sure enough, the crew threw out the anchor and after a few hours a small craft brought out the pilot, a middle-aged hearty sort of man. He stood by the helmsman as the *Sceptre* got under way again and went up a narrow rocky channel with evergreen forests everywhere, right down to the shoreline. There was no sign of houses to be seen, or people, or animals; refugee hearts sank as the Loyalists thought about spending their lives in this wilderness with so little promise.

Before dark, they were at anchor in front of the town, if town it could be called. It was the fourth day of July, 1783, a day of celebration in the Old Thirteen to the South. The African refugees should have felt like celebrating, too, with their dangerous voyage concluded, but their best reason for cheerfulness was for the fact that they were now free to be responsible for their own lives, in a colony where African people, too, could own property, have recognized families, and be protected by the law. It remained to be seen how they could make lives for themselves on this frontier of civilization.

All the passengers felt sadness about the friends and family most of them, both white and black, had left behind and would probably never see again, and they felt some worry about what lay ahead in their new homes. But most of all, they were glad their wanderings in the army and at sea were over, and that they could settle down.

Next morning, they all went ashore. Hannibal determinedly stuck close to Master Clifford as they moved through a crowd of strange people. The new settlers would have to find whoever was in charge of the settlement and report themselves, so as to get registered on the lists of rations, clothes, seed, tools and so forth, all the things they had been promised before they left home.

As they climbed over rocks at the water's edge and up the five-foot bank that served for a wharf, they saw three or four boys watching everything going on. Clifford beckoned one over and said, "Would you like to earn a penny, m'lad? You can have it if you can show us all around the town. I think we might as well begin by inspecting our terrain," he murmured to Hannibal.

The boys talked together a minute then one of them, a yellow-headed boy of about thirteen, sauntered over. He led them around, and talked as they went, telling how he had arrived about two months before, when not a tree had been cut in the forest that covered the town, and the snow lay deep in shady places. Since then, five great parallel streets had been cut through the forest, and he walked them up and down each one. It was amazing to see a city being built in the wilderness, complete with all the comforts of mankind.

Actually, the comforts were not all in place yet. The streets were muddy with the stumps of the trees still standing, save on King Street, where they had been dragged out and the ground properly cleared off and levelled. In other places, teams of oxen were straining to pull out stumps while axmen stood around striking at the stubborn roots as they were pulled to the surface. The many teams of oxen had been shipped down from Lunenburg, a town further up the coast.

Here and there along the streets, the woods had been cleared and people had put up tents or rough huts made of branches and sod or fair-sized logs chinked with moss and plastered with clay.

Connecting the five great streets were narrow lanes, more like paths chopped out of the woods than proper streets, but as they walked around and up and down, the newcomers began to get their bearings. The whole street plan was in the form of a grid, and once they had the picture of it in their minds they couldn't get lost.

The walk was real exercise for them, from having been cooped up on the ship so long. Hannibal had yet to find his land-legs, and had to be extremely alert to the problem of avoiding the stumps without running into the many people who were working on the streets or simply using them to go somewhere. He began to sweat and whipped out his red bandanna to wipe his face as Master Clifford complained, "We've got too many clothes on, Hannibal. Feel that sun… it's as hot as Carolina! Perhaps it won't be too much a shock to our systems to be here after all."

Now, the boy noticed that it really was hot, and that the men pulling on stumps were hotter than he, with their shirts sticking to their backs and chests, and peppered with little black spots that were actually black flies, stinging like red-hot pokers! In between axe strokes at stubborn roots, the men slapped at themselves and killed a multitude of the pesky insects each time.

The yellow-headed boy who said his name was Dan was very proud of King Street. "This is going to be the most important street in all North America," he boasted. "All the great merchants from New York are building their houses here, and the government of Nova Scotia will put its buildings here, too. This is going to be the capital city of the colony, you know, and it's going to be bigger and better and richer than Boston or New York or any of them. It's going to be the best and biggest city on this continent."

"Hear that, Hannibal?" said Master Clifford. "We're in the middle of history, it's being made all around us!" He swung his arm around in a broad sweep to take in the whole busy scene. "It doesn't look like much now, but if we look at it with the eyes of faith and optimism, we can see a big and beautiful city around us. It will come, and we will be here to see it all come into being."

Clifford really was full of faith and optimism. He really was enthusiastic and hopeful; he had to be, or he might have cried. He knew it would be a hard slog before Dan's hopes would be realized, but it was a good thing he couldn't see ahead to the real future of the town.

As the little group walked along, Clifford met old acquaintances from the years of war, and some whom he had come to know in Charles Town or East Florida. Here and there, he spoke to perfect strangers who looked friendly and interesting, for, as he thought, it was a good idea to start making friends of the people he would be living with from here on.

He asked Dan if he could take him to where there was a view, and they climbed to some high ground which overlooked the streets and lanes, and beyond them the broad and beautiful harbour that made the site so promising for trade. They saw the vessels at anchor down there, including the *Sceptre,* where Clifford and Hannibal were due for dinner if they got back in time. Clifford thought he could dispense with Dan, so he paid the boy off with the promised penny and ran down ahead of them, back to his friends on the shore.

When the two got back to the *Sceptre,* it was mid-afternoon and they were certainly ready for the solid meal the galley served up. On the way down through the town, they saw cooking fires being lighted here and there among the tents, and later on from the boat saw clouds of smoke rising from all over the settlement They wondered if some disaster had fallen on the settlement, but soon realized that people were putting green branches on their fires to produce a good smudge to drive away the little black flies and mosquitoes.

That evening, as the long northern twilight deepened into dusk, the refugees saw from the deck the fires among the trees throwing long tongues of golden light across the water. They smelled the smoke which was curling out towards them on a light breeze as the land cooled off, and perhaps that was what kept the mosquitoes away from the vessel.

Clifford decided to go on shore again and found Hannibal in a group of young people. "Hannibal," he said, "I'm going to make a call on the Chief Surveyor tonight, to see about getting some land for myself. I imagine he's too busy to talk in the daytime, so I'll try my luck now and just hope he isn't an early-to-bed man. I want you to come with me, and bring a lantern; it will be confoundedly dark among the trees before we get back."

The ship's boat was continually plying back and forth between the *Sceptre* and the dock, so they had no problem getting ashore. There, they easily got directions to the Chief Surveyor's tent. He was Mr. Benjamin Marston, and his tent was on King Street. Clifford had already found out from his friends that Marston was a man much respected, and believed to be scrupulously fair and honest in doing his job. They soon found his large tent, and he was in it, a large ruddy-faced man working at a desk covered with papers. When he saw Clifford at the door, he stood up and welcomed him in. Clifford introduced himself and mentioned that he had been a junior surveyor back home in Carolina, and wondered if he could be of some use. Marston called to a serving man to bring a couple of mugs of beer, and the two were soon chatting like old friends while Hannibal squatted by the door flap and listened to them, though he dozed off a couple of times.

Clifford explained that he had just arrived from the South on the *Sceptre*. Marston said he was glad to see him, but not sure that he had done the wise thing to come to Port Roseway. He explained himself. He had no great opinion of the abilities of the new settlers.

"These people here are rabble, pure rabble, so what kind of society can they create here? The mob rules. They elect captains for their 'companies,' but the captains are no better than the men. There are very few men of a superior kind here, very few you could call gentlemen. Nobody knows how to command men, or how to 'think big.' They are all barbers, tailors, shoemakers, men of that kind, mechanics, knowing only how to live in great towns and earn an honest living practising their trades. How are they going to live here?"

Clifford was surprised to hear the scorn and anger in Mr Marston's voice; the settlement was only getting started and he was forecasting some kind of ruin for it. He—and Hannibal, listening at the door—didn't really understand the grounds for Marston's dissatisfaction, so different from their impressions of a busy hopeful undertaking, but obviously he felt strongly.

Clifford tried putting forward a more positive view, in the hope that Marston would cool down and indicate reasons for being hopeful.

"Isn't this a great town you are laying out here at this moment? People are telling me it will be the greatest metropolis in America. Isn't it going to be just the place for mechanics and craftsmen? After all, these are the kind of people found in cities, and that is part of what makes cities."

"I hope it may become such a city," replied the surveyor, " but such people as these are only one element in what is required. Have you ever heard of a great town without a group of prosperous merchants enjoying a good trade and bringing in wealth? So far we have hardly any of such.

"Where are our wealthy citizens with money to lend to would-be traders and fishermen? They are not here. And can a great town grow without a rich countryside around to feed it? Around us stretches some of the poorest farmland in all Nova Scotia, and that means it is very poor indeed."

After a little pause, he went on.

"Here's a little story, a true one, that seems to me to be an omen. When the New York fleet, the first to come, sailed in, a little boat came out to meet them. In it was a scarecrow of a man. He came on board. He was old Ebenezer Berry, who had lived across the harbour from here for years, fishing mostly and living in poverty. He told them of his hardships and deprivations; they could see that he told the truth. One of them asked him, 'But how came you to stay here?' 'Ah," he replied, 'poverty brought me here and poverty kept me here.' "

Clifford was silent and thought about what the story might mean, then asked, "If Port Roseway was known to be such a poor place, how is it that the authorities decided to make a settlement here?"

"The short answer is, they didn't. Nobody of authority chose this place. It was a couple of New Yorkers who came up, liked what they saw of the harbour, and decided it would be just the place to base a great fishing fleet, and decided on settlement here, no matter what wiser gentlemen from Halifax tried to tell them about its drawbacks."

"But," said Clifford, "gentlemen from Halifax are probably not unbiased. Perhaps they see a rival town here, perhaps they are jealous. If this town becomes the seat of government, which it ought to do, all the officials will come here and Halifax will be of no account. I suppose people who have property there won't want to leave that place."

"No doubt there is some jealousy among Halifax merchants," said Marston. "Halifax is still a raw town, and has developed very slowly. It may not have been put down in the best spot for success, either. But just the same, there are plenty of harbours as good as this along the coast, with more hospitable hinterland. I very much fear this site is a mistake."

"I hope you're wrong about the prospects here, Mr. Marsden," said Clifford. "At any rate, I'm here and I'm going to give it a try. My father back in Carolina will help me get established in the fish business, when the time comes. But meanwhile, I want to apply for a grant of land and whatever else I am entitled to from the government."

"Every Loyalist, being free, white, and twenty-one, whether a bachelor or a head of family, gets a town lot on one of the main streets, a water lot on the harbour front, and a fifty-acre farm outside the city boundary. I'll add your name to the other applicants on the newest list." Marston pulled a sheet of paper from one of the piles and dipping his quill in a silver inkwell carefully wrote it down.

"Thanks. When can I move on to my town lot?"

"Not for a while. It hasn't even been surveyed yet. When I get another street of town lots surveyed and numbered, then I will put all the numbers on slips of paper and there will be a public drawing for them. Which lot you get will be entirely a matter of chance, the luck of the draw. But I'm afraid it will be a few weeks before that can happen. I'm shorthanded and doing most of the work myself."

"I do have some experience as a surveyor, Mr. Marston, though I'm a bit rusty at the moment. But I'll be glad to give you a hand if I can be of help."

Clifford got up from his campstool and he and Hannibal stepped outside. Marston came out with them. It was pitch dark now and the whole settlement was marked out by rows of twinkling fires among the trees. Clifford admired the cosy looking scene, but once again Marston found fault.

"Yes, it looks very pretty and festive, but all these fires are danger-ous," he said, determined to look on the dark side. "If they were as care-less with their fires before they left New York as they are now, I don't know why the city didn't burn to the ground. We have already had some serious outbreaks; some families have lost everything through nothing but their own carelessness. So they camp with their friends, forcing them to share the little they have."

"Good night, Mr. Marston," said Clifford, and started off, with Han-nibal holding the lantern ahead to show the track. "That was depress-ing," he said to the boy, "but maybe Mr. Marston's digestion isn't in good order. We'll tackle him again when he feeling more hopeful."

Soon they were back at the water's edge, where the ship's boat waited by the rocks, and after about twenty minutes of tossing across the waves were safe in their sleeping quarters below deck.

chapter two
THE TOWN IN THE WOODS

Hannibal," Clifford said next morning, "our captain says he wants to sail at first light tomorrow. He got word they're crying out for more ships at New York. They have to evacuate the city as fast as possible before they let Washington and his Continental Army march in. So get my stuff from the hold and all our baggage from my quarters and have everything ready to be taken ashore when I get back. I'm going on shore to find a spot for us to pitch our tents. In fact, I'll start by calling on Mr. Marston and see what he suggests, and maybe he'll give me a job surveying for the next few weeks. Since I can't get my land for a few weeks, I'd better keep busy in the meantime."

Hannibal got hold of some sailors to help him and located Clifford's belongings in the hold, which was hot and crowded with other people looking for their boxes and casks. Sailors were also lending a hand, as the captain had ordered. He gathered the packages on a clear piece of deck and then brought up Clifford's personal things and sat amongst them and waited for his return.

He was back sooner than the boy expected and said, "We're going to spend the night at Mr. Marston's camp, Hannibal. He was delighted when he heard I was serious about helping with the work. He hasn't explained it all yet, he was rather busy, but I'll get my instructions this evening."

Their belongings were stowed in the ship's boat and carried ashore. Fortunately, there were several gangs of idle boys willing to leave off watching the harbour traffic for a chance to earn a penny. It was just after high noon when Clifford led a line of them up the hill, each carrying a box or crate of the things he had brought for starting life in the wilderness. Hannibal brought up the rear to make sure the boxes went where they were meant to go, and not into someone else's tent. Before he paid them off, Clifford had the lads rig up a couple of tents next to Marston's quarters, and Hannibal set up a camp bed for the master and one out of fir boughs for himself. He covered them with blankets and considered his work done.

Marston appeared from work, hot and red-faced, and with a tin dipper drank liberally from a covered canvas bucket of water hung in a shady corner of his tent. He greeted Clifford as he mopped his red face with a large cotton handkerchief.

"My cook will have some dinner ready for us in a minute," he said. "Come and sit down out here where it's cool." He brought two folding chairs out to a shady spot beneath the trees and they sat down. Hannibal sat on the ground near Clifford. While Marston explained about the work, his servant appeared and set up a small camp table for their use. He served up a reasonable supper, and handed a plateful to Hannibal, which he ate where he was.

"This is the job I'll put you on, Courtney," the older man said. "You probably know better than I do about these people who are called Free Blacks, these African people who were slaves until they joined up with the army. They were soldiers and pioneers, and of course many of them are coming here. Likely there were some on your ship, and there will be more of them. Anyway, it has been decided to give them a town of their own; it would be asking for trouble to have them live in this town. After all, many of your countrymen have brought their own slaves with them—as you appear to have done," he said, looking at Hannibal with an enquiring glance, "and it will be hard enough to control them in the best of circumstances without having Free Blacks all over the place to give them ideas."

"Hannibal is no longer my slave, but my ward," replied Clifford, "and what is this job you have for me?"

"Why, I'll put you in charge of surveying the town for the Blacks I've just been talking about. I thought I was making myself clear."

"I thought that might be what you were leading up to. All right, I'll accept the job and I'll do my best to give satisfaction all around. What exactly have you in mind?"

"Well, Courtney, I've already selected the town site. It's not far from here, over on North-West Harbour in fact, so by water it's fairly close. Naturally it would be longer to go there by land, through the bush, but maybe that will be just as well. You can make your permanent camp over there. Any baggage you don't need will be safe with me. I'll get the Commissariat to supply you with stores.

"How about getting over there in the morning? I'll get a boat assigned to you and I'll go over with you and get you started."

Naturally, Clifford, who was impatient to be doing something useful after the months of waiting, jumped at the offer. Surveyor Marston said a word to his servant, and a short time later announced, "I've sent for the leaders of the Free Blacks and they're on their way now. I think things will go smoothest if we consult with them every step of the way. It doesn't worry me to talk to them man to man. I hope it won't worry you."

Clifford assured him it didn't, and in fact, as Hannibal believed, he was glad to be in a position to help former slaves to be happy as free men. If he had not felt sympathy and respect for poor African people when he was growing up with dozens of slaves around him, he had certainly learned it in the hard days of war when white and black had struggled together against the common enemy.

It was getting on for dusk when the leaders of the Free Blacks appeared. They were headed by a tall and dignified man, Colonel Stephen Bluck, who, it was explained, had served through the war as an officer in the Black Pioneers, and with him were half a dozen tougher looking men, his captains. Their corps had been formed to do labouring work with pick-and-shovel, so they were broad well-muscled men.

But Clifford and Hannibal looked on them with respect. They knew these men had done their share of fighting before the war fell apart. Great was Hannibal's pleasure to see an old friend, Jupiter Brown, among them, and he jumped up and grabbed the big man's hand. He seemed equally pleased to see the boy and gave him a quick hug while the others were exchanging introductions and general greetings.

"Gentlemen," said Surveyor Marston, politely, "this is Mr. Clifford Courtney, a native of South Carolina, a soldier and a surveyor. He will be my deputy in the laying out of your new town. We shall go over to the site and start work tomorrow. You should be at the waterside about seven o'clock, all those who are coming with us."

"How many of us can you take, Mr. Marston?" asked the Colonel.

"Oh, the fishing boat I have in mind could ferry all of you here— probably thirty or more. But do we want to take a crowd over at this time?"

"No, no, sir; but I have twenty captains under me who generally help to make all decisions. I would like all of them to be there to give our town a proper start."

"Very well. You, Colonel, and your twenty captains may come. But there will be no room for any extras."

Next morning, Clifford and Hannibal accompanied the surveyor to the harbour front, where work was at last beginning on a decent wharf of huge timbers. Colonel Bluck was already there, dressed for the occasion; his unusual breadth and height set off by his tight scarlet dress coat and spotless white breeches. His handsome face, light coffee in colour, was framed by his freshly powdered white wig, and a black hat gave him some extra inches on top. His twenty captains couldn't compete with him in dress, but they were looking equally neat and clean. Marston's group included four labourers, all of them white men, who were part of the surveying establishment.

They crowded the boat, which was never meant to carry more than a small fishing crew, and had trouble staying out of the way of the sailors as they got the vessel under way. Fortunately it was a clear run, with the wind more or less behind them, to the inlet where they disembarked.

When all were ashore and had explored the tree-clad slope, those in Marston's party relaxed while Colonel Bluck and his captains held a short conference out of earshot. Then the Colonel led the whole group over and made a solemn little speech:

"Mr. Marston and Gentlemen, we have examined this stretch of land, this area of soil set aside as our property and a home for our people in perpetuity, a gift from our generous and gracious sovereign, King George the Third—God Bless Him!—in recognition of our services and our loyalty to his crown, and in that same spirit of goodwill, we wish to accept it.

"Furthermore, Mr. Marston and Gentlemen, we wish to acknowledge, in naming this our new town, one of those benefactors to whom we owe so much. Among those springs to mind first of all Sir Guy Carleton, who allowed us to board the transports anchored in the harbour of New York at the same time as our former masters, bent on dragging us back into slavery, back into the vile land of Egypt from which we had fled, were actually entering the city and searching for us. General George Washington himself demanded that we be brought back to shore and into captivity. Sir Guy, as we gratefully remember, resisted that demand and by his courageous stand earned our undying gratitude.

"Happily, the name of Guy Carleton has already been commemorated in various parts of this Province, and we have therefore sought to honour another of our New York patrons who has so far not been remembered in any place name. I refer to Governor Birch, the magistrate who gave us shelter when we arrived, homeless and penniless, in the city of New York. He opened up the empty and abandoned houses for us, the houses abandoned by the fleeing rebels, for us, oppressed and fleeing from our oppressors. Therefore we officially request, Mr. Marston, that you give the name of that great defender of the weak and abused to this town; let it from henceforth be known as *Birchtown!*"

With that, he led his captains in cheers: three cheers for Governor Birch and three more and a tiger for Birchtown. Marston, actually moved by their excitement, replied in a few words to let them know that their wishes would be respected and Birchtown it would be as far as he was concerned.

Then Surveyor Marston, Clifford, and the Colonel conferred on the layout of the town and stuck sticks in the ground here and there, while the labourers and a few good-natured captains brought ashore the supplies and erected tents. Clifford, Hannibal, and the four labourers decided to stay in Birchtown for the next few weeks, until the survey of the town was completed.

Colonel Bluck suggested that he could send over some of the Black Pioneers to help cut down trees, and several of the captains agreed to stay and take charge of them. So the boat sailed back to the town, but it came back again a few hours later with more men and supplies. By evening, there was a little settlement of tents and brushwood huts along the shore. The clearing began in earnest the next day, scrubby evergreens came crashing down along the gentle slope, and soon the lie of the land was clear to see. It was fine for a town site.

They worked every day, not stopping even on Sundays, so people would have their lots and houses before winter. Now and again, Hannibal went over to Port Roseway with Clifford or on errands without him, and was amazed to see how fast that city was springing up. Ships came steadily from Boston and Newport with house frames and sawn lumber, shingles for roofs and clapboards for walls, window frames and door frames, and everything needed for proper decent houses—things only towndwellers would have thought of, and things the modest houses in Birchtown would have to do without. All the sawmills in New England must have been hard at work producing what Port Roseway and the other Loyalist towns needed. Times were good for them. Some sawmills had been set up in Port Roseway as well, and were making rough boards that were very useful.

No longer were the main streets lined with tents and huts; handsome townhouses stood along them and there was a bustle of business in the air as crowds went up and down about their affairs. King Street was especially fine, and soon was fit to receive the Governor himself.

As Clifford told Hannibal, having heard the news from Mr. Marston, an invitation had been given the Governor and been accepted, the date was agreed upon (as much as it could be with the chances of sailing conditions being unfavourable), and they noticed the whole settlement buzzing with excitement at the prospect of some great development.

Certainly the Governor would have some important announcement to make, and at the very least confer a charter on the city, so it could hold elections and run its own affairs. Or possibly he was going to declare it the capital of the Province and would choose sites for his own residence, Government House, for a building for the House of Assembly to meet in, and for the Law Courts. People jested and laughed to think of the jealousy it would arouse in Halifax, which would sink into being the fishing village nature meant it for, and even in Boston and New York there would be uneasiness. The new metropolis of the North would outshine them all.

It was on Sunday, July 20, that Governor Parr's little fleet from Halifax was sighted at the harbour mouth and saluted by the cannon of the forts there. At Birchtown, Clifford called all the workers together—Hannibal was one of them by this time—and told them what the rumbling of the cannon signified.

"Tomorrow we're all having a holiday, lads," he said. "We'll sail over to the town early tomorrow morning to see the Governor and all the fun, and we won't come back to work with our chains and stakes until he leaves Port Roseway."

Early the next morning, when the sun was well up, they took their boats and bobbed across the water. They had to steer a way in among the Governor's flotilla, anchored near the now completed wharf. They had to steer clear of the many little boats bobbing out full of well-dressed citizens anxious to pay their respects to His Excellency. When they got to shore, they found the streets decorated in red, white and blue and full of excited people. They were all talking about the surprise the Governor would have for the town. There were all sorts of expectations. Hannibal didn't understand more than half what they were talking about, and doubted that they did themselves. Anyway, in the end most of their fancies turned out to be a long way off the mark.

Alas for their high hopes! When the Governor did come ashore and make a fine speech to the crowd, he did not give the town its charter and did not proclaim it the new capital of Nova Scotia. However, he did give it a new name; it was henceforth to be, "in honour of the great statesman to whom the Empire owes so much, 'Shelburne.'" The crowd cheered and gladly drank the King's health and that of his ministers from casks of rum open in the streets.

That evening, the Governor entertained the important men of the town at a grand dinner, and at intervals the cannon roared, which added to the excitement. Later Clifford heard from Surveyor Marston that this happened as toasts were proposed and glasses clinked; Marston was not impressed by it.

The next day, there was a public supper and a ball thrown by the town. The quality danced on a great platform of smooth waxed planks under a canvas marquee, while everybody else, even the African folks, including Hannibal, danced in the streets. The military band played loudly enough to be heard to the edge of town, so there was plenty of room for all to dance without getting in anyone's way.

Clifford seemed to change his mind about staying on in town. Perhaps the name chosen for the town annoyed him, and he was certainly disappointed that there was no charter and that Shelburne was not to be the capital. As during the war, he seemed to smell the scent of danger or misfortune, so now he showed some of the same signs. He was impatient to leave the town and called the Birchtown captains together and convinced them that two days of idleness were enough. They agreed and they all got themselves back to Birchtown by noon that day. They heard that the festivities continued in town, and it was a couple of days before they heard the cannon booming when Governor Parr sailed out, bound for Halifax, but in Birchtown they were too busy to pay much attention.

Soon in Birchtown they held a drawing for the completed lots, and those who were lucky in the draw moved onto their land and began to clear it. They had to keep at the survey, though, for new men needing land kept appearing all the time.

Hannibal saw a lot of his old friend Jupiter Brown, who was well-suited for the job at hand, and became friendly with all the captains, especially Dixon and Snowball. They were all busy building their homes and he helped first one and then another, where there were things he could do. By this time, their families had come over, boys and girls up to about Hannibal's age, and they worked and played together. It was hard work, because the men of Birchtown could not afford frame houses ready for assembly. Instead work parties trimmed the logs they had felled or went out in the forest looking for more, and dragged them back with their own strength.

To build a house, trenches were dug to make foundations for the walls, then logs were planted butt down in them in a tight row, so they would reach down well below frost level, and were firmly tied with crosspieces to form a kind of log box. A doorway was left, and one or two small windows were cut when the walls were firm. The soil was heaped a foot or two above ground level on the outside, and about half that on the inside. There was a low wet spot nearby and here the women and girls gathered clay and made a smooth floor inside. The chinks between the logs were plugged with clay and moss.

The roofs showed a lot of variety. The men split the driest logs and either used them for the full width of the slope of the roof or sawed them into foot lengths to serve as roofing, overlapping like tiles. Other people cut sheets of birch bark and nailed them on their poles like shingles. Probably they were the wisest, because when there was rain or melting snow, the water found many ways to trickle in between the logs.

One problem the Birchtown community suffered from was the scarcity of good building tools. The government had promised them, along with building supplies, all to be free. But they were a very long time coming. Fortunately, Jupiter Brown somehow had his own set of tools, and as he was a trained carpenter, he built himself the first and best house. After that he was busy helping others, even if only to give lessons in working wood or advice about beams and rafters. He also showed the other men how to knock together rough furniture good enough to make do for the time being.

By the time the days were drawing in (much earlier than those from Carolina were used to), Shelburne and Birchtown were as ready as they could be for the cold weather that was coming. The settlers had caught fish and smoked it, and were learning what animals they could trap or shoot in the woods. They had the promise that the government would provide them all with regular rations and all in all they were confident about getting by pretty well.

Then, on the September 23, 1783, a whole armada of ships sailed up the harbour and filled the anchorage to capacity. They called it "the Fall Fleet," and it was packed with another mass of black and white refugees. It wasn't easy for people to sympathize with them. They had deliberately stayed in the comfort of New York City until the last possible moment. They were afraid to take sail for the northern wilderness, but when they realised that the city really was going to be turned over to Washington, they were more afraid to be at the mercy of his army and the slave-hunters and civilians who would be crowding in behind them.

As Clifford informed Hannibal, some eight thousand people had crowded onto the transports. They were of all types, as the earlier settlers soon saw; the troopers of the Loyalist regiments defending the city, with their wives and children, craftsmen and petty traders of the town, and the runaway slaves who sought liberty within the British lines. When Washington and the Continental Army finally rode through the city, they saw only silent empty streets and empty houses.

Fortunately for those who had already settled in, only half the Fall Fleet came to Shelburne; the other half sailed to Saint John on the northern side of the Bay of Fundy hundreds of miles away. Even so, a way had to be found for four thousand homeless people to survive the winter in Shelburne, and once again canvas tents and rough huts went up under the trees around the town. Fortunately, too many of the transports stayed in the harbour for the cold months and plenty of people found it more comfortable to stay in the gloom and bad smells there than endure the hardships of camping in the woods.

The final fortunate thing was that, by Nova Scotian standards, it was a mild winter. Even so, there was a first snowfall on November 2, and gradually it piled up deeper and deeper through the coldest months after Christmas. Most people had a bleak, uncomfortable time of it.

chapter three
SPRING THAW

The men of the refugee community worked hard all summer, and by the time the days were drawing in, and the sun rose late and set early, Birchtown was complete. The men who had worked so hard brought their families over from the city and they all settled into their new homes. It was a happy community, living in good order under the direction of Colonel Bluck and the captains.

Hannibal had become friends with most of the captains, and looked forward to possibly being part of their community. However, he supposed that Clifford expected him to be part of his household in Shelburne, and his place was with him. Hannibal did not question the fact that in the eyes of the law he was property, that Clifford owned him and had the right to his service, no matter what he said. In any case, his safety and well-being in the confusion of the settlement depended on the protection his master could offer.

He was glad to find as matters developed that he could spend the winter with his friends.

Clifford had found an old friend, Lieutenant Sam Partridge, whom he had known very well during the war, and was invited to live with him in a snug little house he had built in the middle of town. Hannibal discovered that he didn't have much to keep himself busy, because Sam had brought an old couple from his home in the South who had known him from childhood, and who did everything necessary to look after two bachelors. So Clifford let him go back to stay a few days with his Birchtown friends whenever he asked. It was after one such visit in October that they had a serious talk.

"Master Clifford," he said, "Colonel Bluck is starting a school for the young ones over in Birchtown. I would like to go, if you can spare me here."

He thought for a few minutes, then said, "Hannibal, it's time we had a little talk. There are things we need to make clear to each other. You are fifteen now, and almost a grown man. As far as I am concerned, you belong to yourself, but in the meantime it is better for me to be responsible for you. When you are twenty or twenty-one, I'll sign a bit of paper that says you are nobody's slave, but a free man. If you know what you need to do to prepare for the rest of your life, then I'll back you up. I'm buying a fishing boat in partnership with Lieutenant Partridge, and I could send you out to learn that life; Shelburne is going to be a leader in the North Atlantic fishery, and you could have profitable employment for a lifetime in it. What do you say?"

The boy didn't have to think long to know that a life in the fishery did not appeal to him. He had not enjoyed his experiences at sea, and the little he had seen of the fisherman's life had turned him against it. He hoped Clifford would not try to force it on him "for your own good," so he told him that for the moment he wanted to get more schooling. Back before the war he had done some learning alongside Clifford's young brother Adolphus, but after his death he hadn't had any more chances. He had kept up his reading, but he had not had much opportunity to practise writing, and he knew there was plenty he could learn in a few months of attendance at school.

"I agree," he said, "that it would be good for you to have more schooling, whatever you do in life. But how can you go to school in Birchtown when you live in Shelburne?"

"Sir," he explained, "Jupiter Brown says I could live with him, and I've spoken to Colonel Bluck and he's willing to have me in the class along with the Birchtown young ones."

"All right," Clifford agreed, "but these men do not have to deprive themselves for you. I'll pay Jupiter Brown something for keeping you, and he can collect your rations from the Commissariat as long as you're there. Colonel Bluck shall have his fee for teaching you, too; he can't be expected to take you on for nothing."

So it was arranged. Then, before they said goodbye, Clifford said, "Colonel Bluck will have to write your name in his attendance book. What will it be?"

The boy looked at him, wondering. His name was Hannibal Hoops, a name Colonel Courtney had given him when he was an infant suffering from whooping cough. That fact he knew well. What did Clifford have in mind?

"Hannibal, calling you Hoops was my father's little joke, and as long as you were a child it was all right; it was a name that seemed to suit you. But now that you are becoming a man, it may not do. As it is, my friends and most of the white people who know you call you "Clifford Courtney's Hannibal," or just plain "Courtney's Hannibal." That being the case, why don't we do the proper thing, make it official, and call you Hannibal Courtney!"

Hannibal was overcome by an emotion of gratitude and thankfulness that his master was willing to give him his name, as he had never really thought of such a thing. He had always known from his mother's account that his African clan name was Kontay, but he had never told that to Clifford or any white person, and probably never would; but when he compared Kontay with Courtney (pronounced Cot'nay"), it seemed so close that he thought it would be good to be called by it. So from this time on, he went by this name officially, though his friends went on calling him "Hannibal Hoops."

So he spent most of the winter of 1783-84 at Birchtown. In later years, he was told that Shelburne was one of the warmest parts of Nova Scotia in winter (and in fact he indeed later experienced much colder weather on the Minas Basin shore when he lived there), but for those from the South, it was cold beyond their imagination. In fact, the year 1784 was a cold year everywhere. There were weeks after the beginning of the new year when the low cabins of Birchtown seemed to cower nearer to the ground under the pale cold winter sky and people walked only along narrow blue-shadowed trails, pressed down into the deep snow by many feet coming one after another, edged with an icy crust that could rip stockings or bare ankles.

Despite the cold, there was a warmth in the community, a good feeling of friendship and trust, and every day people were visiting one another and thus kept their spirits bright and warm.

From occasional Micmac Indian hunters who visited the settlement and were surprised by the dark faces, the settlers learned about making snowshoes and about the animal life in the dark woods to the North.

Felix Martin, who was about Hannibal's age, was his constant companion many mornings before school when the two went into the woods and followed the line of a dozen traps set where the rabbits liked to run. Often they brought half a dozen home, dangling by their long back legs, and others did the same. It was a tasty change from the salty corned pork they received as government rations. Sometimes the older men made up a hunting party to look for deer or moose, or for signs of beaver; they were all edible, but there were not many of them within hiking distance of the settlement. Sometimes their Micmac friends would appear with a haunch of moose or a tender beaver tail as their contribution to the meal they were invited to share.

Of course, Hannibal's main reason for being at Birchtown was to go to school, and he was glad he did, because he learned a lot from the schoolmaster, Colonel Bluck. He used to begin every day's work with a long reading from his big Bible; the words rolled over the young scholars and went in their ears, through their heads, and then often out their mouths when they spoke or onto their slates when they wrote. The Colonel spoke very much like the Bible himself, so he must have been reading it for years.

They also learned to sing some songs and hymns, to write neatly, to read (from a few books and scraps of newspaper), and to cipher or work with numbers. They all learned to write their names nicely, as Colonel Bluck said they would be judged as literate men by the signature each of them made. He was a man who had learned much wisdom in the world, and sometimes he would just talk about his experiences in the Caribbean and Europe and what he had learned.

The older boys knew they had to help with the hard work of the settlement, too, and when not in class they went along with the grown men as they did what had to be done. The dead trees from the summer were cut and chopped into firewood, fresh trees in the forest were felled and dragged out to season, and the little boats went out when the water was calm and brought back fish and sometimes lobsters, and so they kept busy and were healthy and strong.

At intervals, boats went over to Shelburne, usually taken by the captains who had to get provisions for their companies at the Commissariat or government storehouse and now and again Hannibal had gone to report to Clifford and to hear his news.

Most evenings of the winter were spent by young and old, alike, relaxed and sociable; a group would get together in someone's house to play cards, to dance to fiddle-music, and generally to laugh and joke and talk and have a good time. Jupiter Brown's place, where Hannibal stayed, was a popular meeting place; he had a fine family of boys and girls who seemed to look up to the older boy. At times Hannibal felt he was their older brother and that he had found a real family for himself. He had many a pleasant evening with them and the friends who came in out of the cold.

Sunday was a day of rest for the community, and it had its own preacher who came over in the autumn from Shelburne, built a cabin, and held Sunday services as well as a prayer meeting during the week. This old man was called Moses; he had been born in Africa and was brought across the ocean to Georgia. H had been a Christian then, but after some years, he told his flock, God sent a wonderful gentle Englishman, Charles Wesley, to America, to bring a message of hope to the poor slaves. He was converted and baptized by Wesley, and in his years of slavery had tried to be a witness for the love of God. The war had led to his freedom, and though he was an old man, white-headed and bent, he always rebuked the grumblers of the settlement and reminded them that God had brought them "up out of Egypt" and that they should always be grateful for freedom.

Happy and grateful as most people were, all was not paradise in Birchtown. One Sunday morning, at service in Moses's cabin, Hannibal saw that his friend Felix, standing beside him while they sang a hymn, was swaying back and forth, and then at the end of the first verse he buckled at the knees and fell in a heap. He got someone to help carry Felix out and, on a dry spot of ground, stretched him out and waited for him to come to. In a few minutes, he opened his eyes and looked ashamed when he realized what had happened.

"What's wrong?" Hannibal asked. "Are you sick?'

"I just feel a bit weak," he said, but when questioned further he confessed that he was weak because he was very, very hungry. He hadn't eaten a decent meal for days.

"Why? How could that be?" his friend asked; "Everybody gets rations. You get the same as I do. I know it isn't enough to get fat on, even when we catch rabbits or fish to add to it, but you shouldn't be hungry. Isn't your father giving you your share?"

Felix got angry then and indignant tears filled his eyes.

"It's not my father. He's starving, too. So is the whole family. He can't get us enough food. What we catch in our traps goes mostly to the littlest ones."

A light seemed to shine in Hannibal's head; he understood in an instant. The captains collected the rations from the stores in Shelburne and doled them out to the men in their companies, according to the size of their families. Felix's family was not getting its fair share.

He asked further, "If your father is not getting his rations, then his captain is holding them back. Which of them is it? I'm sure it couldn't be Dixon or Snowball—they wouldn't treat their people like that—but is it Powell? Perth? Hamilton?"

The change in the expression on Felix's face told the boy that he had got it right with the last-named, and then he heard what Felix knew. Captain Hamilton had not handed out any rations to his company for several weeks. No one knew where the supplies were, but they didn't believe he had brought them to Birchtown, and suspected he had sold them off to a dishonest shopkeeper in Shelburne. None of his men knew what to do about it, as they were afraid of getting on the bad side of the authorities, who would, they were sure, stick together.

Hannibal didn't think about it that way. Perhaps he had seen enough of "authorities" during the times he had seen Master Clifford dealing with them to feel no such fear as Felix, his father, and the other men felt. He got an arm around Felix and got him up and held him up while they slowly walked back to his cabin. Hannibal spoke to the father, Pete Martin, who was angry with Felix for his weakness.

"You Black Pioneers are free men, now," Hannibal said. "Captain Hamilton cannot take away your rights, and that includes your food. The government gives him food to give to you. It is not his to keep from you."

"I don't think he's keeping the food," said Pete. "He probably traded it in the town for rum. He likes to drink a lot."

"Well, it doesn't matter what he did, or why he did it. He's a thief in any case, and you have to get the law on him."

"The law!" cried Pete in alarm. "Who would believe me if I went forward with a complaint? Who would take my word against his? Who would even listen to me?"

"Not you alone, man," Hannibal reasoned with him. "Your whole company should go over and find a Justice of the Peace to talk to. He would have to listen and investigate your complaint."

"Well, you're a bold one, young Hannibal," he said, wonderingly, "but maybe you've got the answer. Maybe we just have to show some backbone. It would be better to take a risk than to starve to death."

In a few minutes, ten of the men from Hamilton's company, a sad and bedraggled lot, had gathered together, and Pete made the boy talk to them. It was a bold thing for a boy to do, but he didn't feel timid. He was too angry with Hamilton to have room for any other feelings. He had to argue them out of their fears that it was disloyal to appeal to the white man's law in a matter that was the business of the African community. Colonel Bluck was respected as their leader, but his authority was a moral authority, not an official one, and it did not appear that they had even consulted him about the problem. In any case, the remedy for their plight lay with the magistrates and officials in Shelburne, so they agreed to go and asked Hannibal to come, too.

They sailed across the harbour to the town and he led them to the house of a magistrate he knew, a man who was a friend of Clifford's. Hannibal had gone with him more than once on visits there. As they hoped, they received a courteous hearing from Squire Burden. He heard them out and at once sat at his desk and wrote an order to the Commissariat for replacement rations and another to the constables to go over to Birchtown and arrest Captain Hamilton.

Hamilton didn't try to run away or deny the charges; it turned out that he was very much ashamed of himself for selling the rations and buying rum. Once he had done it, he hadn't known how to get out of his fix. In a few days, he was brought to trial and made a full confession. He broke down in tears and asked the court for mercy. Happily for him, the court put him on probation, thinking perhaps that he would be punished every day when he faced the men and families he had robbed. So he came back to Birchtown, resisted temptation, and cleaned up his tarnished reputation over the next half year.

Captain Hamilton was really very fortunate, because he might easily have been beaten with the lash, as happened to any common pickpocket or shoplifter in Shelburne. Hardly a weekend when by that Hannibal didn't see some poor wretch, male or female, black or white, being dragged at a cart's tail up and down the streets to be jeered at and mocked. And that was not all. At each street corner, the guilty person was lashed on the bare back ten or twenty times, until sometimes they collapsed into unconsciousness, or worse, before all two hundred lashes had been given. Those were the kind of sentences that were carried out, worse than, or at least as bad as anything heard of on plantations or in the army.

In later years, when times had changed, these customs and laws seemed very harsh, but in those days hearts were very hard. The only way to get people to respect the law was by public floggings and hangings. The only police force was half a dozen "constables" at the service of the magistrates; they were old veterans of the wars incapable of doing any hard work. In fact, they didn't get much respect from the citizens, who were a hard-boiled lot. However, law-abiding people liked them well enough. They were decent men, and they carried out their duties as fairly as they could. The army based at Shelburne got more respect than the constables; all the citizens were conscious of its forts around the vicinity of the town. The soldiers were there to keep order if the need arose, and the day eventually came when those soldiers were needed.

During those months of winter, Hannibal began to realize that he was not satisfied with his life. As the snows melted to slush, then froze again, and when rain and fog made the days gloomy, or even when the sun shone on trees and bushes all glazed by a coating of ice that sparkled and glowed like a world of crystals, Hannibal felt a lack of something. He was not satisfied with the daily grind of everyday life and the self-interest that drove so many people. Colonel Bluck's readings from the Bible seemed to say that God intended for people to help one another and share with one another, that spiritual matters were more important than anything else, and that Jesus had told us all to love one another like brothers and sisters. He wondered whether other people heard what he heard, and whether there was a reason for life and a pattern that made sense of what he found so confusing.

Hannibal tried talking to Moses about his feelings, but though he respected the preacher as a saintly soul, he did not seem to understand the boy's problems. Then he heard that the Lord had sent another preacher man, David George, to Shelburne. He built a meeting house on his own land and held services that drew even white people to listen to his preaching and even change their lives. David George called himself a "new light," and though he was not young, he was ageless. His personality was strong and he welcomed Hannibal when he found his way to his cabin. His Sunday services were held at a different time than those of Moses, and Hannibal began to attend them, too. Gradually as spring strengthened and the warm sun melted the ice and drove the frost from the ground, the boy felt himself thawing as well. He spent more and more of his free time talking to Reverend David George, not on religion necessarily, but about life and what made it worthwhile, the "why" of everything created.

The most important day of his life began in late winter when he had gone to the Sunday service in David George's meeting house. For the first time ever, he had to leave before it was over, for he felt suffocated and had to get out in the open air. He wandered along the shore where the waves were dashing on the rocks, and still he was feeling suffocated. He felt as if a wide band were tightening about his chest, making it hard to draw a deep breath. In his mind, some of the familiar words of the sermon were beginning to echo in his mind, words such as "unless a man be born again" and "Lo, I am with you always." Suddenly the iron band around his chest burst and there was a great open space in him, and just as swiftly it filled up with love and happiness; he felt the glow and warmth of an inner fire.

In his innermost being, he suddenly felt that God loved him and that he in turn loved Him and all His Creation, that the Son of God had died to gain immortal life for him, and that he would want to praise God and enjoy Him forever. The whole world was suddenly changed before his eyes, transformed. He was seeing it as if he had never seen it properly before. The birds in the blue sky were singing more sweetly, and the colours of sea and sky and forest were fresher and purer than he had ever known them to be. It was as if scales had fallen from his eyes. He knew that he had undergone what Preacher George called "being born again."

He walked back to David George's cabin as if he were walking on air, a spring of happiness bubbling up inside him and feelings of love rolling out from him. He felt no doubts, no fears, and no ill-feeling towards anyone. When he told the preacher, "I am born again, I am saved," David George's face filled with a great happiness, and he embraced the boy, exclaiming fervently, "The Lord be praised, the Lord be praised."

Then they knelt together and, keeping one hand on Hannibal's shoulder, he poured out a prayer of thankfulness and praise to the Lord. From a full heart, Hannibal could only say again and again, "Amen, amen, thank you, Lord Jesus!"

A few weeks later, on the second Sunday in June, he stood with a group of other people by the cold waters of the stream flowing through Pastor George's land and into the harbour. His friend Felix Martin was there, too, with his younger sister Charlotte, and several other young people, along with some older married people. One by one, they went down with David George until they were waist deep, then, yielding ourselves to his strong arms, they were plunged backwards under the surface of the water, three times for the three members of the Holy Trinity, and were brought up sodden and sputtering and fully baptized members of the body of Christ. They stood on the bank singing hymns till it was over, after which they went to his home nearby as quickly as they could and changed their cold wet clothes for something dry and warm.

chapter four
THE GREAT SHELBURNE RIOT

With the coming of warmer weather, Hannibal left his Birchtown friends, for Master Clifford was starting to build his house, and needed many willing hands. At odd times during the spring, his friends had cleared his town lot and dug a cellar well below the frost line. He had contracted with stone masons to cut and deliver blocks of granite for the foundation, and the same men had built them into walls standing about three feet above the ground. The main body of the house, all wood, would rest on this foundation, and since by early June the masons had completed their work and the stone walls were ready to receive the floor joists, upwards construction could begin.

Knowing what a good carpenter his old friend Jupiter Brown was, Hannibal pressed Clifford to take him on; he did so, along with a couple of Jupiter's friends, and Hannibal worked alongside them as an apprentice, learning the craft. When more hands were needed, a couple of other men were hired from Birchtown; they brought their families over and made a camp for themselves on Clifford's farm lot, still in forest. It was well within walking distance of the job, and suited them very well.

At the beginning of the construction, there was an incident which the workers hardly noticed at the time, but a few weeks later realized had been a forewarning. It happened on a day while they were still grubbing up loose soil to make a tidy cellar and measuring off the large beams of wood for joists and frame. A gang of five strong looking men, all white, came up to Clifford and asked for work. He answered them politely.

"I'm sorry," he said. "I've already hired the men I need."

The men looked them over with hostile expressions and their leader said, rather scornfully, "These are not Shelburne men; they appear to be slave trash. Are they your property?"

"They are all free men, and they used to live in Carolina, like me. Now they live over at Birchtown."

"Birchtown men have no call to take work here," said another of them. "Here we are, good white men desperate for honest work, and you get cheap blacks instead. If you don't send them back to their own place and let men of this town have the work, you'll be looking for trouble."

Clifford was not inclined to bandy further words with them, and they turned to leave. But before they went ten feet, they turned around and told the workers, with insulting words and gestures, that they'd better get back to Birchtown if they knew what was good for them.

Clifford was furious, but faced his workers, who had stopped working and were looking at him, and said, "Pay no heed to that empty bluff and bluster, boys. I have a right to hire whomever I like. Put these rowdies out of your minds and let's get on with this cellar."

For several weeks, the Birchtown men worked away peacefully. Clifford had his share of building material provided by the government and ordered more decent timber from Portsmouth, down the coast. Large pieces of timber easily fitted together to make the frame and there were plenty of government boards to fill in the floors and walls and roof.

They worked well together and it was a time of happiness as well as hard work; nonetheless, now and again mention was made of something wrong in the town. There were too many idle, staring men in the streets—men waiting for their farm grants, or men not entitled to receive land, or men who wanted paid work instead of the unrewarded task of clearing their own farms. There were men who complained about the government and raised a cheer when they heard that some soldiers had deserted from the garrison. Four of these runaways were captured and marched through the streets to be shown off before they were hanged. Crowds of men and boys followed along, insulting and booing the soldiers who guarded the prisoners on every side.

It was clear to Hannibal that Master Clifford and his friend Partridge were worried by the mood of the townsfolk. He was with them in the evenings as they talked it over. The fact was that there were more than ten thousand people in Shelburne, a bigger crowd of people gathered in one place than anywhere in the Thirteen Colonies at that time. These people needed to be kept very busy if they were not going to be discontented and mischievous, but the sort of work they were looking for was not available. They did not have the muscles or minds to be axmen, farmers, fishermen, and shipbuilders; they were tailors, periwigmakers, confectioners, and bakers, not to mention those used to living dishonestly by their wits, such as gamblers, pickpockets and cheats. These were not the kind of fellow pioneers Clifford and Mr. Partridge had expected to live and work with.

One Sunday morning, Hannibal had gone with Clifford to the Church of England service in an empty warehouse—Clifford didn't really approve of the New Lights and did not approve of Hannibal's baptism by David George, and hoped the boy would gradually be content to belong to the Church of England. After service, he sent Hannibal to McTurk's Tavern to get a couple of bottles of Madeira for the dinner table. While the boy waited for attention at the counter in the public room, he noticed some men in a corner talking in low tones, as if they did not want to be overheard. He would not have thought much about it, but as he glanced at them he happened to lock in on the eyes of one of the men who had incuriously glanced at him. Immediately he broke contact and looked away, but Hannibal took a better look and felt there was something familiar about his face.

Then suddenly he placed him; he had been the leader of the group demanding that Clifford send his work crew back to Birchtown. He must have said something to the others, for the boy saw them stealing quick looks in his direction, and their voices sank even lower. He felt very uncomfortable standing there in full view, and was glad when the two bottles of wine were passed over and he could get out the door. He wondered why they were being so secretive, and whether it could have anything to do with himself and Clifford. However, it did not make the impression on him that it should have; he mentioned, when he handed over the wine, that he had received strange looks from a group of men drinking there, but as there was really nothing more to say about it, they all put it in the back of their minds and soon forgot it.

Next morning, Monday, the men were back at work. Clifford stood by and conferred with Jupiter, then went away on business, leaving him in charge of the construction. The first storey had been boarded in and they were busy on the upstairs. Gradually they became conscious of a lot of noise coming from the waterfront and by about nine o'clock a confused roar of human shouting was blown towards them from the direction of King Street. Jupiter stopped his hammering and silenced all.

"I hear Indian war whoops!" he said.

"Have the Micmacs attacked the town?" Hannibal asked in amazement. They had been friendly through the winter, when they could have easily harmed the settlers. It was hard to believe they would attack them now.

"I doubt it," Jupiter replied. "If those are Micmacs, they learned their war whoops from Iroquois or Cherokee! Those are not real Indians making that noise, but white men out for some kind of spree."

They kept on with their work, but in about half an hour or less they were surprised to see groups of people and individuals running past towards the outskirts of the town. They were African people, some of them slaves living in the town and others recognised as being from Birchtown. The workers paused and called down to them to know what was happening.

"They're coming! They're close behind us! Come on, we've got to get out of town before they catch us." That was more or less the reply, leaving the builders no more the wiser.

They all stopped work and gathered around Jupiter, wondering what they had best do. Then they saw a thick pack of white men emerge from the lane that led from King Street. They were yelling curses and Cherokee war whoops and pushing ahead of them, with cuffs and kicks, some African men who had fallen into their hands. Now and again one would fall down, perhaps tripped, and the mob of white men passed over his prostrate form, trampling him into the mud and mire. It was as ugly a sight as seen in all the years of war.

Almost before the workmen realized what was happening, the white men were abreast of them, and seeing them in the half-built house with hammers and saws in their hands howled like blood-maddened animals. They could have been hounds pressing in for the kill. The morning sun glinted off the swords and tomahawks in their hands, and Clifford's workers looked at them in shocked surprise, dazed and frozen for a few moments.

The mob turned to come into the house, shouting things like "Back to Birchtown, you blackamoors!" and "Out, black-trash, out!" Several of the Birchtown men turned and jumped to the ground on the far side and sprinted out of range, but Jupiter said, "I'm not going to run from that trash," and Hannibal stood beside him. The mob came up on all sides against the two of them. The swords and tomahawks were just for show; they picked up bits of timber to strike out at them. Jupiter was hit over the head from behind while he was busy with a couple of tough thugs in front, while Hannibal was tripped up by another pair of men and punched and kicked till he was nearly unconscious. They left him lying on the ground, painfully drawing air into his lungs.

It must have been ten minutes before he sat up. The mob had not stayed to do further damage, but had run on to find more exciting sport. Master Clifford was suddenly beside him with a mug of water. Wherever he had been, he seemed to be aware of what had happened, and concerned about his workers. He felt along Hannibal's arms and legs and was satisfied to find that he had no broken bones.

"I think you'll be stiff for a few days," he said. "You're probably bruised, but I can't see any cuts on you. That's just as well." He turned to tend to Jupiter, who was out cold and lying in a heap. Clifford soaked a handkerchief in cold water and dampened the unconscious man's face and neck. He groaned and began to come to, moving his arms and hands and opening his eyes. Meanwhile Hannibal was responding to Clifford's comments.

"I'm all right," he assured his master. "But those men were out to hurt us. Why? What is it all about?"

"I'm not quite sure," was the reply, "but I expect those men you saw whispering last night at McTurk's Tavern—and probably at other places, too—were cooking it up. They must have spread the word among all the idle loafers of the town. I'll swear there were three hundred men rampaging up King Street. It was like that mob that took over Boston just before the war. Perhaps we have our own Sam Adams here making fiery speeches and whipping up defiance of the law and good order. How ironic, when so many of us here left our homes to escape mob rule. I heard them howling about the bad government and the bad magistrates, but mostly they were complaining about blacks taking food out of their mouths. Luckily the batch that came this way was only a part of the crowd—they've split up to rampage around all the streets."

They looked along the street in the direction everyone had gone and though it was deserted they could see in the distance smoke winding up above the trees.

"I'll bet you they've set fire to the huts up in the woods," said Clifford.

He was referring to the huts the Birchtown men had built for temporary accommodation while they worked in town. Jupiter was recovered enough to understand and with a deep groan, not caused by physical pain alone, sat up.

"Master Courtney," he whispered, "there's women and children there. My wife's there—what can we do?"

"They won't hurt women and children, Jupiter," said he. "They're just out to give you folks a good scare. They want you to go back to Birchtown, but otherwise they mean you no great harm. I never thought of this possibility when I hired you and the boys to work here. Anyway, they've been savage towards you and you've got to get away in case they come back and give you another drubbing. Can you walk over to Lieutenant Partridge's place if Hannibal and I lend a hand? They'll never think of looking for you there."

"I'll try, sir," he said, "but afterwards please go up and make sure our women and children are safe."

Clifford promised to do so, then he and Hannibal helped Jupiter across a couple of intervening streets and over to Mr. Partridge's. Once they had him behind the stout door, they both breathed easier, even though there was no sign of the rioters among the excited men, women, and children who were flocking together in the streets to talk about them. Soon Hannibal was helping the manservant of Mr. Partridge's fix heavy shutters over the downstairs windows, just like other people were doing in their houses and shops along the street. It was apparent that people expected the trouble to continue.

Clifford kept his promise and went to the edge of the town. He came back much later and told Hannibal and Jupiter that he had ducked into an alley when he saw the mob coming back, along with a crowd of admirers, but he hardly needed to take precautions. They were too busy taking over the tavern at the corner to care about observers, and though the landlord was screaming at them, they boldly broached his puncheons of rum and gin and passed the drink out in basins and measures to anyone who wanted it.

Clifford made a slight detour and got to the encampment without trouble; sure enough, the huts had been fired and only ashes were left, but several of the men who had been chased had come out of the woods and were gathering up the few things left. They assured him that the women and children were in the woods on the path for Birchtown, carrying their belongings with them, along with most of the men. Those left were about to follow and would collect any stragglers as they went.

Although by nightfall, there were no African people to be found and in the streets the passions of the mob continued unabated. Clifford and Mr. Partridge talked about the situation that evening and then shared their thoughts with Jupiter and Hannibal.

"This complaint against black people is no more than an excuse for a bunch of criminals to overthrow law and order," said Clifford. "For the moment they control the town; they laugh at the magistrates when they warn them and they beat up the constables who try to stop them. They are seizing the taverns and getting drunk, they are breaking into shops and warehouses to take whatever they feel like taking. I was wrong to compare them to Sam Adams and his Boston mob; they're ten times worse and all they want is chaos!"

Jupiter, the old soldier who put a high value on discipline and good order, was disgusted. "The troops will soon put a stop to such goings-on," he said. "They should catch them all at dawn, while they're still sleeping off their drink, and put them all in chains."

At that point, Lieutenant Partridge came in. He was a friend of some of the officers and always knew what was going on in the garrison. Clifford eagerly asked for the news from that quarter, and in particular, "When are they going to put a stop to this lawlessness?"

"I've just been over to see the Commander," said Partridge. "The magistrates have asked him to send in the troops, but he won't do it. He says they have no power to give him orders, and he cannot do it on his own. He can only act when ordered to do so by a higher authority."

"Surely that is a quibble," Clifford replied. "I'm sure he has plenty of authority to act to keep the peace, especially when the magistrates request it. Why, the whole town could be burned down around our heads if order isn't restored."

The next day, Jupiter was well enough to walk and a small group of Clifford's friends went down to the waterfront and found a boat going across to Birchtown. Clifford thought Hannibal had better go over there, too, lest the mob find him and injure him seriously, so he agreed to stay there until things were better. Later his master filled him in on the chaotic events of the next several days in the town of Shelburne.

Despite Clifford's fears, nobody was so foolish as to try to burn the town, but all businesses were pillaged and laid waste. Apparently the rioters formed rival groups and fought with staves to get the right to sack a particular store or warehouse, or most especially to determine who would have the run of a dram shop miraculously found intact. Dozens of men and boys were laid low with concussions or broken limbs, and dozens of others staggered around dead drunk or fell asleep on the ground. Naturally, all business was at a standstill, and families of the better sort locked and barricaded themselves in their homes. There were women and children in the streets; however, they belonged to the rioters and followed close behind the men to carry home the spoils they took by force.

Although the commander of the garrison refused to stir to restore order, he did at least send a fast craft to Halifax to report events. Meanwhile, during successive days of rioting, he stayed with his men close to the blockhouse. Finally, on the fourth day, the sound of cannon at the harbour mouth brought hope of outside intervention. Sure enough, a small flotilla of ships sailed up to Shelburne an hour or so later and the body of magistrates gathered at the waterfront to tell their story.

Governor Parr himself had come and must have reflected on the difference in circumstances from his visit the year before when he had launched the town and appointed the very magistrates now waiting to greet him. The welcoming committee of men who had been so confident and proud the year before were now broken, harried men who spilled out the story of the uncontrollable mob, the destruction of property and peace of mind, and the strange refusal of the garrison to help them put a stop to it.

"Our streets are battlefields; our town is a captured city given over to plunder," they said. "Only an army can save us from complete destruction."

The Governor had a small force of soldiers with him, and ordered the local garrison out to support them. With them at his back, he proclaimed martial law within the town limits, then had the troops fix bayonets and march in order up King Street, sending the main mob fleeing into the back streets. Then the soldiers split into smaller detachments and broke up the groups they found there and in the alleys. Meanwhile, the town crier was going through the streets relaying the Governor's order that people were to get to their homes and stay there until further notice. Having heard the whole story from the magistrates (as Clifford heard and later told Hannibal), Governor Parr had to be the statesman and determine a way to punish the evildoers without destroying the town. The magistrates had been compiling a list of the ringleaders during the days of riot, so the Governor was able to send the soldiers to their homes and take as many of them as they could find. Some of them were hiding in the forest and had escaped judgment for the time being.

That night, the town slept in peace for the first time since the previous Sunday night. Hannibal felt it was safe to return to town with some others the next morning. He wanted to follow events from close at hand. Soon after he got ashore, he heard the town crier announcing that the Governor would be holding a general reception at ten o' clock to hear complaints and allocate justice. He made his way to Mr. Partridge's house where he found Clifford; Clifford had been asked by Surveyor Marston to accompany him to the Governor's reception, to which he had a special invitation. Evidently he felt he should have a colleague with him.

Hannibal walked along with his master to the house where the Governor was staying. Soldiers were lined up outside to regulate admission through the front door, and were posted at intervals in the street in front of the house. Large numbers of citizens were gathered in quite a bit of confusion, and some of the arrested men were brought past under guard and taken inside. When Mr. Marston appeared, he and Clifford went in together, and were in there for a couple of hours. These few hours changed the course of their lives once again, because of what Clifford witnessed and described to Hannibal later that night.

In a large room, the Governor sat behind a desk and the citizens stood around the walls facing him. They were encouraged to speak up if they had complaints, and it seemed that many did. Mainly they complained about land. Many of them complained that they didn't yet have the grants the government had promised; others complained that though they had received their grants, their land was miserable and not worth working, and that Surveyor Marston had parcelled out the good land to his particular friends. At this point, Clifford noticed that he himself, standing beside Marston, was also the target of hostile eyes. He felt very uncomfortable.

However, there were other complaints, too. One was that the customs dues were unfair and were stifling the trade of the town. Another was about the presence in the town of Free Blacks who were a bad influence on the Africans who were still in servitude. It was said that many of the Africans claimed to be free when they were not, and they were taking the bread out of the mouths of honest white workers.

In dealing with the complaints, Governor Parr commented on several things, but seemed most interested in the accusations that Surveyor Marston was not doing a good job.

He called Marston to the front of the room and asked him to respond to the complaints. Marston did so, and explained that the farms were being given out to people as fast as they were measured out. This was being done in order of their arrival in Shelburne, so the last to arrive would be the last to receive their land. That was why the men who came on the Fall Fleet had not all been dealt with, but he and his helpers hoped to have it all completed within two months.

As Clifford told Hannibal later, "It was no use. The Governor saw he could use Mr. Marston as a scapegoat to save his own reputation, and he did not hesitate. He publicly threw him to the wolves, told him he had not done a good job as Chief Surveyor, and told him to pack his things because he was taking him back to Halifax. That this should happen to Marston, who has been working his heart out the whole time we've been here to help these people!"

Hannibal himself, from a distance, saw the Governor come out onto the stoop in front of the house to talk to the crowd. He looked very pleased with himself and seemed to be playing up the crowd, who, excited and nervous, were ready to be played with. When he told them he had found that Mr. Marston was the cause of their trouble, and was taking him away, they cheered and shouted. He told them they would all have land soon, and that the disbanded soldiers would also be entitled to a share, even if they were not Loyalists. That brought cheers from that group. He said that all Free Blacks were to leave town and work on their own allocations of land, and any who tried to live in Shelburne would be dealt with. That raised more cheering from some people, and looking around, and seeing no other African person there, Hannibal was at pains to shield himself behind a couple of large women on the fringe of the crowd.

Governor John Parr, seen off by the soldiers and the magistrates, and indeed by large crowd of citizens, went back to his ship in a blaze of popularity. Some time later, about dusk, Hannibal went with Clifford and a few others to take Mr. Marston and his baggage to the quay. There were no cheers, but only quiet handshakes and good wishes as the Chief Surveyor of the settlement left the town he had laid out in the wilderness, and which had so ungratefully turned its anger on him.

That night, Clifford made up his mind to leave Shelburne, too.

"I did not turn my back on my home in the South," he said, "to be ordered about in the North by an unruly mob of ignorant ruffians. Anyway, I realize now that I am not cut out for town life or the fish business. After all, I grew up in the countryside and farming is in my blood. So I'm going to look for the best farming land in Nova Scotia. Even if I cannot make a plantation out of it, I can make a decent farm. Of course it is too cold for our southern crops such as rice, but there must be northern foodstuffs we can grow at a profit. We'll stay away from towns, Hannibal, and live a healthy country life."

chapter five
SETTLING DOWN IN HORTON TOWNSHIP

Clifford Courtney had made a hard decision. In his mind, he had shaken the dust of Shelburne from his shoes having lost confidence in its future. Within a few weeks of the great riot, he had sold off his farm and the house lot with its nearly completed house. His friend Sam Partridge agreed to see to his water lot and shares in a fishing boat. Soon the day came when he and Hannibal went aboard a small coasting vessel loading for Halifax and sailed out before evening. They had seen their last of the great Loyalist city.

A smooth voyage with light winds brought them to the entrance of Halifax Harbour early on the second morning. They saw that it was a broad sweep of water, well protected on the seaward side by a large island; though whether it was a better harbour than that at Shelburne, they both doubted. As their vessel came up to the town, a settlement lying on the slope stretching up to a very high hill, they had a good view of its grid of streets bounded by a crumbling stockade. The only landmarks were the steeples of the two churches and the stockade and towers of the fort that crowned the hill.

The streets of the town, as they explored them, seemed wretched compared with those of Shelburne, especially because so many of the dwelling houses were so tumbledown. Outside the town, on the slopes from which the forest had been cleared, were camps where poor loyalists had been living for years; there were old tents and hovels in a wretched state, rotten and falling apart from the wear of the elements. Still there were people living in them, mostly old people and widows and orphans, Hannibal judged, as he looked at them with pity.

They stayed in the town only long enough for Clifford to do some business. He had been directed to a Halifax personage, Mr. Lawrence Hartshorne, who was a young Loyalist businessman with a good reputation. Clifford arranged to bank with him and otherwise use his services and advice. He discussed the possibilities of getting land in the Annapolis Valley, and helped Clifford buy a couple of good horses and supplies.

Finally Clifford and Hannibal set out on horseback, carrying what they could in packs behind them and leaving the rest to be sent by sea to a friend of Mr. Hartshorne's at Windsor. Their route led them through a small village of Dutch folk and then over the crest of the hill where they had a splendid view of Bedford Basin, a vast inner harbour well protected from the ocean's storms. Around the shore of this basin they went, following an old trail. They passed Fort Sackville and the beginning of miles of dense forest and climbed a slow rise of land until they emerged on the crest of Ardoise Hill. From here they saw, in the far distance below the late afternoon sun, inviting views of river valleys and gentle hills. By nightfall they were in open farming country, close to Windsor, and found a public lodging for the night.

Clifford was very serious about finding land which could be made to yield a profitable living, and in the next fortnight he and Hannibal travelled the length and breadth of the interconnected Annapolis, Cornwallis and Avon valleys, visiting the Loyalist settlements of Rawdon and Douglas, still being cut out of the woods, as well as older settlements founded before the Revolution had even been thought of, such as Falmouth, Cornwallis and Annapolis. At Clements and Digby, they found flourishing Loyalist settlements, but in almost every one of the old townships there were also Loyalists mingling with the earlier settlers from New England. Hannibal found some of his own people here and there, too, sometimes in settlements of their own among the white people. In a way the whole scene was exciting, as these many thousands of people busied themselves in taming the wilderness in the space of a year or two. There was a lot of optimism in the air, and hope and good feeling.

Clifford found most to admire in the Township of Horton, where so much of the land seemed to be deep, rich, and free from stones. Here was the "Great Meadow" (or Grand Praye) of the former French settlers. They had been made to leave the country just over a quarter of a century before and, like the Loyalists, had been exiles looking for a place to rest. On their Great Meadow, they had pastured great flocks of cattle and sheep, protected from the high tides (that would otherwise have swept over it every day) by the dykes built by those same people. It was not so unlike the dyked rice fields of the plantation in South Carolina, and Clifford reasoned that if a large-scale crop could be grown in Nova Scotia it would be on such land. He found a suitable farm for sale in Lower Horton, complete with fishing lot, dyke lot, farm lot and wood lot, and so he bought it. Here he and Hannibal lived and worked together for the next few peaceful years.

The farm at Horton Point came to Clifford with the crops growing in the fields, animals in the yard and pasture, and poles and nets off the fishing lot as well as a small sailboat with gear for fishing in deeper water. The owner, one of the original "Planters" from New England, had jumped at the chance of selling out and going back to his old home in Connecticut. The fields lay along the upper slope of a rise of land and faced the west. On the northern side, the farm was bounded by the edge of the line of cliffs called Horton Bluff. The bluff marked the bank of the Windsor River, as people called it. It was a danger to ships coming upriver at night, and a large lantern was contrived and hung from a tree to warn vessels as to the position of the cliffs.

Hannibal would see the light keeper going to tend the lantern each evening and again in the morning; it was a duty of some responsibility, as there was much shipping going up to Windsor and Newport Landing, and down again to Saint John or Boston. Usually, however, vessels coming up at night would take their position from the light and cast anchor. The tides, that turned dry land to deep water within a few hours and then reversed themselves, were a danger to captains who didn't know them and a nuisance to those who did. However, to farmers they offered advantages, such as creating the valuable salt marshes where the tidal waters met the land. Those marshes grew the salt hay that their cattle loved, and though harvesting it could be difficult or even dangerous it was worth the effort.

Clifford and Hannibal soon learned to do as their neighbours did. The farmers would go out on the exposed mudflats to make traps and seines to catch the fish that were so plentiful. It was also said that the mud of the tidal creeks made for good soil for fields, and so the farmers hauled it home on their oxcarts when the crops were harvested and the fields bare. Clifford tried that, but found it excessive labour yielding a doubtful result.

There was a fine view from their house. Sitting in front of it, one could see the broad expanse of the Minas Basin, the marshlands and islands around its rim, the great meadows of the Grand Praye and the distant blue gleams of the rivers draining the Annapolis Valley. But the chief and dominating landmark was Cape Blomidon, the bold forehead of the North Mountain, which seemed to float on the shining waters of the basin like the prow of a great overturned ochre-streaked dory. Behind that blunt prow, the long ridge rippled like an undulating serpent, merging at last with the sky in an undifferentiated blue in the direction of Annapolis Royal. People called this ridge the North Mountain; it protected the valley from cold northern winds and made it mild enough to be the most promising farmland in Nova Scotia.

Hannibal formed a sense of what Blomidon represented in the eyes of the native Micmac people one day when it was looking its boldest and clearest. He was preparing dinner when he heard a knock at the door, and opening it found an Indian mother and her son. They carried huge bulging loads on their backs. On seeing him in the doorway, they untied their large packs and displayed the beautiful things they were selling: baskets woven of thin strips of wood dyed in soft colours from the forest, snowshoes, and best of all, soft doeskin moccasins trimmed with petal-coloured porcupine quills.

When Clifford came to the house, looking for his dinner, he bargained with them for a large and a small basket, and for a pair of snowshoes. Hannibal brought them some food and left them when they sat on the stoop to eat. He decided to come out and eat with them. They wanted to have a conversation, but their English was not very good.

However, Hannibal knew a few Micmac words, learned from the hunters who visited Birchtown, and he managed to get the gist of their story.

The mother pointed to Cape Blomidon, its slashes of raw earth now shining a bright vermilion in the full rays of the sun, and said something like this: "You see that mountain? It is a very holy place. Long ago the god of our people, Glooscap, lived on top there." He was interested in hearing all she wanted to tell him, and heard about how in ancient time this great hero had pitched his wigwam on Cape Blomidon. From there he had ruled over all the people and animals of the lands and waters around.

The Indian boy did his share of enlightenment, too. He pointed to the distant shore of the basin and asked if Hannibal could see five islands. He had never noticed them before, but there they were, red blocks clearly outlined against the distant shore and the blue Cobequid mountains behind. These, the boy explained, were the five great stones Glooscap had hurled at Beaver when he had made a great dam across the entrance to the Minas Basin. The beaver dam backed the waters up and threatened to drown the world. Glooscap had foiled him and saved the world by kicking the dam apart. Its remains could be clearly seen beyond Blomidon.

"Where is Glooscap now?" Hannibal asked.

"One day," the old woman solemnly told him, "Glooscap looked far out over the sea and saw something coming from the east. It was high and white. It was a sail, and it was bringing the white men to our shore. Then Glooscap called all the people together and said, 'I must go now to my kinsmen in the sunset land, for the white man comes to take this country from me. But one day when you need me most I will come back.' So he said and then went away, and the white man came as he said. But one day Glooscap will come with his brothers and drive the pale-faced people away."

She looked at Hannibal with his brown skin, and smiled, and said, "But I think he will let the brown faces stay—and he will love them, too, if they are gentle and good." She and her son stood up, and, slinging their bulky sacks over their shoulders, set off on their road.

Hannibal went back to his chores, but later when Clifford paused to admire the view from the stoop he told him about Glooscap and showed him the Five Islands. He laughed and said it was a pretty tale and one worth remembering.

The farm Clifford now owned had deep soil, red and rich. He and Hannibal spent long hours working it, ploughing it in the spring and removing the larger stones pushed out by the frost, then seeding and planting, pulling weeds out through the summer, and finally in the fall of the year gathering the harvest.

In the winter or early spring, they went to the woodlot or forest that still filled the back corners of the farm and chopped down mature trees. Their team of oxen, called Bright and Lion, dragged them to the yard where the trunks were left to season. There was a woodshed adjoining the house which was well-stocked with firewood, sawn and chopped to a convenient size for the fireplace. The two of them managed most of it by themselves, but frequently men came by who would ask for a few days' work in exchange for food and shelter and a few shillings in the pocket, and if he could use them in any way Clifford would invite them to stay.

Clifford considered for some time what could be grown on a larger scale than the oats, barley, peas and beans that seemed best suited to the climate, along with root vegetables. It was, of course, too cold a climate for rice or cotton, and although Indian corn (maize) could grow, it did not flourish sufficiently to be a staple crop. Neither grains nor root crops could be produced cheaply enough to export in quantity, or at least Clifford did not think so. In the winter evenings before he went to bed, he would talk about various possibilities with Hannibal or with anyone who happened to be there. Finally he decided that the best possibility might be fruit: apples, pears, and plums in particular. The farm had a small orchard of apples and quince, planted probably by the French people who had formerly lived on this land. In fact, there were a few of these apple trees on most farms. Clifford had been pleased, in his first autumn in Horton, to find the trees laden with rosy fruit and he and Hannibal had enjoyed eating them both fresh and cooked. They had tasted good pears, too, from other people's trees, brought as seedlings from New England.

So Clifford had decided to develop an orchard, and he consulted with the farmers around and made plans to buy improved seedlings and to learn about grafting with cuttings from the best kinds of apple obtainable. It was a project that would take years to show results, since these fruit trees grew very slowly.

Meanwhile they endured cold snowy winters in Horton. Their first winter, of 1784-85, set a pattern for those that followed. It was cosy enough in their small wooden house with the brick fireplace and oven taking up most of the inside wall and warming the rooms built around it and the loft above where Hannibal slept. They kept the fire going through the coldest nights and banked it up in milder weather, and the bricks retained the heat and made them comfortable, even though the winter was considerably colder than the winter spent at Shelburne the year before. During the long nights, Clifford read to himself a great deal, and spent time teaching Hannibal, too. After three months of effort, the youth was able to read far more than the simple bits of prose and verse he had mastered at Colonel Bluck's school. They had a number of books with them, a Bible of course, and *Pilgrim's Progress*, and books of sermons and essays, all with difficult words and ideas. Nonetheless Hannibal learned to read them and to understand most of what he read.

Once they had settled down, Clifford regularly received newspapers and journals by way of Boston, and Hannibal took an interest in reading about current happenings, things like matters of war and peace that might affect him and his own people in particular. There was much in these newspapers about political changes in the new United States, but though he searched to see some evidence that freedom would extend to African people as well as white people, he never found it. Even though in the cold winter weather he longed for the warm breezes of Carolina, he knew he would never return there until his brothers and sisters of colour were able to live as free beings.

At odd intervals, letters were received from the Courtney family at Ellenboro Plantation, and there would always be a message from Hannibal's mother, who was still mistress in their kitchen. There was a period of three months when they heard nothing, but that was not unusual, considering how letters were passed from captain to captain up the coast, until they caught a vessel coming to Windsor or Horton. Finally came sad news. Yellow Fever had been raging in Charles Town and all through the tide-water region, and its ravages had been particularly savage at Ellenboro. Hannibal's beloved mother was one of those who took it, and she took it so severely that she died.

When she knew her end was near, she called for Old Master and gave him a message to send on to her boy; it was about a vision she had that she believed would come true. "Tell Hannibal," Old Master wrote, "that his mother wanted him to know her vision, which she believed was sent by God to make her happy in her last moments. She saw him on a vessel with great white sails, much like the one that brought her from Africa. As she told me: 'This ship, like that, was full of black people; but they were not confined below but came on deck as they wished and were full of song and laughter, because they were going to Africa. Then I saw their ship, one of many ships, coming to the great river beside the high green hills that were the last sight I ever saw on that side of the ocean. Tell my son,' she said to me, 'that I saw a true thing, a thing that will be, and when he is a man and goes back to the old home of our people I shall be with him. My spirit will be near him on the voyage and at the landfall, even though he will not see me.' These were her last words in this life."

Hannibal was full of grief for many days, and wept many tears. He had dreamt that when he was a man he would find a way to bring his mother to live with him; he felt full of bitterness against the Courtney family because they never considered letting her come with him and Clifford. He realized then that they had let Clifford bring him away because they considered him Clifford's personal servant and what he chose to do with him was all right, but Hester was valuable family property and belonged in the kitchen of the Big House. As long as she was useful there, they would never let her go, and she was not yet old. In fact, at the time of her death, her son suddenly realized, she was not yet thirty-five years of age. Her market price as a skilled cook was high, but Hannibal had hoped that if he could have made money somehow, they would have taken his offer and let her go. But that had always been years ahead, and now there was no chance at all of such an attempt.

He felt bitterness about the Courtney family, but not about Master Clifford, who was as kind to him as it was possible for anyone to be. At this time he showed the lad an affectionate sympathy and talked to him about his mother, whom he also had known and loved, in a way that allowed Hannibal an outlet for his grief. They told each other stories about her that soothed the raw edges of the boy's strong feelings, and brought her before him so vividly that he could believe her spirit had already come to stay with him.

It was then that Hannibal plucked up the nerve to tell Clifford about the vow he had taken to go one day to live in Africa, and to take his mother with him. The vision she had seen was her assurance to him that it would one day happen, though not altogether as he had hoped. Clifford was moved by the sincerity of his intention, and they discussed it more than once. He probably saw such difficulties in the way that he felt it kinder not to speak of them, but he did tell Hannibal that he understood that Africans had a far better life in America as slaves than as their own masters in Africa.

Hannibal had heard, when amongst coloured folk and mention of Africa was made, that this was a common excuse for the slave trade. He had no evidence of his own to judge the issue; he knew only that his mother had never been reconciled to her life in America and fully supported his dreams of going to the land of his fathers one day, so he did not argue about this. However he told his master about his mother's recollections of her life as a girl and young woman over there, and the burden she felt as a slave, even in a family as kind to her as his family had been, and Clifford admitted that in her case the experience had not been a blessing.

Indeed, this talk made Clifford think more seriously about the nature of slavery than he ever had before, especially as he had come to know Hannibal so intimately and had been moulding him into something other than what he would have been as one of his father's field hands. Then, too, he had come to know and respect some of the Black Pioneers at Birchtown, and he began to realize that his feelings about African people in general had changed. Clifford even began to think that if slavery did not exist, African people would be perceived differently, and would *be* different. As time went on, and Hannibal became full-grown, Clifford began to treat him as an adult, though still as a brother. The youth felt that it was not just because he was growing up, but because Clifford was ceasing to think that people with dark brown skins were perpetual children.

chapter six
HANNIBAL ON HIS OWN

Now and again Clifford heard news from Shelburne and Birchtown, sometimes in business letters from Sam Partridge or another friend there. Sometimes the news came to Hannibal from some of his people, for things were not good there and young men from Birchtown found their way to other parts of the Province, and walked the roads in search of work and food. Many African people came by Clifford's door. Some were slaves, told to look after themselves for a while when their masters could not afford to feed them. Sometimes it was old soldiers who came by, men of the Black Pioneers, who were not satisfied to stay where the government had put them.

One happy day, an African couple coming from Shelburne somehow found their way to the door. Their names were Phoebe and Moses. Hannibal had never heard of them there, but they had heard of him and

Clifford and had come looking for them. They stayed a couple of weeks in the spring and helped with the planting of wheat and oats. They were a source of news about the Birchtown friends and their fortunes. They told Hannibal and Clifford, too, something they were sad to hear: that all over the Colony, greedy white men were trying to re-enslave the Free Blacks, either by trickery or by force. Phoebe and Joseph themselves had only escaped being sold South by the action of the magistrates at Shelburne.

"We come from Carolina, just like you," Phoebe said when getting acquainted. "I used to live near Ninety Six, away in the back of beyond. My master, name of Will Martin, was a real bad man. Oh, he did treat me wicked! He treated me cruel! He used me so bad that I wanted to run away. But I didn't dare do it, I knew he would catch me quick as a wink and treat me even worse!

"Then, you know, during the war Colonel Cruger and his Redcoats came to Ninety Six. I got to know some of them, and when they got ready to leave, I made up my mind to go with them. So then I sneaked away from that old rebel, Will Martin, and the Army carried me safe to Charles Town. I went working for an officer then, Colonel Hamilton. That's when I met Moses here, he was the Colonel's servant. We all went to Saint Augustine together, but no sooner was we settled nicely till we had to get out. We came to Nova Scotia, not to Shelburne but to Halifax. The Colonel didn't stop there, but brought us on another boat to a place along the Eastern Shore, to a fine looking place—but mighty poor all the same—called Country Harbour.

"Bad luck dogged us there in spite of our hard work, and the last straw was when a big fire broke out in the woods back of our settlement. It cleaned out everything—trees, crops, houses—everything burnt up. We had to row our little boats out into the harbour to keep from being burned up ourselves. Then the four of us working for the Colonel made up our minds to leave him.

"We managed to get passage to Halifax without the Colonel knowing, but when he missed us he guessed where we were and swore he'd treat us proper for not being loyal. He found a captain on the shore there willing to buy us, catch us and take us South, so he sold us as wasn't his or anyone's to sell. It was his word against our'n, so you know who people would believe.

"It was a bad man by the name of MacNeil who comes looking for us. He doesn't have too much trouble finding the four of us in Halifax, walking the streets and looking for work. He spoke to us fine and said he had some work on board his boat and would pay us well if we'd put in a couple of hours with him. We didn't think of any danger, and went down into the hold, trusting like. Well, the man pulls down the hatch and then he and a couple of rough tars with him starts beating us with cudgels. They really whales the tar out of us and knocks us out. When we was able to take an interest again, we found ourselves locked into irons in the bottom of the boat, and by the way the boat was pitching and tossing we knew we was at sea.

"To cut a long story short, Captain McNeil put into Shelburne a few days later. I guess he wanted to pick up some cargo there. He wouldn't let us off the ship, but he did let us on deck for air. A passing boat full of people from Birchtown saw us on the deck and, the captain being ashore, heard all our story and went and told one of the magistrates. He thought he'd better inquire and within a few hours McNeil was told to bring us to court so that we could tell our story.

"Captain McNeil didn't want to bring us to a public hearing, and swore that he had the right to take us away. He was called on to prove it, and in front of the magistrates he said he had a warrant from our master directing him to take us to—the Bermudas, maybe it was—or the Bahamas. Anyway, one of those hot islands. The magistrates heard all he had to say and all we had to say, and they believed us and had the constable take the irons off and let us go. They gave McNeil a serious scolding, and told him not to try that sort of trickery again. I wonder if he went back to Country Harbour to get his money back?"

This happy ending left Phoebe and Moses free to travel about, so after spending some time with the Birchtown people, they were moving about wherever their fancy took them. When the pressure of planting was over they travelled on from Horton, following the road wherever it led. Hannibal heard of other African people who were not so lucky, for in their cases the law was satisfied that they really were somebody's property. They were carried back South, where slaves were worth money and not seen as an expense by their masters as they were in Nova Scotia. Hannibal speculated that if Clifford could have had his orchards of fruit planted and bearing, there would have been worthwhile work for slaves. Perhaps that would happen in the future, and Nova Scotia might not be saved from that curse. On the other hand, he realized that the severe winter weather made it extremely unlikely that plantation-type slavery could ever be profitable in the Province.

The curse of slavery was brought home again some time later that year, when in one of his letters Colonel Courtney asked Clifford to keep his eyes open for any prime slaves he might see for sale, as some of his neighbours had bought some from the North and were very satisfied with their health and energy. Hannibal was shocked when Clifford told him about this request, and was relieved when he was assured by his master that he would never act as an agent to send men back to the South.

"This country can never benefit from the labour of slaves," Clifford said. "It costs more to feed and shelter a slave here than he is strictly worth. If a man needs to employ labour, he will do better to hire free men. For them, he has less responsibility and ends up paying less. But if a black man wants to stay here and be free though hungry rather than eat the bread of slavery, then I shall never try to dissuade him, nor buy up any slave here to go South, whether or not it be against his will."

When they had been living in Horton a couple of years, Hannibal realized that Clifford was spending more time away from home. He had become friends with the family of a retired officer living at Apple Tree Landing, in the neighbouring township called Cornwallis. Colonel Manners had six daughters, and Clifford soon decided that the eldest, Lucy, was the loveliest and best-natured of the six, and would make him the perfect wife. They were married by Mr. Wiswell, the Rector of the Parish of Cornwallis, in the presence of her family and friends, and after that Clifford's household changed.

Before the wedding, Clifford had had several rooms built on to the house, so there was room for Miss Lucy and the small girl she brought with her to help with the housework. Clifford and Hannibal could spend all their time on the outdoor chores without taking time out to cook meals or wash clothes; however, there were always things to do in the autumn evenings, like tying the ripe ears of corn in bunches to hang from the ceiling, there to dry out and keep good, along with onions, apples, and pumpkins and other food to live on all winter. Under Miss Lucy's direction, the two males did a better job of having good stores than they had ever managed in their hit-and-miss bachelor existence. They tried their hands at whittling and carving when there was nothing else more pressing, making fresh wooden spoons and prongs and attempting bowls, with mixed success. Then Clifford decided he would carve a cradle "that might come in useful sometime!"

The years passed and as Hannibal grew towards manhood, Clifford's family grew, too, until three little ones played about the yard and called him Uncle Hannibal. The youth felt almost as much a father to them as Clifford did, and kept as good an eye on them. He felt that he did a better job of telling them stories before bedtime, and Miss Lucy much appreciated his help at that time of day.

They were part of the community now, fully accepted in spite of their "funny way of talking," their attendance at the services in St. John's Church of England instead of the meeting house, and Hannibal's complexion. The families of the neighbourhood, the Witters, the Bacons, the Lockharts and the Fullers, all stiff-necked New Englanders, welcomed them to their working bees and frolics. All of these "Bluenoses" turned out to make a frolic of helping Clifford build a good new barn, with stalls for cattle and a great hay loft for fodder.

Some of these people had been sympathetic to their kinsmen, the rebels in New England, during the war, and made sure that Clifford knew it. Others went out of their way to say that they had always supported the King and Empire. Needless to say, it was usually with these latter people that Clifford and Miss Lucy were invited to dine, or went to visit on a Sunday. If Hannibal went along, it was as a groom, to stay with the horses, but the meal sent out from the kitchen was pretty much the same as that in the dining room. In Clifford's household, he was treated like Clifford's younger brother by Miss Lucy. He knew he was blessed, for she might easily have disliked him, or been jealous of his closeness to Clifford, or scorned him for his colour. She didn't do any of these things, but seemed to him like an older sister, and the boy loved and honoured her as such.

Evidently, after a few years, the old hatreds were dying down in Carolina, too, for broken friendships were repaired, and men who had been loyal to the King found it possible to again play an active part in public activities along with those who had been their bitter enemies. His father's letters reaching Clifford from the South made the drift clear, for it was his habit to comment as he read passages to Miss Lucy (and Hannibal) in the evenings after mail had arrived on a trading vessel. He often expressed surprise, for the rifts had seemed so deep he had thought they would never heal.

Then a new element appeared in his father's letters; the Colonel was urging his son to come home, if only for a visit. He wanted to see Clifford again, and to meet his wife, and he wanted to embrace his grandchildren before he died.

Clifford talked it over with Miss Lucy and sometimes with Hannibal, until at last he decided they would go South for the winter. He would leave Hannibal in charge until their return in the spring, and told Squire Lockhart, the local magistrate, about his plans so that there would be no misunderstanding in the neighbourhood. A few days before their departure, they borrowed a two-wheeled cart (there were no four-wheeled wagons in Horton Township) and, with Hannibal holding the reins, carried their baggage and their children in it to Apple Tree Landing. Clifford and Miss Lucy rode their horses a little way in front, watching for any difficult passages, especially where they had to cross rivers and streams.

They all stayed with Miss Lucy's parents and their household until the little schooner *Joy*, chartered by Clifford to deliver him to Charles Town, was loaded with the cargo of apples, winter pears, and cabbages he and Colonel Manners had gathered together in Cornwallis and hoped to sell in South Carolina.

"It will be a good test," he said to Hannibal. "If they sell well, we'll plant more orchard in the spring when I get back." Once the cargo was safely stowed away, the family's personal baggage was carried aboard and they said their goodbyes on the little wharf.

Hannibal's heart was buoyed up by excitement and effort until the ropes were cast off and the little vessel tacked back and fourth as she proceeded down the twisted channel of the Habitant River. Along with the Manners family, he waved and those on the boat waved until they could see one another no more. For years his life had revolved around Master Clifford, and the longest they had been apart was from week to week when Hannibal spent the winter in Birchtown. Now he felt quite alone, and began to realize the responsibility he was shouldering for himself and for the farm. Did he have it in him to look after the farm and its animals, and to keep himself nourished and healthy through the long cold winter days and nights that lay ahead? He was not sure he did, but he was going to do his best. Likely, he thought, it would make him or break him.

It was a hard winter for him, that of 1789-90, and the spring was slow and long, though folk were kind and he had friends keep him company. But he was anxious to see his "family," for that was how he thought of Clifford and his wife and children. Every day, as May drew along, he watched for sails on the basin, and whenever he saw one coming closer on the rising tide, he would think, "This will be the one." Every time he was disappointed. Clifford's letters, not very numerous all winter, were normally sent enclosed in those to Squire Lockhart, and Hannibal began to call on him to find out if he had news he hadn't passed on. Finally, at the end of the month, the Squire had something to communicate.

"Hannibal," he said, "they ain't a'comin' this month—or next month—or ever. They're going to stay down South. Mr. Courtney's going to look after the plantation for his pa, for the old man's about past it, you know, and the brother was wounded in the war and has never been well since. He's not up to running things, so young Mr. Courtney's got to stay and look after them all. He says it all in this letter that just came in for me, and this one for you will say the same. And I guess it will say more, that you go on looking after the farm and doing a good job of it, and one day it'll be yours to do with as you like."

Sure enough, the enclosed letter said these same things, as well as enclosing a legal certificate, all signed and sealed and looking very impressive, releasing Hannibal from bondage and certifying him as a legally free man. Amongst other things in the letter, Clifford wrote, "Although I cannot help being a slave owner here, I shall do my best to see that all the slaves on the Plantation are fairly treated. As much as I am allowed I will, when I see those who show the ability to support themselves and prosper as free men, set them free just as I am doing for you. If at some time a way can be found to return such worthy men to Africa, then I shall support it. If there were any way I could help you, yourself, Hannibal, to accomplish the voyage prophesied by your mother, then I would help you. But although I know that ships sail to Africa from many ports, including Charles Town, I do not know how I could send you by one without the strong risk of your being enslaved again.

"For the moment, look after the farm. I shall send you some seedlings for apples and other fruit. Plant them the way we did last spring. I can send you suggestions for what crops should be planted, but I think you can do just as we did last year. Make improvements as we have been doing, but I cannot direct you from here to try anything new. The real responsibility to make decisions will be yours, for I will gladly transfer the property to you as a small thanks for the debt of my life, which I still enjoy thanks to you."

Hannibal was now a well-grown man of twenty-two years, though strangers usually judged him to be about eighteen, and ready to take on responsibility. He knew he could manage the farm work all right, with the help he could easily hire, but he was not sure about the business side of it—the buying and the selling. Still, he felt in his bones that he could be a good business man if he really tried, and he did. He made decisions whenever they were needed. He hired the men he needed from the many who came to his door looking for work. He supervised them and got value out of them. So that year, he harvested his cabbages and potatoes, his barley and oats, and sold what he didn't need for himself at good prices. He sold fat young cattle, too, and was satisfied that he did well. By the time the days got really short and frosty, he was sure that he could stand on his own two feet and look any man in the face.

It was as well, for the time was coming when he would be faced with another of the important decisions in his life: whether to stay in the security he had won in Nova Scotia or to gamble it all to attain his deep desires to find his way to his own country in accord with his mother's dreams and visions.

chapter seven

"SETTLERS WANTED FOR SIERRA LEONE"

The autumn of 1791 was dry and warm in Nova Scotia, and Hannibal regarded his fields with satisfaction. He had gathered in his cabbages and made a cask of sauerkraut with those not sold. The turnips had done well, and were only waiting for the first frost to sweeten them before being brought into the earthen cold cellar, where a few barrels of potatoes were already waiting to be eaten through the winter. The apples were mostly harvested from the orchard Clifford had set out, so were the grain crops from their fields, and all in all Hannibal was happy with the year and proud of what he had accomplished. His animals, cattle and pigs, were in good condition, too. He had sold the horses, with Clifford's permission, and his team of oxen did all the hauling and carriage work necessary.

Oxen were slower than horses, but that was no great matter, and they were cheaper to feed. Moreover, he had an experienced young ox-driver to get the best out of them. Gus was a young man of about twenty who had drifted about the province until landing at Hannibal's door, where he was taken on to help with the planting. He was so helpful, as well as being so friendly, that once the young farmer got to know him he didn't ever want to let him go. So he became the junior partner in the running of the farm. He had learned to train and handle oxen in the early stage of his life, which had began, like Hannibal's, in South Carolina. Unlike Hannibal's story, though, his included a sojourn in New York. There he had been somehow separated from his parents, and though he had been looking for them ever since, he had never seen or heard from them again. He was beginning to think they had somehow been taken back into slavery in the South, since if they had got to Nova Scotia or one of the other colonies, he should have had word of them by this time.

Gus had stayed first in Digby with his friends, Free Blacks who had come from New York, and could have remained with them if he had been ready to settle down. He couldn't settle. He felt he had to travel, in his search for his parents, to every community where Loyalists were living. So he wandered, staying a week here or a month there with Free Blacks or others who welcomed his company. He first arrived in Horton in the spring of 1790, just when Hannibal needed help with the planting. Though he drifted off in the slack times, he turned up again and again, and now Hannibal counted on him being around more than he was away. He seemed to be so fond of the two oxen, Bright and Lion, and of their owner also, that he more or less looked on the farm at Horton Bluff as his home.

Hannibal was happy with his farm and with his neighbours also, good-hearted New Englanders. As he looked over the brown autumn fields and thought with satisfaction of his preparations for the winter ahead, how little he knew how much his life was about to change. It was a day in late October, full of sunshine but with a hint—in the freshness of the air—of chilly nights; it was invigorating and made the blood flow faster in the veins. He was on his way down to Squire Lockhart's provision shop, which was also the post office, in right good humour. He had in mind to see if the squire cared to barter with him, to take some of his surplus for several things he needed, and of course to see if any letter had come in from Master Clifford.

A wide stoop that ran across in front of the door to the ell sticking out from the main part of the house served as the squire's business premises. As usual a group of male idlers of all ages, both black and white, were gathered there. Some of them, especially those of colour, were intent on studying a large notice posted on the board.

"Here, Hannibal Hoops!" one of the older men greeted him. "Have a look at this and tell us what you make of it."

People in the community knew that Hannibal could read, and that he did a lot of reading. They seemed to pay him some degree of respect because of it. The group at the board gave way and then gathered in close around him as he read what he saw in as clear a voice as he could manage. It seemed important that everybody could hear him.

"Free Settlement on the Coast of Africa," said the headline. In smaller print, it explained that Free Blacks who could give satisfactory testimonials about their character could, if they applied and were accepted, be carried to Sierra Leone in Africa to form a colony. There, each man would receive twenty acres of land, with ten more for a wife and five for each child. They would receive free provisions and other supplies until they were self-sufficient.

Hannibal was especially interested to read the assurance "that the civil, military, personal, and commercial rights and duties of Blacks and Whites shall be the same, and secured in the same manner."

When Hannibal finished, there was silence.

Although everyone who could read had already read it, and those who couldn't just heard him read aloud, there was uncertainty in their faces about what it meant. The white men present were only interested because of the strangeness of the offer and the reference to Africa. But the several who were African wanted to know if it could really apply to them. Hannibal had understood what he had read, and was so excited by its possibilities that, as he tried to explain, all people of African origin now had a chance to return to the land of their fathers. His voice trembled and he was on the verge of tears.

He turned then to hear what his white neighbours were saying about the announcement. Squire Lockhart was at the centre of the group facing him, and looking straight at Hannibal he spoke to him and the half dozen African men around him.

"Well, that's a very interesting offer for you coloured people, isn't it? What do you think of it? Myself, I'd say you're best off right here. Yes indeed, Sierra Leone is no great bargain. My cousin Rathbone, over at the landing, sailed along that African coast when he was a young fellow afore the mast. As hot as Hades, he said it was, and he tells stories of cannibals and savages and poisonous bugs and fevers. In fact, he was pretty glad to get back to this side of the ocean in one piece and still alive. No proper food to eat, too, he said. I don't recommend it to you, boys, not one bit."

That was a splash of cold water on his excitement and Hannibal felt it was no time to talk to the squire seriously about applying to go, though he knew in his heart that he must do so or hate himself ever after. He beckoned to the several boys who were his friends to walk away.

He wanted to talk about the offer with some of his own people out of earshot of those white people, who, however kind, could never think about the concerns of the African people the way they themselves did. A short time later, they were gathered, four of them all together, on a little wooden bridge spanning a small stream all shaded by old willows planted long ago by the long-gone Acadians.

The group which came together were all in their early manhood, and as free as Hannibal to make plans for their own lives, but it turned out that there was no agreement about the government's offer. To his surprise, the others found arguments against it. They didn't trust it; probably it was a hoax, or the motives of the men who had put it out were not honest. They thought of many possibilities of evil intention and said the best thing was to pretend they had never seen the notice. However, Hannibal's arguments had an effect and it was agreed in the end that it could not hurt to find out more about the offer and the motives of the people who had sent it out.

Hannibal went home in a state of high excitement to consider the possibilities. He had known as soon as he saw the notice that his fate was written on it. Whatever the conditions, whatever the motives of those making the offer, he knew he had to seize the opportunity which came so unexpectedly and would probably never come again. If his mother's vision of him arriving on African shores was ever to become real, it would be by this means, a means he could never have imagined. It seemed like magic, employed for him especially. There was no way he could ignore it or pretend he was indifferent.

But it was a very strange offer, as his friends had said. How could the practical side of it be arranged? It would certainly be expensive, and the African people of Nova Scotia were too poor to pay passage. Was the offer a sincere one? Could it be a plot to take people back into slavery down South? It would be best to enquire carefully into it. And if it was sincere, was there room for all who wanted to go, or only for a limited number? Should he get his name on the list before it was filled up?

Such were the thoughts running through his mind as he walked along the red clay road toward home. In another month, the ruts and hollows in it would be full of ice, crackling and groaning under his feet. The fields and trees would be white with frost and snow. The nights, as he remembered well, would be thick with the arctic chill that penetrated men's bones, especially bones used to the gentle warmth of the South. He shuddered as the memories of past winters crowded in on him, and drew his shoulders together involuntarily as if feeling already that cold that cramps human flesh and squeezes it to the inner core. He felt passionately that this country, so desolate and gloomy, and dead half the year, was not his country, and that he would find a true home in the perpetual sunshine and warmth of Africa.

His former satisfaction with life as a farmer in Nova Scotia was gone. As he came up towards his house, he suddenly felt how small and naked it looked. The shingled roof and walls seemed as thin as paper when he thought of the winter winds blowing across the ice-filled waters of the Minas Basin. The maple and oak trees Clifford had planted for wind break and shade were still small and spindly. A few surviving red and gold leaves fluttered sadly in the breeze. Their colour was fading, and in a few days they would fall to the ground and the branches would stretch out naked and without a sign of life for six months or more. He was sure that in Sierra Leone the trees were always green and leafy.

He opened the kitchen door and walked into the glow from the big fireplace. In front of it, Gus was sprawled on the floor, holding with one hand a large hollow orange pumpkin while with the other he was cutting out the face of a "pumpkin grinner." The two men had had a good crop and thirty-five or forty-fine round specimens were in the storeroom waiting to be cut up and dried for eating over winter. They could spare one or two for Halloween fun, the festival being just a bit less than a week away. It was an event that gave great delight to Gus, and he entered into it each year with zest. He would carve a particularly frightful face in the largest pumpkin he could find, and as dusk deepened on the night of October 31, he lit a strong candle in it and put it on the front stoop by the door.

However, once night had really fallen Gus would not go out that door again. Somewhere in his past he must have spent times with Scots and Irishmen. As a result, he believed that the graveyards released their dead that night, and that folk out on the roads might well meet them. He believed that imps of Satan appeared and did all sorts of destructive mischief, such as setting fire to haystacks, pushing over privies, and taking the wheels off wagons. He believed that on that night the howling in the chimney was that of doomed souls on their way to hell, and tappings on the window came from the skeletal fingers of the dead, strayed from their graves. For these reasons, Gus would not go out into the darkness of a Halloween. But he put his pumpkin grinner, or, as some called it, "Jack o' Lantern," outside the door to welcome any friends foolhardy enough to venture out. He had invited a few to come and play some games, and most importantly to tell some scary stories about ghosts and goblins.

When Hannibal came into the house, he was far from thinking of Halloween observances. "Gus!" he cried out in some excitement, feeling his friend was one person he could really share his feelings with. "Do you know what? We have a chance to leave this land and to go back to our own people! Back to Africa! It's true, it really is! What do you think of that?"

Hannibal grabbed Gus by his shoulders and tried to shake a little of his excitement into him. Perhaps he was too abrupt. Anyway, Gus shook his hands off and kept on cutting out the sharp teeth of the pumpkin. He seemed to become very sulky, and asked, "What's so wonderful about going to Africa? And how could we anyway? You know there's no chance of such a thing."

Hannibal sat down in a chair close by and told him about the notice asking for settlers for Sierra Leone and how it was the answer to his prayers, but he couldn't infect him with any excitement. When he had finished his arguments and spoken of his intention to apply for passage, Gus just said, "Go if you like, but I won't go with you."

Hannibal could not believe he meant it. He went on:

"I'm sorry if I caught you by surprise, but don't say things you'll have to take back later on. Isn't this what you really want, the same as I do? We are really Africans, Gus. We just happen to have been born in America. It was not our fault, or the fault of our parents. They belonged in Africa and so do we. My mother was always homesick for her own people and her own land, and I feel the same, even though I know it only from her stories. I know I will never really be home until I am in Africa."

"Huh," said Gus very rudely. "I've heard all about Africa from folks who came from there—the snakes! The hard work in the hot sun! The fierce wild animals! And oh! The hungry times when the food is all eaten up and the new crops are not ready. My mother remembered Africa, too, and she worked harder there than she ever did in Carolina and got less for it. She was never sorry she exchanged one set of masters for another. She was glad she'd been brought away. No, Hannibal, I can't help it. I wouldn't ever want to go to Africa. But don't be angry with me for that; I have a different picture in my mind than you do, and I know it wouldn't work for me. If you want to go, then I'll be happy for you. I'll hope your picture of it comes true for you and that you'll be happy. But it all sounds very fishy to me. I heard lots about Africans coming to America, but I never heard of any of us being taken the other way."

Hannibal became angry with the youth for spoiling his excitement and joy, and seriously scolded him. He said, "Gus, Gus! It is there in black and white! I saw it! It is official. You have to believe it. 'Free Settlement on the Coast of Africa,' that is what it says. The trouble with you is you have no faith. I do. I believe God has looked after me these many years and I'm sure that with His help I'll go over safely to my Promised Land, and there I will have a happy and useful life."

Then Hannibal made an appeal to his feelings as a Christian. "Gus," he said again, "think of what we could do! My own people, perhaps my relatives, live there in ignorance and doubt. They know not God. They don't love Him, and they don't know of His love stretching forth to them. They don't love their fellow men—they sell them into bondage— as they sold your mother and mine —into bondage to the white man! And they fight amongst themselves, not so different from the white man there. And I've heard things from the preachers about abominations, human sacrifice, burying people alive, tortures and wicked practices, so many abominations!

"As I see it, Gus, not only is it the right place for us black people, there under the warm sun, but also there's work there for us as Christians! Perhaps God brought black people here for a purpose: to be messengers of the Gospel back to our own people. The white men are not taking that message. They don't want many blacks in Heaven, I guess. Think now: when the last trumpet blows and the blessed get swept up, how many will be blacks? Not many, not many in Africa especially. The white people know about God, but they aren't telling the blacks, so we must. We must go and show them what God wants of people. I want to live a Christian and civilized life there, and perhaps I can preach and teach a little, too."

Gus told him rudely that he had already preached too long at him and that a lot of what he was saying was nonsense. Although Gus was impatient, Hannibal tried to explain why he felt so strongly. "I can't forget what my mother used to tell me about the village. Things like the *juju* and things I don't have the words to explain in English. False gods and false men and false spirits, and powers that keep men's souls in bondage. She believed in them, and so did I, when I was a child. But I know better now."

More things were said between the two young men, but Hannibal did not any longer try to persuade Gus that his destiny lay in Africa. Dusk was falling and they had to get busy with the evening chores. They settled the animals for the night, and Gus milked while Hannibal fed them all and gave them clean straw. Then, as was their custom, when the animals were all settled they went back to the house for their evening meal.

It was warm and comfortable as Gus took supper off the fire and stirred it up to fresh life. A pot of succotash had been bubbling over the fire a few hours, and the beans and corn had softened and cooked together to make a tasty dish. As they ate, Hannibal's mind was busy thinking over the efforts they had to make to feed themselves through the year. All around were the fruits of harvest that would keep them fed until a new food cycle began when the fish began to run with the winter's snow melted. The beans and corn in the stew they were eating had been dried weeks before. Hung up high around the kitchen was a goodly supply of the best cobs of Indian corn, tied in bunches of half a dozen, the faded leaves pulled back to reveal the dried golden kernels. Near them, hanging by their long faded stalks, were pale globes of onions, clean and dry. In the pantry off the kitchen was a barrel of dried beans threshed out a week before on the kitchen floor. In the store cellar dug in the ground under the kitchen where the men sat (with a trap door in plain sight and a ladder leading down) were barrels of apples, potatoes, carrots, and open heaps of pumpkins of various colours and shapes. In the smokehouse were smoked fish and hams and bacon. In the fields there were still parsnips, turnips, and carrots to be gathered in.

Hannibal knew they would not go hungry, and that he could make a go of farming this northern land with its heavy clay soil and the limitations of its climate. He thought of the possibility that his hard-earned knowledge and skills would be useless in making a living in Africa. Nonetheless, he felt that he would never be at peace with himself if he held on to what he had in Nova Scotia and did not try for a life in Africa.

The evening for Hannibal passed like so many others, sitting in front of the hearth and chatting occasionally with Gus, working on a piece of pine wood he was carving into a masher, while Gus played softly at times on his flute or took his own knife and carved at a hard piece of apple tree wood he had come by somewhere. Later, as on every night, Hannibal read aloud a chapter from his little Bible. Usually he tried to explain its meaning to Gus, but on this night he didn't feel like doing so, and without a pause went right into a customary evening prayer.

It was time to go to sleep, but he sat and stared for a while into the depths of the fire. In those white and yellow and scarlet jets of flame, he saw the glowing sun of Africa and the white mists rising from the steaming rivers, the flame trees of the forest, the dazzling brightness of the green leaves of luxuriant vegetation. And above all, he saw the gleaming eyes and teeth of a laughing brown people, exuberant in their welcome, people full of friendship… his own people!

chapter eight

THANKS TO A SERGEANT
OF THE BLACK PIONEERS

A few days after the people of Horton heard about the chance to become settlers in Sierra Leone, a messenger came around to all the African people in the district and told them that the rector, the local church missionary, would explain fully. Hannibal knew Mr. Twining a bit, though he was new to the township, and sometimes went to his services at Muddy Creek, a couple of miles away from home. More often, he went to the New Light services, a little further along the Annapolis Road. The messenger told him that Mr. Twining had a special interest in African people, having been a missionary in the West Indies previously, and that he knew all about the Sierra Leone proposal. So it was that on a Friday afternoon Hannibal and a few others walked briskly to the meeting house at Lower Horton. By the time the rector was satisfied that he had a full audience, there was quite a gathering of Free Blacks from all along the shore and back into the South Mountain area.

Mr. Twining stepped up to the pulpit and looked around at the twenty-five or thirty persons carefully. They were all men, mostly young men. Some were married and had children at home, some still lived with their parents, some were there purely out of curiosity and for something different to do with their evening, while others seriously wanted to know more about this strange project. The rector was a good-hearted man, more like a Methodist preacher than the missionary he replaced, and he spoke to them like a father to his children. He had grown up in Wales, and that showed in his musical and friendly way of speaking.

"My friends," he said, looking around the room, "a fine Christian gentleman newly arrived from England, Mr. John Clarkson, has written me from Halifax to ask for my assistance in this matter that is, or could be, so important to all of you and your community here. Ah, my humble friends, your race may well praise now and in the future, the names of a select group of fine men who are spending their time and money in your cause. Besides Mr. John Clarkson, who is a lieutenant in the navy, there is his brother, Mr. Thomas Clarkson, and to name two others, Mr. Granville Sharpe and Mr. William Wilberforce, who is a Member of Parliament. There are others, but it is needless to name them all. I am sure that in years to come, whenever representatives of your sable race are gathered together, you will have cause to laud these gentlemen for the things they have accomplished and will yet accomplish. They have declared war on the slave trade, and before long, I verily believe, their determination will bring to an end this blot on civilized society."

Many of the men present were not familiar with some of the words Mr. Twining used, and were not sure just what he was leading up to, but they got the general drift of his admiration for the people he named, and his belief that it was important to them. He went on: "Now to details. I believe you have all seen a copy of the notice sent out by the Sierra Leone Company, and you are wondering what it is all about. Perhaps you may know that of late years there have been many poor Africans wandering the streets of London, formerly slaves like you and like you, now free. Many of them, like you, formerly lived in America. The gentlemen I have just named, with their associates, took pity on their destitute condition in the unfriendly English climate and decided to return them to Africa. The most suitable place was determined to be Sierra Leone, in West Africa, where probably the finest harbour in the whole of the African continent is to be found. The British government—that is to say, Mr. Pitt—contributed the transport, and so, over four years ago, in 1787, some four hundred pioneers chosen from amongst the thousands who are in England sailed to Africa and established a town in Sierra Leone.

"Now, the sad news. This settlement, I am sorry to say, has not been a success. The settlers, as I have been told, instead of being a good example to their brethren, the natives of the country, have either reverted to their unenlightened ways or have joined forces with the slavers who live nearby and are now doing to more innocent people what was done to them years ago. But this has not discouraged these English gentlemen who are determined to accomplish something good, and they have organized the Sierra Leone Company to undertake to plant a colony in a more systematic way. They are inviting you, as their notice said, those of you of good moral character and regular habits of work, to form a new colony, a colony of such virtue that it will be a beacon in the darkness, or perhaps I could liken it to a torch that will set all Africa alight. Those of you who choose to go will be, in many ways, missionaries of a kind."

He invited questions, and one of the first asked was how these men in England had become interested in the Africans in Nova Scotia.

"Ah, yes, I wondered about that myself," he said, "and Mr. Clarkson himself explained that they knew nothing of your existence here until one of your own people, a sergeant in the Pioneers, came to London to make complaints to the government. He found his way to some of these gentlemen, and volunteered to find black settlers for them here. However, as you see, they sent Mr. Clarkson to manage things on an official basis."

After answering a few more questions, from which the gathering learned little more, Mr. Twining asked their intentions. "You have heard all I can tell you," he said, "and it is time to take some action. What do you wish to do about this proposition? I am prepared to write to Mr. Clarkson on your behalf, giving him the names of all interested in joining his expedition, and asking for further instructions. I am not sure how many people he is prepared to accept. There may be limits on the numbers. But if you have made up your minds to try for it, I am ready to make a list now."

There was a general murmur of approval around the room, but one of the older men, a short stout muscular man known to all as Tom the Blacksmith, got to his feet respectfully. In a loud and rough but kindly voice, he bellowed, "Yes, Mr. Preacher, we's ready to give our names. But before we gets caught up in something', we wants to know a bit more about this business. Now that doesn't mean we don't trust you, or that we think a fine gentleman like you wouldn't tell us everything we need to know, but I surmise we should speak to this Master Clarkson ourselves."

Everybody seemed to think this was a good idea, but the missionary looked a bit doubtful. "I don't believe Lieutenant Clarkson will be along this way," he said. "I know he plans to visit somewhere on the South Shore and Digby next month, but I don't believe he'll have any time to come to Horton. Most of his time will be taken up dealing with the authorities in Halifax."

"In that case," said the persistent blacksmith, still on his feet, "why don't we send one of our own men to talk to him there? You write a letter speaking for us, with our names, and we'll pick a man to carry it by hand. Then he can have a good talk with Master Clarkson and really find out if it's all right. We'll know what we want to do when he comes back and tells us what he's found out." Then Tom glanced over at one young man and seemed possessed of another idea. "That young Hannibal Hoops over there is a bright lad," he said. "We wouldn't go far wrong sending him to talk to the big man, eh, Hannibal my boy? What say ye?"

There was loud applause at the suggestion, so the rector had to give his approval, though a bit unwillingly. "It would be easy enough for me to send a letter on your behalf by the regular post," he said, "and that would be the most satisfactory way of proceeding." However, it was clear that having decided on sending Hannibal the interested men would stick with their decision. With a stifled sigh, Mr. Twining sat at the table, sharpened a new quill carefully, opened his ink pot, smoothed a sheet of paper out carefully, and began to write. He carefully and precisely noted down the names of all who said they were interested in applying to emigrate, along with details of their families, their possessions, and their occupations. These details were provided by the men themselves who came up to the table one by one. Hannibal was almost the last, and when he gave his name, Mr. Twining looked him in the face and asked, "When will you be going to Halifax to find Mr. Clarkson, Mr. Hoops?"

He had been thinking about that and had an answer formed in his mind.

"I'll be ready to start early Monday morning, sir," he said.

"Good!" said the rector. "I'll write my letter tomorrow and send it along to you on Sunday, or if you come to church, you can collect it from me."

Hannibal felt the last remark was in the nature of a question, and as he had no objection to coming to his service, replied, "I'll be there, sir."

After everyone who wished had given his particulars to be written down, Mr. Twining stood again and addressed the group who were hanging about uncertain of whether to go or stay.

"Now, my good fellows, I have all the information I need for Mr. Clarkson and it will be sent to him in the manner you have requested. I want you to realise, however, that only men of industry and good character will be accepted by him for this venture. If any of you are not of that quality, you need harbour no expectations in this matter. Now, let us kneel together to ask God's blessing upon this work."

After a brief prayer for the Sierra Leone Company and its good works, the group broke into a cheerful chorus of "Good night" and once out of doors set off in various homeward directions. It was already dusk and there was no sign of a moon. Along the Ridge Road Hannibal walked, at first with company but gradually his companions turned off towards their homes and finally he went on alone. On the high ground, there seemed plenty of light, from the fading glow of the sky behind him and its reflection in the mirrored surface of the great basin of water in front.

Then his steps led downhill, the sky darkened, the wind rose, and the few stars in the sky were scarcely seen between the scudding clouds. The last mile or so was uphill again, up the slopes leading to Horton Bluff, and dark and lonely it was. It was a road Hannibal had walked perhaps a thousand times or more, yet he was always to remember this particular walk along this road, on October 31, 1791, with special vividness.

Perhaps this was because of the emotional tension he felt, knowing that he was, in a few days' time, to undergo what would be one of the most fateful days of his life. There had been other days in his life of great importance, but they had come on him unexpectedly, like the night when Master Clifford had ordered him to follow him to the war. It was not something he had known beforehand. But this time, he did; he knew that his meeting with Mr. John Clarkson would mark a turning point in his life, either a swift passage to Africa or, probably, a permanent exile in Nova Scotia and a life of bitterness and dissatisfaction.

The night was dark now, and there was nobody about. Fleetingly, it crossed his mind that this was the night called Halloween, when the graves were supposed to open up, and ghosts and worse things were believed to roam about doing evil things to the living. He trusted too much in the protection God gave the righteous to feel any fears, but he was uncomfortable in the darkness of the night. He walked as fast as he could, looking forward to the warmth and light of his own hearth and the company of his friend Gus.

He realized that soon, perhaps, he would be walking this particular road for the last time and became conscious of the familiar features of the land and sea barely visible in the faint light of the stars. The earlier cloud cover was rolling southward and the Big Dipper, and beyond it the North Star, were clearly revealed in the northern sky.

On his right hand was the very black masses of the forest climbing the South Mountain, forests never yet cut, full of the wild animals of the region, from bears and foxes to hares and squirrels. This forest clothed the whole width of Nova Scotia until the land ended and the ocean began, but for Hannibal its black mass was bounded by the curved bowl dome of the starry sky.

More interesting, always, was the great round basin to his right, a depression in the earth full to its brim, at this point, with ocean water pouring in from the Bay of Fundy. Faintly it gleamed with reflections of the stars; dimly the familiar lounging shapes of Blomidon and the Cobequid Mountains supported the pale glories of the northern sky. These things he had seen every day for years, and he wondered whether he would miss them when grown accustomed to other mountains and other bodies of water.

Conscious of these distant shadowy landmarks as he was, he was even more conscious of the faint light and shadow of the track ahead, dark where a rut threw a deeper shadow, light where rainwater glimmered in puddles and tracks. At times he had to jump smartly to avoid stepping in water up to his ankles, or in order not to splash himself with liquid mud. He came past a hedge of small spruce trees that meant he was home, and was just ready to relax, when suddenly, turning into the yard, he stiffened with surprise and fear.

A ghastly visage with fiery features was standing on the stoop, in front of the door he had to enter. He was petrified, to his intense shame a moment later when he recognized it for what it was. Gus had refused to come out with him, because he had invited some other boys in for Halloween fun, but after they had gone home he had spent some time arranging his Jack o' Lantern as a welcome for Hannibal. He had stuck it on a small barrel so that it seemed like a dwarf from the inferno, the candle guttering inside illuminating the truly diabolical nature of the features he had cut in the pumpkin.

Standing on the doorstep, Hannibal laughed at his momentary fright, and asked himself whether he was as free from superstitious fears as he wished to be. He went inside and found Gus already asleep, so it was not until next day, when they were out harvesting in the root field, that Gus was told all about the meeting.

Hannibal was disappointed when Gus still refused to be impressed with the Sierra Leone Company's offer. "All very strange," he said. "How do you know this isn't just a trick to get you back into slavery there? I've heard there are slaves in Africa just like here. It wouldn't surprise me any to know that the Nova Scotians have hit on this scheme to fool us and have us go peaceably away. They're not very keen on having African people here; we all know that. Maybe this way they'll be rid of us and the price they get for us will pay for the cost of shipping us, or maybe more. How would good people in England ever hear about our predicament anyway? It must be these same people in Halifax who are arranging this that told them!"

"Oh no," Hannibal said, delighted at the chance to put him straight, for he had fortunately remembered what the rector had casually mentioned. "I can correct that aspersion on these honest people. It was one of our own, a sergeant in the Black Pioneers, who went over to England and got the Sierra Leone Company people interested in us."

"The Pioneers! A sergeant!" shouted Gus, slapping his leg with the bunch of carrots he had just pulled and then, taking a little leap into the air, "Why, that must be my old guardian, Tom Peters! Oh, that man! Mark me, Hannibal, if that's the man you're going to get as leader you'd better not go for sure. That's the most unluckiest man I've ever had the bad luck to be with, and I can tell you I got away from his company as soon as I could. And what's more, he hasn't got the nature to be a good leader. He's too impatient and hasty, and he thinks a good sight of himself, too."

He stopped talking for a moment and went on with his work, throwing the carrots into a basket and pulling it along the row between them.

Hannibal felt that Gus had somehow got hold of the wrong end of the stick and tried to straighten him out. "No, no, Gus! I don't think this Sergeant Peters is to be our leader. Nobody said that. Anyway, he may not be the same as this Tom Peters. Who is he, and what makes you think he would be the man who went to London?" He went on pulling carrots as he talked; they came easily from the damp soft earth.

Gus straightened up, banged his heels together and stood ramrod stiff at attention. "Sergeant Thomas Peters of the Black Pioneers reporting, Sah!" He burst into loud laughter as he stooped to the carrots again. "Why, old Tom Peters was the man that took care of me when I was all lost in New York. I fell in with a couple of young chaps who turned out to be Pioneers and they took me along to their leader, old Tom. He was mighty kind for a sergeant, I'll say that for him. He looked after his men first rate, and I wasn't the only orphan they picked up and took care of. No, he was a good kind man.

"Well, when everyone was leaving New York, our batch went along with Tom on a boat called the *Joseph*. They counted me as one of the detachment by then. Well, of course we'd all had our fill of hard times; I've told you lots about that, but I didn't tell you that our bad luck became serious after we left New York. We ran into a storm, and while everyone else was getting safely to Nova Scotia that summer, the old *Joseph* was tossing us all over the Atlantic. No fires, no hot food, no dry clothes for weeks and weeks. Well, the storms finally died down and we sailed along and struck land, and do you know where we found ourselves? It was the Bermuda Islands, the same ones they call the Summer Islands.

"Our captain wouldn't take his ship any further on account of he was afraid of more storms, and the ship not being seaworthy, he said. So we stayed there for the winter while the sailors patched up the vessel, and I can tell you they really were summer islands. My, now I look back on it I just wish I'd stayed there. But if I had, I guess, someone would have sold me down South. Anyway, some of the fellers did; they just said they wouldn't go any further. They said they could take care of themselves and I guess they're not worrying about winter coming on or anything much right now. And, my oh my, it sure was pretty there!"

He paused, remembering the beauty of the Bermudas and Hannibal rather impatiently told him to get on with the story. He wanted to know whether this Tom Peters really was a person who attracted bad luck. If he indeed was that sort of person, and if he were to be the leader of the expedition to Sierra Leone, then definitely he, Hannibal, would be leery of being a part of it.

"Oh, yes, well," continued Gus, "we had to leave there in the spring, of course, and we sailed along till we came to the Bay of Fundy and put in at the port of Digby. I guess you know where that is, all right, sitting on the westward side of the Annapolis Basin. Well, we found a lot more of the Pioneers there and we joined 'em. Tom wasn't in charge there, 'cause of course he was months late a'coming and they already had a leader. He was a sergeant, too, Joseph Leonard. He's still the boss there, I 'spects. I reckon from what I saw that he's a mighty smart man, smarter than Tom Peters, I'd say. And he doesn't seem to think so much of himself, neither.

"You asked about Tom's bad luck. Well, I suppose it was bad luck not getting to Digby in time and having to take second place to Sergeant Leonard. But the next thing was that he settled on the land and then lost it. It happened this way. When the Pioneers applied for land, they were told to pick out the place they wanted. They picked out a good place and called it Brinley Town.

"They—maybe I'd better say we, because I was doing my best with the rest—built nice houses and good gardens and had a good summer free and independent. It the first time in our lives that we were not being ordered around by some white master or officer. There was good fishing, too. Digby's the place for that: lots of herrings. Of course, the woods thereabouts is thick with game—more than around here—bear and moose and such. So, we were all right.

"But the bad luck came just when we were happiest. We were told by the authorities that we couldn't own that land, 'cause it was for the glebe and school! It was all surveyed for that in the township plan. Well, they should have told us that 'fore we went ahead and did so much work. Anyway, it made Sergeant Tom Peters kinda mad—angry mad and mebbe a bit crazy mad—I suppose he had a lot on his mind, with about two hundred of us to look after, counting soldiers, women and young ones."

"Tom up and left us with hardly a goodbye the day he got the news. Our gardens were coming along nicely, the fish catches were good, the weather was warm and sunny, and right at that time the Surveyor told our captains, including Tom, that we couldn't have the land. Well, didn't he create a fuss! I declare, the young ones got out of the road fast when he came storming back to his cabin after the meeting. He was kicking everyone out of his path and breathing hard. He told his wife to pack everythin' up. Said they were going across the Fundy, over to Saint John, to see if people over there wouldn't act more civilized and kindly. He left that same day, just with his own family.

"He told me I could come with, but I was helping someone else anyway and to tell the truth was glad of the excuse not to go with him. I didn't shed any tears when he went away. Maybe that sounds ungrateful. He'd saved my life, I suppose, and been plenty good to me, but at the same time he had a quick temper and a swift foot. I'd felt his boot where it didn't feel good lots of times, and it looked to me like that ole boot was going to do lots of kicking before Tom found what he was looking for."

"Everyone else stayed put at Brinley Town and we had a good summer as we expected. Sergeant Leonard took care of Peters' detachment as well as he could. He asked the Surveyor to find some other good land for the Pioneers, land that would be theirs to keep. Well, he did find some, a few miles away at Bear River. Sergeant Leonard himself got a hundred acres, I heard, but I don't think he's on it yet. The last time I was at Brinley Town everyone was still living there; nobody has tried to push them off yet.

"That was not the end of Tom Peters, though. I guess he found troubles at Saint John, a lack of civilized people perhaps. Anyway, he was back in Digby the next summer—that would be about '86—and he fought with Commissary Williams and Mr. Brudenall and some other big men around Annapolis, because he said they were robbing him of his share of rations.

"That was the time when I began my roaming life, and started to travel up and down and around this country. I wasn't around to see if he tried to settle down again there. But the last time I was in Digby, they told me Tom Peters had got some of the Pioneers to give him money so he could go to England and see the King and make him keep his promises. So that is why I am sure the Sergeant of Pioneers you heard about is this same unfortunate Tom Peters. I guess he got more from King George than he bargained for! I wonder if he's happier now?"

Hannibal wondered, too. It seemed to him that the trip to England might have changed the Sergeant's luck. He said, "If it is your Sergeant Peters that got the government to help us, he ought to be happy now. It sounds as if he is considered an important person, with lots of officials and government people taking him seriously and listening to what he has to say. Tell you what, I'll write and let you know how important he gets to be, if indeed we ever get to Africa together."

chapter nine
THE HALIFAX ROAD

Hannibal went along to church on Sunday morning and heard a good and thoughtful sermon from Mr. Twining, and after the service was finished collected the precious letter from him. He had written the address on it, "To John Clarkson, Esq., at Mr. Hartshorne's chambers, Halifax," so boldly that there would be in no danger of forgetting where to find the gentleman. It was well sealed, stamped with the rector's own signet in the wax, and Hannibal was anxious to have it reach Mr. Clarkson's hands in the same state, so he locked it in a cupboard for the night. He need not have bothered. Gus was quite indifferent to its contents and the several well-wishers who came to bid him a safe journey did not even ask to see it.

Hannibal was resolved to start out on foot early the next morning, and had been thinking about his route. The main road to Halifax turned up the South Mountain a few miles away and led to Falmouth, through forest and bog. Then it forded the river and rounded back along its upper reaches to the town of Windsor, and then by a superior road to Halifax. It would take a day to walk that road. He thought to himself that if he could go directly up the river he would reach Windsor in the easiest and quickest manner, in an hour or less.

He persuaded Gus to come along with him in his little boat, from which, at idle times during the season from May until September, they spent profitable hours with a fishing net out in the river. Late in September they had laid the boat up above the high water mark, planning to leave it there for the winter. Now Hannibal decided he would use it one last time.

He knew that the tide would be full at about ten o'clock on the Monday morning, but the boat could be launched on the rising tide a couple of hours before that. So late on Sunday afternoon he and Gus pushed it down into the bare mud and left it well anchored so the night tide wouldn't pull it away. That done, they spent a quiet evening and turned in earlier than usual.

They were up early in the morning and had time for breakfast and for Hannibal to tie up some provisions in a handkerchief before heading down to the shore. They squished through the mud to where the boat lay close to a familiar little creek, which was now filling up with a slow but steady flow of rising water.

They pushed the boat off, raised her sail, and upstream they went with some speed, borne by the tide and the slight breeze from the North. They passed along the steep shale cliffs of the bluff, bordered by its beach of broken flakes—known to everyone, from its colour, as Blue Beach. After that came banks of red clay, followed by green fields and marshes where the Halfway River came in to join the main stream of the

Windsor River. A few more miles of clay banks and marshes and they were touching the public wharf at Windsor. They had taken little more than an hour to bypass the miles of rough road that would have taken Hannibal half a day or more to walk or ride.

Windsor was the largest town in the region. It was dominated by the stockaded walls of Fort Edward, where that great lady Flora Macdonald and her Highlanders from Carolina had stayed one winter after the war had been lost. At the opposite end of the waterfront was Ferry Hill, below which the ferry boat plied back and forth to Falmouth, and the town lay between the two, facing out on the wharves along the river and running back from them. They were supposed to be building a bridge to replace the ferry, and that would certainly improve the town, but there were no signs that any work had begun.

They tied up at the public landing and Hannibal pulled himself up the ladder and with a word of farewell set out for the Halifax Road. Gus would wait for the tide to begin to ebb and would have no difficulty getting back home within the hour—unless the wind set in against him. If that happened, he would have to tack a bit, but there was no doubt he would have landed safely in the creek before the tide went out.

Hannibal had no time to stare at any of the sights of the town, but passed through the bustle of Water Street and through the several quiet residential streets, and then past meadows and the graveyard and was out in the open country within a few minutes. He stretched out his legs to a comfortable stride and headed for Halifax forty miles away. The road was in a miserable condition because of the October rains, and the going would get tougher, especially beyond the Newport turnoff as the road climbed up the long steep stretch of Ardoise Hill. His last view of Windsor, before the forest trees obscured it, was of the block houses and stockade of Fort Edward on the hill above the town; the rest was a haze of smoke from the chimneys of the town, amidst which the bright autumn trees glowed like dying embers. He paused there and ate the lunch he carried in his handkerchief.

By late afternoon, with the shadows lengthening fast, he was still short of Ardoise Hill, but that had not been his goal. He was hoping to find a bed for the night near its foot, from which he could make an early start the next day. In his travels, Gus had stayed several times in a settlement of African people on the road there, and he had provided the names of several people who would, he was sure, be glad to take his friend in and put him up for the night. The air was getting colder and the sun was low on the horizon when Hannibal found himself there.

The people of this hamlet, of course, were not well-to-do; for the most part they were day labourers who walked the long road to Windsor every morning and came back each evening, particularly in summer when there was always work in the town. However, there were also some who worked on their own farms, and his hope was that one of these, a Christian named Solomon Bates, would offer him hospitality. Gus had praised him as the best man in the settlement, and Hannibal was anxious to make friends with him. He soon found his home by inquiring from the first boy met on the road. The Bates family lived in a neat-looking cabin on a small hill some distance from the road. Their home was well-sheltered by a small grove of forest trees on one side and a barn and other outbuildings behind.

There was nobody around as he walked up the lane, but he saw smoke coming from the chimney and knew someone was home. He knocked at the door and it was opened in a moment by a young girl with a very pretty face, marked by particularly large and beautiful dark eyes. Hannibal had the feeling of being jolted by a shock to his chest, and hardly knew what was happening. However, she welcomed him in and made him sit down, and the conversation they had during the next little while was forever engraved on his memory, though really nothing of great importance was said.

Her first words were, "Come in, please," and she held the door open in a generous and inviting manner. He walked in feeling very awkward and almost stumbling over his feet. Shyness and confusion were unaccustomed feelings for him, but he encountered them then. He found himself in a kitchen much neater than the one at Horton Bluff, and very comfortable, too, with the little touches women added when they made a home.

"Pray be seated, sir," she said very politely, as if Hannibal were an old man with feeble limbs. Disregarding that thought, he did sit down, but he chose a stool near the hearth rather than the inviting armchair beside it. It was not a time to show that he was tired. It was time to state his business.

"I'm looking for Mr. Solomon Bates," he said. "I hope I have come to the right house."

"Indeed you have," she answered. "This is his home, but he is out at work just now. He will be in soon. You can wait for him here if you are not in a hurry. I am his daughter, Evalina Bates."

She moved gracefully about her household chores, stirring the stew in the black pot over the flames, laying a cloth on the table by the window, and setting dishes out on it.

"You're not from around here, I think," she said.

"No, I'm from Horton Township," he replied, beginning to control his beating heart and breathlessness. The peace and calm in the room had a pacifying effect on him, and he began to feel at home, so much so that he began to tell all about himself, about the farm, about the Sierra Leone expedition and his reason for going to Halifax, and finally he mentioned Gus, who had told him to look for the home of the Bates family.

"Oh, of course we can put you up tonight," she said warmly, "and I know my father will enjoy talking to you. We don't often have interesting company here, and Papa loves to hear about things and to talk, too."

While they waited for her father to return, Miss Bates chatted easily until Hannibal felt quite comfortable. He had never known a girl quite like her before, and as he listened and talked to her, he felt a warm glow in his chest that was new to him, except that perhaps it was a bit like his sensations when stirred by religious experiences—like it, but not the same. He realized that Evalina Bates was creating this internal glow. Later in the evening, when all was quiet and he was alone, he knew that he was feeling the new sensation of falling in love.

As it was, his time alone with Evalina was all too brief, for soon her father and brother appeared. Solomon Bates gave him a hearty welcome to his house and to the table which was soon spread with the tasty meal cooked by Evalina. The four of them sat around it, and Hannibal had to tell about himself again.

Later, after the evening chores were done, they sat by the fire and Solomon Bates told of his experiences while Hannibal filled in more details about himself. Solomon had been living in Virginia as a free man, following the blacksmith trade, when the war began. He had thought he was lucky when his work pleased a British officer whose horse had lost a couple of shoes on the road and who had brought him in to be shod, because the officer spread the word of a good and reliable smith and the officers kept him busy.

This was fine while the British controlled the neighbourhood. But his luck turned around when they moved on and the rebel forces moved in. They decided that Solomon Bates had not acted like "a patriot" and a petty persecution of him and his family began. Threatening letters were found on the smithy floor when he opened in the morning, insults were scribbled on it with charcoal, and it was clear that he had enemies around.

These things worried Solomon, but he regarded himself as a neutral in the struggle that was going on, and felt that as long as he did honest work for the community he would ride out the storm of ill-feeling. However, he was to find that he had more enemies than he realized. After the defeat at Yorktown, when Loyalists and runaway slaves in his area cautiously made their way to Charles Town, he stayed where he was. But one evening, when he was shutting up shop after the day's work, a sack was thrown over his head and he was taken—as he put it—"to a tar-and-feather party." He was one of several treated like that, but he was the only man of colour there and they seemed to hate him more on that account. He heard several saying, "Why don't we finish him off for good right now?"

They treated him terribly. He refused to go into the details, but if he had not been a man of immense strength, this abuse would have probably brought about his death. As it was, he was laid up for several days. After that he collected his tools from the shop, packing them and all his household effects on a wagon he was able to borrow, and slipped away by night. The wheels were bound in cloth and the axles well-greased to give no notice to their village of their departure. After some day,s they reached Charles Town and were recorded there as Loyalists, and like Hannibal they eventually arrived in Nova Scotia. They came in a vessel with the disbanded troops being settled in the new townships of Rawdon and Douglas, and for a time he lived among them and took up his trade again. However, their circumstances were bad, and the hardships killed Mrs. Bates. When Solomon gained the grant of a small farm, they had moved here and were doing well. Solomon farmed when the weather was good and operated the smithy at other times.

Hannibal was, all the while, very conscious of Evalina's bright face in the fireside circle, and when he told about his experiences on the battle-field and in camp, she seemed to find them more exciting than her father's story. Her eyes glistened and her breath quickened as she heard of his narrow escapes and desperate forays in the war.

At last it was time for all to go to bed. They spread a mattress for their guest on the floor near the fire and departed elsewhere. Hannibal was tired and went to sleep at once, but his last thought was of Evalina, and his hope was that he had made the impression on her that she had made on him. He knew he wanted to see much more of her.

Nonetheless, he set out again early next morning, before the house-hold was up. He walked for miles along the rough road that wound eastward through a narrow valley, then up and down hills with ancient forests on either side. He crossed the St. Croix River by a sturdy wooden bridge and beyond this began to climb a long slope leading on to the central plateau, or heartland of Nova Scotia. Halfway up this slope, he saw in front of him a two-wheeled cart drawn by a team of horses. They were resting when he saw them. The farmer who sat on the seat had tossed them some hay to munch and he himself was eating his breakfast. The vehicle had a load of sacks, probably oats and wheat for sale in the town.

Hannibal had always thought that one lost nothing by being polite and gained nothing by being surly, so as he walked past he respectfully said, "Good morning, sir," to the sturdy red-faced farmer.

His discouraging reply was an "umph!" and then he shook the reins and said "Giddap" to the horses. The beasts threw their heads back and, still holding wisps of hay in their great yellow teeth, stepped out, with a jingle of metal, groans of the leather harness, and a squeaking of the ax-les as the wheels turned reluctantly. Hannibal decided that the farmer would not be very friendly to him, so kept ahead of him at a good pace and ascended the crest of Ardoise Hill well before him and his team.

He turned around for a look at the view, one he had seen years before when he with Clifford, both on horseback, first found their way to Windsor. It showed a scene which, he could better judge now, went down and on for miles and miles. In the blue distance, he was sure he could make out the Annapolis Valley, but he did not recognize any particular landmark for certain.

Everywhere, westward and northward, were forests, fields, hills, and mountain ridges, with glints of water reflecting the sunlight amidst the blue-green masses of forest. Somewhere down there, down at sea level, was Horton and the community he had come to know so well. For years, he had never ventured this far away from it. Directly below, the road ran straight down and then took a twist and went behind the trees. Now he saw the team of horses labouring up the slope and catching up to him. The farmer was walking beside them. Hannibal stood his ground as they came abreast and slowed to a halt.

"Going far?" the farmer asked.

"I'm on my way to Halifax," Hannibal replied.

Evidently the farmer had had a change of heart

"Oh? So am I. Hop on if you want to ride."

The man swung himself onto his seat and Hannibal got on, too. The horses ambled along easily now that the crest was gained, and went along steadily for the next couple of hours. Now and again, when the road was cut up or full of potholes, and the vehicle careened sideways and nearly tossed him off, Hannibal preferred to get off and walk, but even then he stuck close. He liked having company and it was pleasant, when the road improved, to travel sitting down and resting his legs. When the sun was at its zenith and the farmer reached in a small sack for his dinner, he looked in his pack and brought out a lunch Evalina had prepared for him the night before. It was delicious, not least because her hands had prepared it, and he enjoyed every scrap of it while he thought gratefully of her kindness and her interest in him. In fact, thoughts of her all day long made the long miles go more quickly.

Finally, by nightfall, they reached Sackville, not far from Bedford Basin. There was an old inn there for just such travellers as farmers going to market. It was not much to look at—weathered clapboard on the walls, curling shingles on the low roof, and a yard that could have been more neatly kept—but the stable was tight and solid and the public room was large and warm.

The proprietor and his wife questioned him closely, and he was half expecting them to tell him to sleep in the haymow above the horses—if they let him stay at all—but when he told them his errand in Halifax and showed that he had money, they accepted him as a guest for the night. They seemed particularly interested in hearing about the Sierra Leone expedition and said they wished the African people well. Indeed, he felt he had made a very good impression on them, because after a good supper he had to amuse them with tales of life on the old plantation and his adventures during the war and since. In fact, the details of the kitchen and larder on Ellenboro Plantation were of more interest to the landlord's wife than any of his more exciting stories.

The farmer smoked silently on his battered corncob pipe, interested in all that was said around the hearth, but never speaking himself and refusing to be drawn into anything but the briefest replies to the landlady's questions. Now and again, he smiled at the stories or observations, but it seemed he did not believe in wasting words on idle chatter.

His orders to the landlady about his meal and bed were given clearly and concisely, and she seemed to be in awe of him, for everything was done just as he directed without needless question.

At bedtime he, as chief guest, went to the one private chamber, while a straw-filled tick was brought in for Hannibal and spread near the fire. Then the landlord and his lady retired to their own private quarters. Hannibal was left alone, and for a few moments watched his own visions in the fire until he suddenly closed his eyes and was asleep.

chapter ten
MEETING WITH MR. CLARKSON

Early the next morning, after a good night, the farmer and Hannibal continued on their way along the rough and rocky road leading to the capital. The road wended its way close to the shore of Bedford Basin and then onto the peninsula, in the far edge of which lay Halifax. The farmer was bound for the public market on the waterfront, which suited Hannibal very well. When he reined in his donkeys, there they prepared to go their separate ways.

Hannibal was sorry to leave his friendly company, but he had spoken so little that they had not established a friendship; there had been an unspoken barrier of some kind between them. It may have been a matter of age, of skin colour, or it may have been because the boy had been a slave, but there was a distance between them that sitting together in a cart, even for hours, could not bridge. So Hannibal parted from him with warm thanks and without further ceremony pushed among the produce stalls, having a look at the activity while making his way in the general direction of the Grand Parade, in the heart of the town.

The market was a hive of activity. From the fringes of the city and from across the harbour, farmers had brought in their produce. Their stalls displayed potatoes, carrots, turnips, cabbages, enormous wine-coloured beets, large orange pumpkins, and all the bounty of a Nova Scotian autumn. The thrifty housewives of Halifax had ample opportunities to lay in a winter stock of provisions if they had commodious frost-proof cellars. However, Halifax was perched on a great mass of solid bedrock, and that led to problems. In Horton, it was an easy matter to dig a good root cellar because of the deep soft soil.

Hannibal saw many men of his own race working in the market; generally ragged, some of them had things to sell, but most were selling their labour. When a housewife purchased a sack or so of vegetables, a fortunate African man would be chosen from the number standing around and beckoned over; he would put the sack or sacks on his head and follow the lady to her home for the sake of the few pence she would give him. There were coloured women there, too, squatting behind the array of vegetables they had grown or fruit they had gathered, or perhaps shellfish found in the mud at low tide. In some cases, they must have had husbands with fishing boats, because there were lobsters and finned fish, too. These people looked better off than the porters.

Nor were these all who sold in the City Market. There were Indians there, too, Micmac men and women. The men stood around in small groups, smoking steadily in silent communion with each other. The women, on the other hand, sat amidst their wares, such as small game animals they had trapped or shot in the forest (one Indian woman even had a live young deer for sale). Their bright-coloured baskets were woven of thin strips of wood dyed with the juices of tree bark and forest plants. Their expertly crafted moccasins and leather clothing was fringed and decorated with bright porcupine quills. Snowshoes were offered, for the sporting classes who planned to travel outside the city walls when the snow was deep. Hannibal even noticed toys for children, such as small bows and arrows, model wigwams, and small birchbark canoes.

Years later, in Freetown, Hannibal remembered the Halifax Market. How like the market in Freetown it was, but what a difference in the commodities offered for sale and in the people selling and buying! Still, a market was a market, and though it was carrots and turnips in Halifax and kola nuts and coconuts in Freetown, it was the same kind of activity taking place. Strange it was to think that the common vegetables of the Halifax market would be luxuries in Sierra Leone, and its plentiful supply of nuts and fruit the reverse.

After wasting a few minutes in refusing the offer made by a lady to pay him a few pence to carry her vegetables home, Hannibal got away from the confusion of the market and found his way to the Grand Parade, which was the central square of Halifax. Standing there in front of St. Paul's Church, he proceeded to get his bearings. The midday sun was flooding the shabby streets with clear light, stirring his memory. It was still a dirty, dingy-looking place, compared with Shelburne, with a confusing network of short streets.

However, he only wanted to find his way to Duke Street, to Mr. Lawrence Hartshorne's office, as indicated by the directions on the outside of the letter he brought from Pastor Twining. The minister had told him how to proceed from St. Paul's Church, and by going along Barrington Street, on the lower side of the Parade, he counted openings as instructed and so discovered Duke Street nearby. He had no difficulty finding the clearly marked nameplate that showed him his destination. After entering the office, he explained his business to a clerk, who brought back word from an adjoining office that Mr. Clarkson and Mr. Hartshorne were busy, but would soon see him.

Hannibal sat on a bench and contemplated some of the notices posted around the room, thinking how blessed he was that he could read them and so pass the time in a self-improving way. Soon he heard the door to the inner room open and it seemed, by the sound of chairs scraping and boots hitting the floor heavily, that some gentlemen, whose voices had been a low rumble, were now on the verge of coming out. Fortunately for his understanding of the issues involved in the emigration scheme, they did not come out, but carried on their conversation with the door wide open and perfectly audible to him. Now one voice was now distinctly heard as a loud roar, and no wonder, because its owner was accustomed to making himself heard through howling gales on the high seas.

"I tell you, Gentlemen," he roared, "that though there are elements here, aye, and in *England*, too—in the very office, it may be, of the Secretary of State himself—who would like my mission to fail, yet it shall *not* fail. What I am doing is what any Christian man should approve, and although governments and powers may resist me, the Almighty, with *His* Power, stands behind me."

Hannibal's suspicion as to who was speaking was confirmed when a high-pitched Yankee-type voice cried, "But, Mr. Clarkson, how can it be God's desire to carry these poor people back to a land of heat, savages, and disease? If the British government wishes to be kind to these people, it should leave them where they are, but provide them with some useful livestock, animals like sheep and cattle, along with farm implements and seed, so they can be prosperous and happy here."

Mr. Clarkson had probably already heard this kind of argument more than once. He retorted confidently, "Mr. Smith, I do not think that the lot of Negro people in Nova Scotia or in any other part of the Americas can ever be better than life for them on their own continent. After all, these people have been adapted by God for that life. They are strangers here and it would take, perhaps, centuries for them to change. Not only that, but since every white man makes it his business to degrade and keep subservient every black man, the Negro race can never hope to be happy or respected here."

A chorus of outrage and dissent seemed to follow these remarks; then a new voice broke in. "Suppose we concede you the argument, Mr. Clarkson—though in point of fact I wager that half your colonists will die of fever in the first twelve months, and the other half be sold as slaves again—why then do you not take away the whole population of black people in this Province? It is obvious, surely, that we dislike your mission because it creams off the best of the blacks among us, the most honest, industrious, and ambitious. You are going to leave us to deal with the rubbish, the riffraff, without their natural leaders and those of better quality who would otherwise guide them to a better life here. Do you call this fair, either to them or to us?"

"Captain Peebles," replied the voice of Mr. Clarkson, "there may be something in what you say. But I have not come to solve the problems of you gentlemen of Nova Scotia. Rather I have come with the explicit mission of helping worthy Africans willing to help themselves, to go to a land where they can be free and unhampered in their own development. You yourselves will have to deal with the Negroes who are left behind; they are your responsibility. My task is to help my friends of the Sierra Leone Company and other supporting Christians to establish a beacon in the darkness of Africa that will lead, step by step, to its enlightenment and awakening. I think that if you will take the larger view, you will see that your arguments to the contrary are basically unworthy of you. Our aim is, in time, the complete abolition of this dreadful slave trade and, in the long term, of the very institution of slavery itself. With Mr. Pitt our firm friend, we are confident that our aims will soon be accomplished."

This provoked another explosion of dissent and expostulation, and Mr. Smith voiced his violent disagreement with these sentiments. "It is impossible, Mr. Clarkson, that the West Indies should ever stand for such a development. Anyway, I am sure that the Carolinas and Georgia will still buy slaves, even if the whole British Navy stood off their shores and tried to stop the traffic. And why should they not? Slaves are not only money in the master's pocket, but in the course of time they are elevated and become civilized and refined under his watchful eye!"

Another voice, belonging, as the silent listener learned later, to the merchant Lawrence Hartshorne, now broke in for the first time. "Really, Smith, you are uttering preposterous propositions! Have you any experience of plantation life down South?"

"Well, no, but in Boston—"

"But Boston nothing! You have seen house servants in Boston, I'll wager, leading a very different life than the brutish existence of plantation labourers. In Boston, they can aspire to be human beings. A slave woman can be a poetess, as was that woman Phillis Wheatley who was all the rage reciting her poems in fashionable circles a few years back. How many female slaves in Carolina do you suppose have the time to think poetic thoughts, let alone to write poetry and get anyone to listen to it? I can tell you that the field work comes first, and most of the rest of the time is taken up in looking after their little ones. Neither the women-folk nor the men have a chance to become refined beyond what Nature has already done for them. Boston, indeed! Go South and see for yourself what real slavery is like! Don't ever judge it by the parlour maids and grooms you've seen in Boston—or in Halifax, either."

"This is all beside the point," spoke up Captain Peebles again. "If the Parliament in London comes to seriously contemplating cutting off the slave trade, then we can bid farewell to the prosperity of the British Empire in all its parts. Bristol and Liverpool would stagnate, the manufacturers of Great Britain would be unable to sell their trade goods to Africa, and the West Indian planters would have no labour for their fields. English trade would slump if there was no West Indian sugar and rum. In fact, we ourselves would be finished here in Halifax!

"What! No regular shipments of rum? I don't believe we'd get any effort at all out of our working people if we didn't have the rum puncheon open and handy when they wanted refreshment. And just imagine the state of the Navy without rum! It doesn't bear thinking about! Pfah! It would be impossible! So, Mr. Clarkson, sir, with all due respect, we must agree to hold differing opinions on these important present and future matters. Good day to you, sir. Come, gentlemen, let us away!"

The door which had stood half-open all through this conversation was suddenly pulled back and three Halifax gentleman, somewhat red in the face with agitation, walked past Hannibal without a glance and on out into the street. The boy's heart was pounding as he stood up at the clerk's gesture and came towards the door. Either their agitation had communicated itself to him, or perhaps it came from deep inside himself. He perceived these three prosperous merchants as heartless enemies who would deny him his heart's desire if they could.

On the other hand, he felt better now about facing Mr. Clarkson. His emphatic words in refusing to give way in the least to the merchant's arguments showed that he really was a friend to him and his people, and a true hero. From the moment the boy entered the room and shook

Lieutenant Clarkson's hand, to the last day of his life, he never had any reason to change his mind.

Hannibal had expected Clarkson to be bald, red-faced, middle-aged and portly, but to his surprise the hand he took was that of a lean young man. Tall, fair and well-built, with a complexion darkened from wind and salt spray, and with the roll of the sea in his walk, he gave an impression of a large and kindly nature. His blue eyes beamed warmly on the boy as he walked through the door of the room, and when he held out his hand Hannibal at once held out his own in response and they shook hands.

Such a normal thing to do! But he had never shaken hands with a white man before. African people shook hands with African people, and white people with white, but hardly ever with those of the other complexion. This simple handshake was a final proof that this man really believed in equality between the races, and that if he had any influence in Sierra Leone, there would be equality there. Hannibal took to him from the start, and later, as Clarkson asked him about the circumstances of his life as if he really wanted to know, became ever more attached to him. After a few minutes of conversation, Hannibal had no misgiving about going with him to Africa, no matter what savage beasts or murderous vermin might lurked in the forests there.

Clarkson's first words to him were, "Are you coming to Africa with me?"

Hannibal had practised in his mind how he would state his business, so the words came readily to his tongue. "Indeed, sir, I hope so. I have come to enquire, on behalf of a group of us living in Horton, into the details of your plan. I bring you a letter from the missionary at Horton who has also made a list of those who would like to know more and are considering becoming colonists in Sierra Leone. Here it is, sir."

Clarkson looked at the superscription on the letter, where Mr. Twining had written, "By hand of Hannibal Hoops," and asked, "And are you Hannibal Hoops?"

"Yes, sir, Hannibal Hoops Courtney; that is to say, I was part of the Courtney household in Carolina. They gave me the other names, but my mother called me Kanday. That is an African name, a name among my people there."

"That is very interesting," he remarked, and then motioned the boy farther into the room where another gentleman was sitting at one of several desks. "This is Mr. Lawrence Hartshorne, who is helping me with the great enterprise," he said.

Hannibal recognized Mr. Hartshorne as the businessman who had been so helpful to Clifford when he had come from Shelburne. He was a soberly dressed young man who gave a friendly nod but showed no sign of remembering the boy and did not rise or speak.

Mr. Clarkson sat down behind the other desk and motioned Hannibal to the chair in front. In the next hour, he asked many questions and heard Hannibal's story, about going through the war with Master Clifford, and about coming to Nova Scotia and his life in Horton.

Then Clarkson explained that he had just come back from a visit to Shelburne and Birchtown, and had no doubt that many of Hannibal's friends from former days would be among the several hundred he had agreed to take with him. But some were choosing a different life. "One of my companions on the trip," he said, "was a recruiting officer from the West Indies. He signed up a dozen or more young men in Birchtown; they will be soldiers in the West Indian Regiment. I don't suppose you would want to be a soldier? No?

"In fact," he added, "it seems to me, Hannibal Hoops, that you are very comfortably situated where you are. Life in Sierra Leone could be uncomfortable and even dangerous for you. Why do you want to go?"

"Because, sir, I want to be a free man in my own country. They call me free here, but I feel they look on me as little more than a slave. I am damned in all eyes because of my race alone. I want to be in my own land where I will not be looked down upon and where I can live in peace and happiness, the equal of anyone I meet."

"Reason enough, young man, for undertaking a journey that may include danger and hardship. Now excuse me while I read the letter."

When he had glanced through Mr. Twining's letter, he passed it over to his friend and said, "I gather you have some questions to put to me. Ask me whatever you wish, and I shall answer to the best of my ability."

"Sir, the people who sent me want to know if there are fierce animals and dangerous snakes there. We want to know whether the native people there will be friends or enemies. We want to know if the soil is good, and whether we can grow good crops there. We want to know whether we will be able to keep in touch with the Christian part of the world, and with our friends and relatives here. Can we educate our children there? Can we better ourselves according to the standards of civilized men?"

He smiled and said, "Those are all very good questions. I am glad your friends sent you with such practical queries. From what I have been able to learn, there are few animals there that any prudent group of people need fear. There are snakes, of course, but they are easily avoided. We hope that the native people will be friendly to our settlers, but of course that will depend on circumstances and we cannot be sure about it. The settlers themselves will really be responsible for building up friendly relations with the native people. Until they succeed in doing so, the colony will always be in a dangerous position. As a matter of fact, the first group of settlers whom we sent from London a few years back were attacked and scattered by unfriendly natives. I fear the settlers were at fault in the matter; they were not carefully chosen and included some who had a wrong outlook on their mission. That is why we are being very careful about the type of people we are inviting and accepting from Nova Scotia.

"Now, as to the rest of your questions, our intention, speaking for the people of good will in England who are founding and supporting this settlement, is that Sierra Leone will be in close touch with Europe, and thus with civilization. It is our dream that, from Sierra Leone, Christian civilization will penetrate into the unknown and unexplored reaches of Africa. The Company in England will buy produce from the colony and in return protect and encourage it during its infancy, until in the fullness of time it becomes self-supporting, self-governing, and an important element in the transformation of Africa."

As to whether the land would support good farming, he was hopeful, since the soil of Sierra Leone normally supported luxuriant vegetation. "When the forest is cleared, I am sure we will find the soil to be of the utmost fertility."

Hannibal, from disappointments already met in farming, had some doubts on that score—and later experience confirmed them—and said, "Here in Nova Scotia, sir, much fine looking forest has been cleared in the past five years, in the hope of making good and fruitful gardens. But in many places the earth has been only a thin layer over the bedrock, much too slight to grow crops. After a rainstorm or the spring runoff of melting snow, there is really nothing but rock left."

"Indeed?" Mr. Clarkson was not surprised by any revelation of false expectations in Nova Scotia and obviously thought its problems would not be found in Africa. He went on to say, "I hope all the settler families will bring quantities of good seed with them, and I am sure they will find their foodstuffs flourish very well. Of course, they should also bring their tools and other useful articles. Any articles useful in Nova Scotia should be equally useful over there. Except things for winter, of course; people won't need snowshoes there, to take an obvious example."

Hannibal thought to himself that probably things that had been useful in Carolina would be equally of use in Sierra Leone.

Mr. Clarkson by this time had another appointment and the boy left, after arranging to call on him the next morning at about ten o'clock. By that time, he would have written an answer to the missionary's letter, and probably some of the points raised in conversation. It seemed to Hannibal that the officer became very tired towards the end of their talk, so he bade him goodbye without further ado.

But for that hasty exit Hannibal might have asked his advice as to a place for the night, and probably he would have sent the boy to a shelter set aside for use in such a case. As it was, he was on his own, and during the next few hours wandered about the town that still compared badly with the Shelburne he remembered. It had changed little since he passed through in '84, though there were more little wooden houses, the tents were gone from Citadel Hill and Camp Hill, and the dockyards were beginning to bustle again because of the new war against the French. But after the quiet years in the country, the number of people gathered in this one spot, with all the bustle and variety it brought, was of great interest to the boy, and he gawked his way like any country bumpkin from one end of the harbour front to the other and all the streets running up from it.

He was ripe for plucking, though he thought himself wise and vigilant.

chapter eleven
FOUL TREACHERY

All the while Hannibal explored the town, he was keeping his eyes open for signs of a suitable lodging for the night. Walking along Upper Water Street, he was particularly on the lookout for a friendly and honest face, of African background among the towns-folk walking or standing about. He found the person he was looking for leaning against the wall of the Blue Bell Tavern. He was a bright-looking lad of his own race, neatly dressed but with a sad expression on his face. Hannibal went up beside him and caught his attention. As he introduced himself, the youth brought his thoughts back from some faraway journey and looked at him with interest.

"I came in from Horton today," Hannibal said, "and I'm looking for a lodging for the night. I can pay. Can you direct me to a place where I can eat and sleep?"

"Certainly I can," said the youth. "Call me Randy. You're welcome to come stay at my place for the night."

"Will your family mind you bringing in a stranger like this?"

"Oh, no," he said. "I don't mean it's my place like that. I mean it's the boarding house where I stay. They'll give you good grub and a good enough bed, if you ain't too fussy."

"No, I don't mind, just so long as it's dry and warm."

So he led the boy off along Water Street and then took a turn up the hill, and after a few more turns Hannibal lost his bearings and was not at all sure that he had ever seen the shabby lanes and yards through which they were walking. Meanwhile, Randy was keeping up a continuous tale about himself and his exciting adventures; he apparently was a seafarer and was with a small ship moored in the harbour and waiting for cargo. He was a confiding young man who treated Hannibal like an old friend, and seemed interested in hearing about his errand to the city and the meeting with Mr. Clarkson.

"I have to report back to my ship this evening," he said. "Perhaps you'd like to come along and have a look at her. She's a nice little vessel, snug and seaworthy."

But Hannibal declined. He felt tired, suddenly, and wanted to relax. Moreover, a fine drizzle had developed and once the daylight faded it was going to be a dirty night. He didn't want to get his feet wet in the muddy streets or sit uncomfortably in a ship's boat rowing around the harbour when there was nothing to be gained by it.

"I just want a good hot meal, Randy, and a quiet talk by the fire, and then a good night's sleep. Tomorrow I have to see Mr. Clarkson again. If I have time after that, I may be able to visit your vessel."

Randy didn't seriously mind. "All right," he said, "we can do that. Anyway, here we are at the Bonny Brier Bush." He knocked with an odd rhythm on the door, which apparently was locked. In a moment, it opened and a worn-looking woman looked carefully at them before moving aside to let them enter. Then, to Hannibal's astonishment, she shut and barred the door behind them. He was puzzled and said to Randy, "We never lock doors in Horton."

"This town is a bad place for thieves," Randy explained. "They might break in anytime if they see easy pickings. That's why old Nannie keeps it locked all the time."

They had walked down a short corridor and into a large public room by this time. Gratefully, Hannibal warmed and dried himself in front of the huge fireplace, where great birch logs were burning briskly and throwing out an abundance of heat. He took off his damp boots and jacket, putting them where they would dry nicely. There was a large black iron pot slung over the fire, bubbling away contentedly, wafting out delicious homey smells that reminded him that it was a long time since breakfast. He was glad when the old woman came back with two bowls into which she ladled large quantities of an appetizing stew. Randy got them each a mug of small-beer from a cask in the corner. There was a table in the room, but the two youths stayed close to the fire and sat in its warmth with their bowls on their laps and were content to clean up their bowls and help themselves to more.

As they ate, the two youths got better acquainted, and Hannibal liked Randy better and better; he was so interested and approving of the idea of going to Sierra Leone. He did not argue with Hannibal or scoff at the whole scheme the way Gus had. Of course, having met Mr. Clarkson Hannibal was more confident of the future of the colony than ever before and happier than ever that he was to be part of it, and he decided to make a convert of Randy. He thought he might be an excellent partner for him over there; the two working together could do so much together that one alone would not be able to manage.

He brought out the arguments he had used on Gus and even mentioned some of Mr. Clarkson's views, and felt he was getting somewhere until after a time Randy stopped listening. At any rate, he became silent and his mind was obviously far away. The sad look on his face noticed earlier returned; Hannibal stopped talking and there was a silence in the room for a while. Suddenly Hannibal realised that he was very sleepy, and saw through the window that it was quite dark outside.

"Time for me to report aboard ship," said Randy, and he stood up. "I may be gone a while. If you want to go to sleep, don't wait up for me."

He opened a door in an inside wall and revealed another room with straw mattresses on the floor. "We'll sleep in here; take whichever you like. Here are some blankets," and he brought a couple from a dark heap in the corner.

Hannibal thought he seemed troubled, and said sympathetically, "I'm sorry you have to go out and get wet all over again."

"It's all right," he said, managing a smile. "It's a sailor's life to be wet more often than he's dry. Don't wait up," he said again, and in a moment had his outer clothes on and was gone.

Hannibal stayed sitting near the fire, thinking his own thoughts. The room was very empty with him in it alone. Now and again, he threw another log on the fire. Outside the night seemed to be a rough one; the wind blew in gusts, shutters banged against walls, and signboards creaked and groaned. Even the timbers of the house seemed to be grating against one another as the wind tugged and twisted the structure. He felt sorry for Randy out on the harbour.

The old woman came in and out of the room at intervals, intent on some evening tasks, but she only mumbled to herself and did not speak. Eventually she settled down in a corner and worked away at some knitting. She was no company for Hannibal. He kept expecting that other people would come as the evening wore on, and began to think that Randy and he would be the only ones sleeping there that night. He went to the bedroom and brought out several blankets to warm by the fire. They felt cold and damp, so he was glad he was showing some foresight.

While the blankets toasted away, he got out his little Bible and read some beloved passages again. His favourite chapters were in Exodus, and he quite naturally turned to that book. Once again, he read about the struggle of the Children of Israel to leave the land of bondage and return to the land from whence their ancestors had come. He could understand that from the time African people in America first heard of the enslaved Hebrews, they felt a special kinship with them. Hannibal always pictured the Hebrews as being Africans, with all their physical characteristics; it was they he saw toiling in the brickyards of Egypt and scouring the countryside for straw; it was they he saw being whipped by Egyptian overseers who looked like certain brutal white men he had seen in the South or even in Nova Scotia. He liked to read about how Moses struck down the brutal overseer, and how in time God called him to lead his people out.

Hannibal asked himself who the Moses of his people in Nova Scotia might be. He looked into the orange flames and saw the face of John Clarkson. Was he their Moses? Could he be a Moses for all oppressed Africans in North America? Truly, he was a prince among rulers, just as Moses had been when he lived in the palace of Pharoah, so that was a hopeful parallel. On the other hand, the Bible made it clear that Moses was really of Hebrew blood, and certainly John Clarkson was not an African. He might sympathize with the oppressed brethren, but he was not really one of them. On the other hand, he thought, thinking of what the New Testament taught, Clarkson could perhaps claim to be a brother in a spiritual sense, since he evidently took his Christian belief very seriously. He clearly felt his brotherhood with all God's children, both black and white.

He was a Christian not by his tongue alone but in his heart. Yes, he had the possibility of being called by God to be a Moses for the oppressed African of Nova Scotia.

Hannibal began to fall asleep where he sat, and even though his new friend had not come back, he had to lie down. Taking his warm blankets into the sleeping room, he wrapped himself in them and lay on his mattress. He left a couple of blankets for Randy near the dying fire and thought he would be grateful, for they were now warm and dry. The wind still roared outside as he closed his eyes. It had been a long day, and before he had been there many minutes, he was deeply asleep.

Morning seemed to come very quickly. He woke from a deep sleep and found the sun already up. For a moment, he did not know where he was, but then he remembered the events of the day before and recognized the room with the straw pallets scattered about, on one of which he had slept so comfortably. From where he lay, he could see out of a dirty window and into the cold grey light of another Halifax dawn. He was warm in bed and for a moment thought he might catch another forty winks. Why get up too soon? There were no hungry animals waiting to be tended to; he was on a holiday. Then he scolded his slothful self. He was supposed to meet Mr. Clarkson during the morning and had better rise and prepare himself in good time.

Hannibal sat up and saw the pallet meant for Randy. There were the blankets tossed on it, so it had been used; Randy had been careful not to waken him, he thought, which was kind of him. "What a thoughtful young fellow indeed. He knew I needed a good sleep." He found his jacket and boots on the floor, so Randy had brought them in from the other room. Hannibal put them on and went to the door, and then realized that something was wrong. The latch string that should have been on the inside was not there, and on the other side the latch in its groove held the solid door as well as any bolt. Whether his captivity was accidental or not, he felt a gust of terror run through his body. He suppressed it and tried to slow down the beating of his heart. There was surely no reason to feel danger in the company of his new friend. But was he a friend?

He put his eye to the small hole where the latch string normally passed and could discern the glow of the fire and human figures in front of it. Randy must be there.

He called to him.

"Randy! I cannot get out. Something's wrong with the door!"

A moment later, a dark shape stood between his eye and the firelight and Randy was speaking through the hole. "Go back to sleep, Hannibal. You need a good rest. I'll open the door when it's time for you to get up."

Hannibal, of course, had no way of knowing just exactly what time it was, but at this season of the year, when the days were short, he was always up well before sunrise. He felt sure he had overslept and that it must be at least nine o'clock, and that was very late. In fact, it was strange that he had not wakened at his usual time, and he wondered if he had eaten or drunk something to make him sleep longer.

It was obvious now that Randy wanted to keep him a prisoner in the room. Why? How could it be to his advantage to do so?

He called again, "I want out now, Randy. I don't want to sleep anymore. I've got things to do and people to see. Let me out, please, at once."

"It's best for you to stay there, friend," came the reply.

Hannibal had nothing to gain by playing the innocent any longer and said, "Look, Randy, I haven't done anything wrong and I'm not afraid of anyone. Why are you so anxious to keep me in here? What are you trying to do to me?"

The door was not as sturdy as it appeared and there was actually no problem in speaking to each other through it. So the two youths had a strange conversation in which they could not see each other but Hannibal learned very clearly that he had fallen into a trap.

Randy gave it all away when he said, "Believe me, Hannibal, I'm doing the best thing I can for you. You'll thank me for it when you think it over. I know you don't like this cold country anymore'n I do. You told me yourself how you want to live in a warm country. An' I know Africa is a bad place to live, so I thought about it and I told Captain and he said it would be alright to take you with us when we sail South. Ain't that good, Hannibal? We'll take you to a place that's a lot better than Africa."

A cry of anguish broke from Hannibal's lips before he could contain it. Explain it however he might, Randy had somehow betrayed him back into slavery, and if he could not find some way of helping himself in the next few hours, he would be carried away and doomed to the lifetime of servitude he had believed he had escaped. The frightened youth now wished he had kept his thoughts and plans to himself the previous day; but how could he have believed that a brother of colour, and one of his own age to boot, would ever betray him to such a fate? He ruefully admitted to himself that perhaps he was more of a country bumpkin than he wanted the world to know. What could he do? The only answer to that question seemed to lie in making Randy see that he was doing something very wrong, but what could he appeal to?

"Randy, I thought you were my friend. I cannot believe that one person of colour would treat another like this. Come on, Randy, let me out and we'll treat it like a joke. It is a joke, isn't it, and we'll laugh about it later. But let it end now, Randy, before it goes too far."

There was no response and he continued, "After all, Randy, it's not likely your captain really wants to go to a lot of bother for me. He may want to do nice things for you, because he likes you. But perhaps he won't mind me doing nice things for you, too. I can take you over to Horton and show you how nice country life is. In fact, you could stay there all winter with me and my friend Gus, if the captain doesn't need you."

In a croaky voice, as if something was squeezing him inside, Randy said in broken phrases, "I cannot go anywhere with you. I am still a slave. Captain bought me a long time ago. I cannot leave him."

Hannibal saw that Randy was only a pawn in some kind of game. Perhaps he had been sent out to watch the streets for strong young fellows who would fetch a good price as plantation workers. His mind raced as he thought of how to cut himself out of the trap. The key, so far as he knew, was Randy. It seemed he was alone at the moment. He had to be alone. If his captain and other crewmen were in the building, he wouldn't be afraid of letting Hannibal loose, so he had to keep him confined and a prisoner until the others were ready to come get him. Maybe he could be shamed into doing the right thing.

"So, Randy," Hannibal sneered, "you, a slave, want to see me become a slave, too. Don't you see you are just like the fox in the old story, the fox who froze his tail in the ice and lost it, then wanted all the other foxes to freeze theirs off, too? You are a traitor to me and to our people. You are a Judas! Is it envy of me that makes you do it, because I am no longer a slave and you are? Are you doing this because you don't want anyone to be free unless you are free, too? Don't you see that you are not hurting just me, but all our people? For so long now, all of us have been looked down on as the lowest people on earth, fit only to work for other people. You know full well that up to now you can nowhere find black men respected by whites.

"But now we have a chance, Randy, to go to Africa and make our own nation of black men. We will show these white men that we can work as hard and be as clever as any of them. But it's people like you, full of envy and jealousy, pulling your brothers back, who may not let us do that. Are you not ashamed? Wouldn't you rather help your people? Don't you want to work towards making Africans respected so that one day no one will think of enslaving them?"

"I'm a slave," Randy replied bitterly, "and I'll always be a slave. What difference does it make to me if you and all the world are free? What have Africans ever done for me that I should care whether they are slaves or not? I wish my skin were white. I wish my eyes were blue and my hair straight and yellow. I wish I didn't have to be a slave, but that's the way I was born. That's the way you were born, too. You don't want to be a slave, but you are going to be. People like us are meant to be slaves. It's foolish to talk as if we weren't. You are a slave now just the same as I am and if you got out of the habit of knowing you were, you'd be better off shutting up your mouth and getting used to the idea. I'm not listening to you anymore."

When Hannibal looked through the latch-hole again, he saw that Randy had moved away from the door, since he could see the flames on the hearth again. His reaction was one he was later very ashamed of. He became a maddened creature with but a single thought, to attack Randy and kill him. He had heard of people "seeing red," and this is what happened to him. He kicked at the door without making a dent in it and then tried to get a grip on it to pull it from its hinges, but there was nothing to grasp hold of. He literally threw myself at it, but only bruised himself.

When he saw that nothing would succeed, he put his mouth to the edge of the door and shouted the foulest abuse he could call to mind. He was full of the rich juices of youth, after all, and let them recall to mind and voice the curses and oaths he had heard among the soldiers in the army and among the sailors aboard ship. There was a great and varied vocabulary of them, colourful, sulphurous and supremely insulting. Since arriving in Nova Scotia, he had never had any reason to want to use these words, and had lost sight of them in the dark recesses of his mind. Later he was ashamed to realize how easily he dragged them into the light and hurled them through the door with such facility. He later thought to himself that he may not have frightened Randy, but he certainly amazed and shocked himself.

Harsh words were no more successful than reasonable arguments or kicks and blows in getting the door, and he realized very quickly the futility of going on with his hysterical outburst. His anger ebbed and suddenly he felt cold and tired. He went back to his mattress, rolled himself up in his blankets, and thought hard.

chapter twelve
RESCUED

Hannibal calmed himself and thought about what was likely to happen to him. It seemed to him unlikely that he would be taken from the house in full daylight, and he wondered why they had not collected him before dawn. Perhaps that had been Randy's plan, and something had gone wrong. He did not think that even in Halifax a struggling man, even an African man, could be carried through the streets without it being noticed and the authorities making inquiries. In the darkness it would be another matter. For example, they might pass him off as a drunken sailor needing help from his mates to get back to his ship. If he was on the right track, and his kidnappers intention was for him to play the part of a drunken sailor, he probably had most of the day to wait for further developments.

However, he could not afford to relax and go to sleep again, if indeed he could have. He had to think of a way to escape by broad day-light. He looked around the room more carefully. It was as bare as he thought; however, the night before he had not noticed the window, and now it might be his only chance. He rolled out of his blankets again and went to study it. It was a small window, consisting of four small panes of glass held together with thick strands of lead. The glass was not of very good quality, but peering through the miniature whirlpools between himself and the outdoors he could make out a gloomy back alley.

The window could easily be broken, but it was certainly not a big enough opening for him to wriggle through. But since it seemed to offer his only possibility of changing his situation, he thought he had better break it out and see what followed. With the blanket over his hand, he punched at the centre where the two lines of lead made a cross. The blanket stifled the sound of the blow, the window fell outward, and there was only a faint tinkle as it met the hard ground. There was no sound of anyone coming to the door, so Hannibal was sure nobody in the house had heard anything.

He now had an opening to the outside world, and tried to put his face out for a good look. It was of no use. His ears caught painfully on the jagged edging of lead around the opening, and he had to be satisfied with the little he could see with his nose poked out.

As Hannibal adjusted to the outside light, he was suddenly riveted by shock. Not ten feet from him was a boy, a raggedy blond boy, who had been turning over trash in the hopes of finding something useful. He was thin, with a determined and serious face; Hannibal felt that he was a boy largely on his own, with an independent mind. If so, he would not run away when spoken to from a broken window, but would listen and consider where his own advantage lay. Hannibal didn't have to yell to attract his attention. It had already been caught by the tinkle of the window hitting the ground.

Now he was gazing silently at the window and seemed astonished but not alarmed when Hannibal's brown face appeared in the opening.

Hannibal backed away from the window and, taking one of the precious silver coins from his money belt, held it out the window and wiggled it to catch the light. The boy took this as intended and came closer to have a look. Holding it out where he could see it clearly, Hannibal said slowly and clearly, "This is for you if you will do as I ask. Run as fast as you can to Mr. John Clarkson at Mr. Hartshorne's chambers on Duke Street. Tell Mr. Clarkson or Mr. Hartshorne that Hannibal Hoops is locked in this house and cannot escape. Hurry. This is yours," and he dropped it into his hand, "and another like it when you bring help."

The boy's solemn face brightened somewhat and he nodded and stumbled away over the clutter almost obstructing the alley. Hannibal went back to bed, rolling himself up in the blankets again. He reckoned that nothing would happen against him in the next few hours, and before that he would—if all went well—be rescued by his friends. He couldn't think of anything else he could do to get out. Now he could only pray, for the rest depended on God.

After the passage of time, when he had prayed and then listened at the window opening several times over, his faith weakened and he began to imagine that things had gone wrong. He was sure it would take no more than fifteen minutes to get to Duke Street. Maybe the boy had been waylaid by friends or by his parents. Perhaps the thrill of a silver shilling in his hand put his task and the promise of another out of his mind. By Hannibal's reckoning, several hours had gone by, but perhaps it was no more than an hour. He couldn't tell.

At last to his great joy he heard sounds in the alley, and finally the burly form of Mr. Clarkson and the more slender one of Mr. Hartshorne appeared within his restricted range of vision. They were following the boy, and appeared to have other large men in tow.

Mr. Clarkson raised his eyebrows when he was face to face with Hannibal, through the window opening, as if to ask, "What kind of pickle have you got yourself in now?" Hannibal told him everything, keeping his voice low so as not to be heard in the other room. He looked very serious when he heard the full account, and as Hannibal learned later, such kidnappings into slavery were not unknown in England, even in London itself. Suspecting the worst, Clarkson had hired a couple of stout labourers to give him a hand. He also brought Mr. Hartshorne, who incidentally was a magistrate and brought all the power of the law with him.

Having heard Hannibal's tale, Mr. Clarkson stood back and looked up and down the building. He could see that the only opening in the wall facing him was the same small window they were talking through.

"What does the front of the building look like?" he asked, for the houses in this area were built against each other and their entrances fronted on another alley. Hannibal had to admit that he had not noticed anything distinctive.

"Randy called it the Bonny Brier Bush, but I didn't notice any sign; he gave a special knock at the door, though," and Hannibal put his hand out and gently tapped it on the wall until Mr. Clarkson caught on.

"Well, we'll find the Bonnie Brier Bush one way or another," he said, and led his party out of sight down the alley. Now the imprisoned youth felt a profound relief, knowing that rescue was only minutes away.

His complacency was short-lived, for as he stood by the window he felt a heavy hand on his shoulder and a gruff voice growled in his ear, "What are you up to, young varmint?" The next thing he knew was that the hand and its twin had pulled him violently back, twirled him around, and dashed him against the wall. His wind was partly knocked out and the blow to his head made him blink, but he was able to see that his attacker was a sailor of middle stature, about his own height, but extremely solid and broad. It seemed probable to Hannibal that he whetted his appetite and built up his muscles by knocking down less fortunate seamen.

"So! Busted the window, eh?" went on the big man, peering out. "Much good that'll do you! We'll take it out of your hide when we get you aboard ship. Wake up there, Randy!" he bellowed. "Randy! Get in here quick! Bring a piece of rope."

"Yessir, Captain. I'm a'coming."

"Now, young fella," he growled. "We'll see how much damage you can do with your hands tied. We're all going to take a little walk, since you want fresh air so much. We'll all walk along nicely as friends, and I'll have a knife ready to stick in your side if you so much as speak a word or make a move I don't like. Now where's Randy? C'mon, Randy, don't just stand there. I want you to tie his hands nicely behind his back."

Hannibal had his wind back now and, knowing that rescue was close at hand, was in no mood to submit easily. In any case, Randy's treachery still maddened him, and when the boy appeared he thought only of dealing him punishment.

"If you come near me, Randy, I'll knock your teeth out! In fact, I think I will anyway!" He leapt towards Randy with all his strength, but the captain, for all his weight, was fast and had him by the collar just as his fist was about to connect with Randy's head. The captain said not a word, but jerked Hannibal back and this time threw him against the wall with such force that he slid down it to the floor and lay there half-stunned. Before he could collect his wits, the two were on him, had rolled him over, twisted his arms behind his back, and tied them tightly with a coarse piece of rope.

"Now," said the captain to his slave boy, lifting Hannibal up as if he had been a piece of timber and putting him back on his feet, "just fetch that cloak from the other room and put it around his shoulders. It will cover his arms and no one will have the least idea of anything wrong. We had better go down to the ship as soon as George gets here; there's nothing to be gained by putting it off. That must be him knocking at the door now."

Away in the distance, the muffled sounds of a knock at the street door could be heard, the same signal that Hannibal had shown Mr. Clarkson at the window. Which man was it, John Clarkson or George? Hannibal prayed very hard.

The old woman was apparently not around and so Randy went out and down the corridor to remove the bar and open the door. Hannibal heard him do so and then cry out with fear and surprise.

"George?" cried the captain. "Is that you, George? What's the matter?"

He had no need to call further, for in a trice Mr. Clarkson and his rescue party were in the big room and looking around for Hannibal. Mr. Clarkson called his name.

"Here! Here!" the boy shouted before the captain knocked him down again. In an instant, Clarkson and his companions rushed in. With an oath, the captain sprang to meet them. He fought well, though the stout working men were both at him. Even Mr. Clarkson had to get involved before the villain was thrown to the floor, held down by force, and finally secured with stout ropes holding his arms to his sides. He was, of course, both surprised and furious.

"What does this mean?" he screamed. "By what right do you break in on an honest man and assault him in this way? I'll have you up before the magistrates tomorrow, as sure as my name's Tobias Smith. Curse ye, ye rotten swabs! Let me loose and get off my premises at once, ye idle lot of landlubbers!"

By this time, Mr. Hartshorne had put Hannibal on his feet and cut his wrists free. Despite the ringing in his ears and bruises on his body, he was beginning to feel more like himself. Randy, who had been knocked to the floor when the rescue party forced their way past him, and who had arrived in the room too late to help in the fray, looked to his captain for orders. "Cap'n Smith, sir," he panted, "should I run and get the constables?"

"Don't bother to look for constables," said Mr. Clarkson. "These men are my constables under my orders, and they have just secured a blaggardy villain who deserves to dangle from the yardarm." Then he spoke directly to the captain, who had been lifted to his feet to face him. "Captain Smith, if that is really your name, don't call me a landlubber. I have served my time in His Majesty's Navy and I suspect I know a great deal more of the Seven Seas than you ever will. And I wouldn't bother to send for a regular constable, if I were you. I have not brought one of those with me because I do not want to involve the law in this matter. I do not want any distraction from my mission at this time, nor any excuse that might be used to detain me in Halifax.

"But Mr. Hartshorne, my friend here, is one of the leading legal gentlemen of this town and if need be his testimony could have you put behind bars for a long, long time. We came, Captain, to rescue from your criminal clutches our young friend here, this young member of the long-suffering African race, whom I see you have assaulted as well as confined unlawfully. He appears to be merely shaken up, but if he has been seriously injured, Captain, I will have no mercy on you but invoke the full power of the law against you."

The captain spat out a few blood-curdling expletives that showed the complete foulness of his mind. A few of them were insulting references to Clarkson's interest in Negroes, too vile to be repeated.

Mr. Clarkson, being the naval officer and gentleman that he was, remained calm and unmoved. "Go ahead and call me a friend to the black man," he said, "for in fact that is what you are doing, however foully expressed. These names you call me honour me. I am proud to be on God's side in this business. If men like you hate and despise me, the more certain I am that I am doing what is right. Why do you and others of your kind hate these fellow creatures so? I wonder if you have a dog that you regard with as little esteem as you do your young servant there." He pointed at Randy, who sat sadly in the corner.

"Randy's a good lad. He knows his place and does what he's told, and I don't know what you're kicking up such a fuss about this young sprat for. If I'd knowed he'd cause so much trouble for me, I wouldn't have got interested in him at all. Randy must have lied to me for once. He said this lad didn't have any friends or masters here, so who are you? Are you wanting him for yourself? Why? What's so special about him? I could buy you twenty boys in the market in Savannah that would be more use than this'n."

Clarkson replied that he did not own any slaves and would never want to own any.

"Then what do you want to interfere in my affairs for?"

Then Mr. Clarkson tried to explain that he was taking some of the free African people of Nova Scotia back to make their own settlement in Africa. It made no more impression on the captain than Hannibal's own account had made on Randy. Captain Tobias Smith had never heard about the founding of the Sierra Leone Colony, though he knew that slave ships came from the Sierra Leone River. He could not grasp the utility or purpose in carrying African men the other way. "It don't make no sense to take them from this side back to that one," he said. "It just don't make sense."

"Captain Smith," said Clarkson, "I could bring serious charges against you, as you know. However, as I said, I have my own reasons for being prepared to ignore this matter. I will not inform the authorities of this attempt of yours to kidnap this young man and sell him as a slave down the coast, provided you get out of this town at once—tonight. If I find you still here tomorrow, I shall take all necessary steps to have you arrested and a case brought against you, not only to punish you, but as a warning to all vampires who prey on the weak and vulnerable.

"I know that a detestable traffic goes on here all the time, that slaves are constantly purchased here and taken South. I know that even free men, like Hannibal here, are carried into captivity by wretches of your ilk. I make one condition about letting you go: this boy you have, this Randy, shall—if he wishes—be allowed to come with our expedition to Africa. I presume he really is your property. I demand that you release him and give him the chance of a free life in Sierra Leone."

What Captain Smith would have replied to this demand was uncertain, for Randy uttered a heartrending cry and settled the matter by running to his master. Sinking to his knees and grasping his master around his legs, Randy burst out: "Don't want to go to Africa! Don't want to leave the Captain! Don't let them take me, Captain! I belong to you."

Hannibal was puzzled by this behaviour, because he had thought Randy's whole treacherous act towards him was prompted by envy of the fact that he was a free person, but apparently it was not as simple as that. Apparently Captain Smith was the nearest thing Randy had to a father; he was used to his rough ways and rough tongue to the extent that he could imagine no other kind of existence. He had no conception of being his own master and was a willing partner with the captain in enslaving other people as a way of pleasing the older man and perhaps earning his affection.

Perhaps the captain did value Randy, as much, at least, as if he had been a faithful hound. His face worked with emotion as he looked down at the boy embracing his legs.

"Eh, Randy," he said, "what's this? I thought you'd jump at the chance to leave me. D'ye really want to stay?"

"I don't want any other master. Only you, Captain."

Mr. Clarkson, amazed, interrupted. "But I'm offering you a chance for a new life, boy, a new life as a free man in a free country!"

"Freedom!" said the boy bitterly. "It's just a word to me! What can it mean to how I live and what I do? I don't want your freedom. I don't even believe in it. I want to stick with my master and go on the same way as I've been doing."

Mr. Clarkson was baffled, but simply said, "Very well. Captain Smith, you may keep the boy and I hope you will value his loyalty as it deserves. But I advise you to keep to honest trade and not attempt any more kidnapping. Whenever you return to this port, eyes will be on you, is that not so, Mr. Hartshorne?"

"That is so. I will notify the customs officers and constables to keep a close watch on the actions of Captain Smith and his crewmen whenever they are in this port."

Thereupon, Mr. Clarkson led his party out of the Bonny Brier Bush, leaving Randy to untie his master. Clarkson paid off the men who had been so helpful. To the boy who had carried Hannibal's message to him, who they found hanging about at the door, he gave two silver shillings, twice what had been promised. Then he and Hannibal made their way to Mr. Hartshorne's chambers, whither that gentleman had already preceded them.

As they walked, Hannibal tried to find the words to thank his rescuer for his prompt and effective response to his cry for help, especially as he felt he had been responsible for getting himself trapped.

Mr. Clarkson understood his feelings and assured him that he was not annoyed. He felt he should have realized that such traps existed and should have warned about taking precautions. As it was, he said that Hannibal had given him the chance to make an impression on an enemy he could actually see. "That kind are not the most dangerous, I've discovered," he explained. "There exists a whole legion of enemies, hidden and secret, who are trying to frustrate my mission here. In the larger world, they are keeping the slave trade respectable and legal. They refuse to recognize its inhumanity and injustice. They will be much harder to vanquish than Captain Smith and his kind."

chapter thirteen

WHY THE SIERRA LEONE COMPANY?

Well, Hannibal Hoops," said Mr. Clarkson, back in Mr. Harts-horne's chambers on Duke Street, "this has certainly been a morning of surprises and excitement. We had better get you off home before somebody else tries to kidnap you. I have looked through the list of names you brought and on the basis of the account the rector has given of each one, I have marked the ones I think would make good settlers and whom I am ready to take. I need hardly say that you are among them. I am enclosing with the list a letter for Mr. Twining, in which I am asking him to issue each of these prospective settlers with a certificate to that effect. It should be clear to him, but it is as well for you to know, too, in case some of the applicants do not understand, especially those whom I have to refuse to take.

"Now before you depart on your way, is there anything more you wish to hear from me?"

"Sir," the youth said respectfully, "you have been very good to me and I can see clearly that you are a sincere friend to my people. But there are some in Horton who will be shy about trusting you; they will say that you are a rich man and an officer, and that you have no reason to befriend poor black folk. I want to know what I can tell them to change their minds. As well, some of them think the Sierra Leone Company is set up to trick us back into slavery. I would like to be able to tell them the truth about that."

"I'll be glad to tell you everything you want to know. At least, I will if I know the answers," he said. "I have not belonged to the Company very long. In fact it is really a new organization. Before I begin to talk, let me be clear about something. I think you told me yesterday that you had been saved and baptized some years ago. Is that correct?"

"Indeed, sir. I was converted seven years ago in Birchtown and baptized there. I have tried to live a Christian life ever since."

"Then you will understand when I tell you that I too love the Lord and try to do what is right. It was not always so. I was only a young boy when I became a midshipman in the Royal Navy. I grew up as an officer on ships of war and took part in sea battles and blockades. I think I was a good officer. I loved my life at sea and I loved the fighting, too. I was proud to serve my king and ready to give up my life in his service, but then one day when I was reading my Bible I saw more clearly what the King of Kings demanded of me.

"As I thought about it, I came to realize that the fighting and killing of my fellow men was finished for me. God hates and abhors war, Hannibal, and though priests and prelates bless us and send us off to battle, we are still committing sin when we engage in it. When I studied my Bible seriously enough, I knew what I had to do. I sent in my resignation to the Admiralty and I left the Navy. I have never regretted it, though there are lots of men who scoff and jeer at me for my 'principles.' And now, since I have the time to do God's work wherever I see it, I volunteered to help the new Sierra Leone Company. You see, my brother, Thomas Clarkson is one of the chief men in the Company. He felt that I was well-equipped to arrange this affair in Nova Scotia, and though now I begin to have doubts, at the time I was happy to take up the task of gathering your people together and taking you to Africa. It is the least I could do in personal restitution for the crime committed against Africans this past century or more.

"I think that is enough about me and how I come to be here. Now to explain about the Company, I must first talk about the slave trade in general. But perhaps you know all about the slave trade?"

"No, sir," Hannibal admitted. "I'm very ignorant about the trade. I know a little from my mother and other people who were brought from Africa, but it was so horrible they did not want to say much about it. In any case, they only knew what they saw and heard themselves. Of course, I have seen the slave market in Charles Town, where slaves fresh from Africa would be sold."

"Well, at least you have an insight into some of the unpleasant aspects of the trade from one point of view. By the way, Hannibal, before I go on talking, I have another question for you. Have you eaten today? I don't believe you have."

Hannibal agreed that indeed he had not eaten since the previous evening.

"By Jove, think of that! You must be starving!" Turning towards the door, he called out, "Mr. Sparrow! Mr. Sparrow!"

"Yes, sir," and the trim dark-clothed figure of the chief clerk appeared in the doorway.

"Send out for some food for this young man—bread, cheese, ale, whatever you can get at this time of day. Bring it in straightaway when it comes."

"Yes, Mr. Clarkson. I'll attend to it."

Then Mr. Clarkson resumed his account, and continued while the food arrived and Hannibal sat gratefully eating every crumb of it.

"Slavery, you know, is as old as mankind itself," Clarkson began. "Do we not read in Holy Scripture that there were slaves amongst the earliest people, as well as amongst the Hebrews and Egyptians? The earliest records of the Greeks and Romans show that among them slaves were held as necessities, for all that their orators prated a great deal about liberty—for themselves. In Asia, the situation was even worse, with the great majority of people being as slaves to their rulers.

"These slaves, of course, were not usually Ethiopians or Africans; that must have come later when the Arabs began that trade in the parts of Africa near them. So far as Europe is concerned, the trade in Negroes began when the Portuguese explored the western coast of Africa beginning about three hundred years ago. They bought slaves in Guinea and brought them back to Portugal, from where they were carried to other countries. But really, Europe had a large labouring population and did not want the labour of slaves. They kept them more as curiosities than anything else.

"Then the Spanish settlers in the West Indies found out that the Africans served much better as labourers than the native Indians, who were weaklings and died too fast. The Portuguese began to send shiploads over. I am ashamed to say that Englishmen engaged in this disgusting traffic, and that some African rulers have not proven themselves honourable in the face of the temptation of guns and whisky. If all the rulers on the African coast would themselves refuse to sell their subjects or to allow slave dealers to pass through their territories, I believe the trade would stop tomorrow.

"It is only within the last few years that some people in England have realized how disgraceful this inhuman traffic is in this day and age. Many think it is permissible because the Bible speaks of it and because it has lasted so long, but of course in England we don't see the kind of slavery you knew in South Carolina. Lots of rich people in England have owned one or two African slaves, but usually as exotic ornaments, like the little page boys dressed in silks and satins who are kept close by lovely ladies to set off their own beauty. And of course gentlemen from the colonies have often brought their personal servants with them when they visited England."

At this point, Clarkson's account became more personal.

"It was on a day shortly after the end of the Great War against the French, the Seven Years War as we call it now, nearly thirty years ago, that my friend Mr. Granville Sharpe met a man who changed his life. The man he met was a slave, and his name was Jonathan Strong. I think I've heard Sharpe tell the story a hundred times—it will be in the history books one day I believe. What he saw in Jonathan Strong's case was the evil men do to other men, and he has been fighting that evil ever since.

"Jonathan Strong had been savagely beaten by his master, so badly that it seemed he would die. So of course, that brute of a master did not want the trouble of a dead man on his hands, so he turned him out of doors, to die like a dog in the streets! Sharpe came across him in the way, took pity on the poor fellow, and carried him to a surgeon—to his brother, William Sharpe, as a matter of fact—and the two of them nursed Strong back to health and then found him a job. That seemed like the happy end of his story, but there was more to come. A few years later, his master saw him restored to life and actively working, and without saying a word to him sold him to a planter going to Jamaica. Thirty pounds was the amount paid by the planter—thirty pieces of silver! It was easy money in the pocket of the old master, for the new one had to secure his new property himself. He had Strong kidnapped, and to hold him safe bribed a jailor to lock him up in prison until his vessel was ready to sail.

"Like you, Strong was able to get word to his friend. Mr. Sharpe got in touch with the authorities and they ordered the jailor to free him. Still it wasn't over. The captain of the ship tried to seize Jonathan Strong and carry him to the ship by force. He didn't desist until he was warned that he would be charged with assault. Then the man who had sold Strong, and the man who had bought him, brought a suit against Granville Sharpe. But he was ready for them and they soon saw it was not worth pursuing the case. The publicity was becoming highly damaging to them. So they more or less gave up and Jonathan Strong continued to live and work unmolested.

"However, the principle was not clear. The law still considered a slave to be an item of property, not a person with rights. Other cases came before the courts, and finally, in 1772, Lord Chief Justice Mansfield ruled that slavery was an institution so odious that unless a positive law establishing it were enacted, it could not be said to exist in England at all. In short, men and women may be brought to England as slaves, but once they set foot on the soil there they are slaves no more. The whole weight of the law stands to prevent them from becoming slaves again. You may easily imagine that there were a large number of Africans in England who claimed that freedom!

"My brother, Thomas Clarkson, who vowed to fight for the abolition of slavery and the slave trade while he was still a student at college, was one of those who befriended these poor strangers and tried to look after them. Perhaps you have heard the name of Mr. William Wilberforce? He is a Member of Parliament and is leading the fight for the end of this criminal traffic. I expect him to be successful soon, because Mr. Pitt is his friend, and William Pitt is the real ruler of England just now."

The names were not unfamiliar to Hannibal, who said, "I think, sir, that Mr. Twining mentioned those names when he talked to us at our meeting."

"Very likely, because Mr. Wilberforce and other gentlemen have set up the society called the Sierra Leone Company. It has been organized specifically to help settle former slaves and other homeless Africans in England back in their original homeland. Somehow the existence of your people in Nova Scotia was forgotten until Sergeant Thomas Peters from Digby came over to London and made us aware of it.

"It was then decided to include you Nova Scotians among the possible settlers. The British government is giving the money and every other assistance to us, and, as I may have said yesterday, there is no end in sight to our ambitions for Sierra Leone and for Africa. You and your friends may be assured that whatever you find on the Guinea Coast, England will be watching over you and guarding you. I hope that many of you will decide to come with us."

As Hannibal had now finished his bread and cheese, and had learned all that he needed to pass on to his friends in Horton, he was ready to start on his return journey.

Mr. Clarkson was surprised that he would think of setting out so close to the end of the day.

"Where will you spend the night? Surely it would be better to start early tomorrow morning."

"No, it is better to go now," the youth said. "I will get out of the town and a few hours' walk around Bedford Basin will bring me to a good inn. They'll look after me all right there, and certainly they won't sell me to any slave dealers." He packed Mr. Clarkson's letters in his coat and as naturally as breathing he shook hands with his new friend.

"God bless you," Clarkson said. "I shall look forward to hearing from you and your people by December. Then we must bring everybody together here in Halifax and, if possible, get away before the onset of winter."

chapter fourteen
BLIZZARD

Hannibal felt a sense of relief as he prepared to leave Halifax with its contrasting groups of good and evil men, and to set out for Horton where people were individuals, where if some were not as good as they thought they were, the evildoers were not very evil, either. He walked at a good pace along the same streets he had explored the day before, crossing the Grand Parade at St. Paul's Church where the wind blew unimpeded. Thence he walked past the market and around the lower slopes on the north side of Citadel Hill, crowned with its ramparts of wood and stone. Once past that, he was walking into the open country of the common lands where the townsfolk had their gardens. The gardens, in many cases, were brown with the decayed remains of plants and weeds, but a few were raw with exposed earth where some energetic men had dug over the ground before the winter had really set in.

Thinking serious thoughts inspired by the events of the past twenty-four hours, Hannibal stepped along the road, which soon led off the peninsula and into a wilderness of rocks and stunted trees he had barely noticed when riding through it in the cart. He seemed to be the sole traveller on the badly rutted highway as it followed the contours of Bedford Basin, where the waves sparkled in the waning sunlight. He paced on, despite some soreness from his bruises, during the greater part of the rest of the day, stopping occasionally for a short rest and to eat from his pack.

At last as the ice-clear dusk thickened, he saw the friendly shape of the rambling roadhouse where he had stayed two nights before. He entered the public room and was glad to see there not only the ruddy-cheeked proprietor and his comfortable wife, but also the farmer who had so kindly given him a lift in his wagon. They all greeted him warmly and the farmer told him that although his cart was loaded with winter stores for himself and friends in Newport, he could still find room for a passenger. Hannibal was glad to accept his offer; he thought that perhaps he could have made better time on his own feet, but it would certainly be less tiring to ride. Moreover, he preferred company when travelling through the dense forest ahead, even if the company was rather silent.

They started off very early the next morning, while it was still dark. The landlord was still sleeping, but his lady was up early to give the travellers a good breakfast of oatmeal porridge, bread, cheese, and ale, and to present her bill. Eventually, as they laboured along the road, the darkness gave way to the dim dawn. Then a wan sun finally came up behind and they saw their shadows cast weakly before them. Looking around to the east, Hannibal saw that though it glowed fiery-red, like an ember;

there was no strength in the sun, and he was able to look at it quite steadily without strain. As it rose higher in the sky, it began to fade, and then simply disappeared. Clearly there was solid cloud above, and their occasional glances up as the morning passed showed the travellers a sky sinking towards them with the weight it carried.

The air was very still, and the heavy cart moved slowly. The squeal of the axles, the squeaking of the harness, and the assortment of sounds the wooden boxes and barrels made as they incessantly rubbed against one another provided all the sound.

Finally, the taciturn farmer broke his silence. "There's a lot of snow in those clouds," he said. "It is bound to catch us somewhere on this road. Gee-up!" he called to the horses. But the beasts were doing all they could to pull the load as it was. Even a touch of the whip had little effect as the vehicle slowly gained the high ground that ran like a backbone along the middle regions of Nova Scotia. Hannibal could not but take notice of the universal greyness that pervaded the scene. Sitting beside a man who would not talk, and having nothing else to do, he took note of the unusual drabness of the atmosphere. It stayed in his mind long after he had left Nova Scotia as yet another typical picture of his winters spent there. He seemed to be moving through a world with light and colour all washed out. Everything was grey: grey horses, grey driver, silent grey landscape. The trees, half dead in the swampy soil, looked as though flat and pasted on a wall; there were no shadows to give them form and depth.

Hannibal smelled the odour of winter in the still grey air. This greyness so struck him that he took off his glove and looked at the back of his own hand to see if he also was becoming grey. It was its normal rich brown colour, but he had a sudden fear that the cold would turn it grey, too, and he pushed the glove back on. In later years, living amongst the bright colours and warmth of the African world, this scene came back to him as a picture of what he had escaped when he left Nova Scotia. It would seem that Nature was determined that he should have an experience that day and the next that would make a lasting impression on him.

The snow began falling at around noon, very softly and sparingly at first. For a time, the sun was visible again, its white disc as pale as the full moon at dawn, The first tentative flakes of snow, crisp and dainty, appeared to be falling directly from it. Then Hannibal noticed that the nature of the snow changed. It became puffy, and fell on his nose like clumped white cotton. The sun absolutely disappeared and the sky was blotted out completely. The snow clung to the animals, to the clothing, to everything. Then a rising wind blew it off again and sent the blobs of white whirling along the grey road, like the white cotton of the Balm of Gilead trees that stood along the roads of Horton.

Soon, however, the snowflakes whirled no more but clumped together to form a smooth carpet across the road. The horses stepped silently along on it, and the wheels ran as smoothly as on air. The jingle of the harness and the scraping of the axles sounded more distinct, yet more tuneful, in the tunnel of silence created by the snow. It was a kind of music with all the unnecessary noise absorbed by the snow falling all around. Hannibal began to realize that this was an experience he would, in future, never have again once he arrived in a southern land where snow never fell and the peculiar silence of its fall was never heard.

By mid-afternoon, the animals had performed a good day's work, and the travellers appeared to be getting close to the crest of Ardoise Hill, after which the road would be easier. However, the horses were now moving at a snail's pace, virtually swimming in the heavy snow. Their hooves were caked and heavy with the stuff, which clung in masses to their feet and impeded every step they took. The cartwheels were turning with difficulty and the snow was so deep that frequently the axles were brushing it aside.

"This is going to keep up for a while yet, and probably get worse," announced the farmer finally. Obviously he had been hoping for a brief sample of winter weather, not the full-blown storm this was shaping up to be. "I'm not going to try to go further today. This is probably as good a place to camp as any in the next mile or two. We can spend the night here anyway; the storm cannot last longer than that. Ah, here's an opening in the trees. Lets find shelter."

He took for granted that Hannibal was in agreement, and he was. It would have been foolish to try to walk to the nearest house, which was probably miles away. Although he had never camped in the woods in winter, he knew that lots of people, especially hunters, did. It was unusual, but not impossible. Once off the road, they found themselves sheltered by some thick spruce trees. The air was calm, and the snow not so deep as in the open. Nonetheless, stray gusts blew flakes into their faces and through gaps in the branches.

"It's going to blow up rough, I'm afeared," the farmer said, as if thinking aloud. "A blizzard is in the offing, or I'm no judge of weather. Come on, boy. We've got some work to do before dusk." He took his axe, and they had a look around amongst the thickly growing spruces, firs, and other evergreens. They spied a young pine standing straighter than its fellows and together they fashioned a shelter, thatched with spruce and fir branches, around it. Some boxes from the cart were brought in and stowed.

At first the roof was not tight, because snow was filtering through the fat green needles of the evergreen boughs, but all the time some of them were being caught, and bit by bit delicate bridges of snow were built from needle to needle and from twig to twig and the gaps were closed in. The snow, continuing to fall, made a solid covering. Hannibal swept up the snow on the ground as well as he could with a thick branch of evergreen and pushed it to the edge. He spread two heaps of thick fir branches to make mattresses, remembering times in the war when his bed had been made like that.

The cart was put close to another good sized tree, and the animals unhitched and tethered in a sheltered spot close by, with their own warm blankets thrown over them and feed put in front of their noses. Their master was obviously fond of them, and spent half an hour putting up a windbreak for them, while Hannibal was gathering together dead trees and other dry material to make a fire.

The darkness had come by then, and the wind had risen with great force. It was well that they were in the heart of a group of thick evergreens, for when Hannibal went outside the thicket in his search, he realized that the snowfall had become a blizzard of fierce winds. After nearly getting lost a few feet from the shelter of the trees, he retreated to safety among them and stayed there. He lighted a small fire just outside the entrance of the lodge, and his travelling companion, satisfied at last with the situation of his animals, came inside and from his boxes produced blankets, food, and a kettle. Hannibal took the kettle out and filled it with clean snow and slung it over the fire. As the snow melted, he added more fresh clean white crystals to it until at last there was enough water for a good pot of tea. Soon it was boiling. The farmer produced a tin of well-filled tea caddy and in a few minutes they each held a mug of the scalding and invigorating brew in one hand, and washed down a meal of hard-tack and slices of a large homemade sausage in the other.

Hannibal still had no idea of his companion's name, and in fact never did. He called the older man "Sir" and he called Hannibal "boy." They ate in silence, and though the man passed occasional remarks, he did not seem to expect any reply. He seemed to be a silent brooding type of man by nature, so the youth kept his mouth shut for the most part. Still, when two people were alone together for a prolonged period, sharing primitive conditions and dependent on each other, they were bound to relax their guard and communicate more than they intended to. The farmer and the youth were trapped for two whole days by that blizzard.

The farmer puffed on his pipe, and Hannibal dreamed his dreams. Each time they left the shelter of the woods and felt the full fury of wind and snow, they knew they had to stay put. The wind blew from the northeast and roared continuously in the trees. Fortunately the farmer had bought a batch of heavy woollen blankets in Halifax. Well wrapped in them, with a thick cushion of fir boughs between their bodies and the ground, they were warm and reasonably comfortable. However, even with the dreams in his head about Evalina and their future happiness, time passed slowly for Hannibal. At intervals, one or the other of the two went out with the axe and found more fuel to keep the fire going, or they went out together and tended to the horses; at other times, they lay silently in a doze, or, if awake, looked up and found patterns in the branches and snow of their ceiling.

Finally the farmer began to thaw out, in a manner of speaking, and really began to ask about Hannibal's experiences in the war, and to tell about his own. He already knew about Hannibal's adventures from hearing his story at the roadhouse, but asked the occasional question while describing his own history, which followed a common enough pattern. He stated that he was well aware of what it felt to be a slave, for he had been an orphan boy in Scotland and had been sent out to America with other boys as indentured labour. Their passage across the Atlantic, he felt, was in many particulars as bad as or even worse than what African slaves had endured on the infamous Middle Passage. He knew too, as Hannibal never did, what it was to be inspected and handled, and then auctioned off to the highest bidder. But he admitted that he had had one consolation: hope of a better future, for his slavery was for only seven years, by law.

So he worked hard for seven years for an honest farmer, and then he was a free man. He was able to get a grant of land and make a farm for himself in the backcountry of South Carolina, and he had been doing well until the Revolution came. Then he discovered, as things moved along, that he was more a Loyalist than otherwise, and he found himself at odds with his neighbours. Finally, he joined the 84th Regiment, the Royal Highland Emigrants, when it was formed, and fought through the war. He was especially loyal to his commander, Lord Rawdon, who had been a hero in so many battles. Hannibal of course remembered Lord Rawdon and easily recollected him galloping recklessly everywhere on his horse. At the close of the war, the commander of the 84th, Colonel Small, had got a grant for his men near Windsor, and they named it for Lord Rawdon, while another grant next to it was called Douglas.

The farmer took up a grant in Kennetcook, but then, like many others, had grown dissatisfied with the poor soil and managed to buy an abandoned farm in a more fertile area, near Newport Corner. So many of the single men had left their grants and gone away that the townships were underpopulated, and without neighbours to give a hand, life was harder than it should have been. He was happy to be in Newport where the farms were occupied and the people, even if they were Bluenoses— by which he meant old settlers—were friendly and helpful.

"Many of the men who were with me through the war have gone somewhere else," he said, "and I wish they hadn't. But as for me, I am staying where I am. I won't let anyone ever say that Nova Scotia got the better of me."

On the morning of the third day, Hannibal awoke from a dream of the old days in Carolina. In the dream, it was a warm summer's day and he was taking a nap against a great tree trunk when his playmate, Adolphus Courtney, came up and splashed water on his face to wake him. Then he really woke up and was several minutes understanding where he was; Adolphus had seemed so real that he felt he had gone back many years to the time when the little master was his constant companion. Then he felt another splash, a real one, and opening his eyes properly, found himself in the makeshift shelter with cold water dripping down from the branches and along his cheek and under his collar.

Gone in a flash were the verdant sun-filled Carolina scenes and he lay on prickly evergreen branches in the cold snow-filtered light of a winter morning, bathed by trickles of water running down the branches where the roof of snow was fast melting. In the early hours of the morning, the weather had changed, the air had warmed up, the falling snow had turned into light rain, and the snow was melting rapidly. As he struggled to his feet, Hannibal heard dull thuds where heavy chunks of snow were falling from the pine trees and crashing to the ground. His friend the farmer was just waking up, too, and they speedily packed up their boxes and put everything back on the cart.

The deep snow on the ground was already getting sodden and heavy and their feet and legs were soon soaked as they thrust their way through it. It was heavy work harnessing the horses, and just as heavy work pulling the cart back onto the road. They did it, though, and were making some progress along it when the drizzle ceased, the sun came out, and theirs spirits rose.

"At least now we can see where we are going," said the farmer. "I only hope we don't get a freeze up again until all this stuff melts off." In fact, the blizzard had been rather local in its intensity, and as they descended to a lower altitude, they could see that ahead, down the slope, the road was open and bare.

Within a couple of hours, they came to the Newport Road, and there the farmer had to go off to the north, so the two travellers said their brief goodbyes. Getting down from the cart, Hannibal thanked the farmer for all his kindness; he in turn said, "God Bless… and good luck." Then he drove on towards Newport Township and Hannibal struck out west along the main road.

He was determined to be at Five Mile Plains before dark. He did it easily. The snow had receded to such a shallow depth that it was no impediment and he struck out at a lively pace through barely an inch of the soggy stuff. His cold wet feet were an annoyance, but their condition had to be borne, and he hardly noticed their complaints because his heart was so warm with the pleasure of anticipation. The image of Evalina went before him, hastening his step. He was bursting to tell her of all that had happened to him, thinking what he would say first and how he would phrase the more exciting bits, building up her fears for him and then suddenly putting it all right with the happy conclusions to the episodes of peril and discomfort. The story of the kidnapping would certainly excite all her concern for him.

The two days pent up in the snow had given him many hours to think about her and he wondered whether she had been thinking of him, perhaps even fearing he had been lost in the storm and wondering if she would ever see him again. In fact, Hannibal cruelly hoped she had been worrying, and that she was hoping they would meet again soon as much as he was.

The hours passed quickly, and near dusk Hannibal arrived at the Bates' door. He was soon sitting close to the kitchen hearth where a good fire was blazing. Evalina did not make him wait for her father to arrive; when she realized that he had been camping in the woods, she was quick to heap him up a plate of hot food. He was glad that they had the house to themselves, for he wanted to tell his story only to her. He would have had to tell the tale of Halifax and his dangers there differently if her menfolk had been in the room. As it was, he was able to tell her fully of his terror when he discovered he was a prisoner and realized that he might end up as a slave sold down south. She not only sympathized with him, but became very upset, as though she had been in danger herself. He had to put his plate down and go to her and put his arms around her to assure her that he was safe and sound. Her agitation was such that he took measures in soothing her that he would have otherwise been too shy to offer. She did not resent his efforts, but was soothed, and was finally able to smile at him. Hannibal went back to supper and turned his tale to the happier subject of Mr. Clarkson and his plans, and she became interested and even excited about the expedition to Sierra Leone.

"Oh, Hannibal!" she said. "What a wonderful man he must be! And how brave you are to have gone through so much danger to be part of this expedition! You must be very anxious to go to Africa."

"Evalina," he replied in deadly seriousness, "I believe we will never be equal citizens here in Nova Scotia, never, never, never! Even those of us who are free men are thought of as slaves, and that is the case everywhere in North, South, and Central America. And in the right circumstances, if we stray from where we are known, we can be kidnapped, and without any proof that we are not slaves we will be assumed to be slaves and we will be made to be slaves. The burden of proof will always be on us here to show that we are not some white man's property. Maybe in two hundred years' time, after a hard struggle by black people which will change the hearts of white people, black and white may live together as brothers; though I doubt it will ever happen.

"But even if it does, it will be of no use to you or me. That is why I cannot stay here. Not when I can go to Africa now and be as good as or better than any wandering white man who ends up there. We will be in our own country then, and they will be the outsiders and strangers."

Hannibal went over all the reasons for going to Sierra Leone, but more intensely than he had in arguing with Gus. He didn't mind that Gus refused to be won over, but he felt he had to win over this lovely young woman. He felt that she had to be on the vessel carrying him away, or his happiness at being on his journey at last would be more like grief.

Evalina did not fight against his arguments; she was excited by what he said and seemed to approve his plans. With a flushed face and trembling voice she said, "You are right, Hannibal; I quite agree with everything you say. Oh that I were a man! Then I would go to Sierra Leone, too."

He immediately felt that she was bringing matters between them to a head and it was important that he find the right things to say, and quickly.

"Evalina," Hannibal said, "the colony is not just for men. There will be plenty of women and girls going with us."

"Ah, but Hannibal," she said, "they will no doubt go with their fathers and brothers, and I know that my father and brother are not going to stir from here to wander any further. Do you think any women are going alone?"

"No, I don't suppose they are," he said. "They will be with fathers, or brothers, or husbands."

"Well, then I cannot go. I haven't got a husband, so there is no way for me to go. I had better not think of living anywhere else. I'll live out my days here in Five Mile Plains."

There was a pause in the conversation, and he struggled to find the right words to break the silence. She was not looking at him, but out the tiny window, perhaps avoiding his eyes.

Very softly, he said, "There is a way for you to go to Africa, even if your father and brother stay here. Will you come to Africa with me, Evalina, as my wife, and share my dream?"

She turned her face and looked into his eyes. He was standing now, and holding out his arms towards her. She came to him at once and embraced him and held her cheek against his.

"Yes, Hannibal. I do want to share your dream and Mr. Clarkson's dream. Your vision of the future is a true vision, and I want to be a part of it. But most of all, Hannibal, I want to be with you. You have won my heart. It seems so strange; this is only the second time we have been together, but I know it is right!"

At this point, they heard sounds outside, indicating that her father and brother were home. He quickly said, "We will not tell your father about it tonight. I will have to leave early tomorrow, but I will come back soon and ask him for your hand."

He had only time to press that kind hand before her kinsmen entered with expressions of surprise and pleasure when they saw their visitor. The evening passed very pleasantly, though the young couple kept their secret. If the others had been suspicious of an understanding between them, they could have confirmed it by noticing how often and how long they looked into each other's eyes.

Hannibal told his story again, somewhat re-edited, which led to a general discussion of the slave trade and its cruelties. They concluded that they were fortunate that none of them knew about it from personal experience. Although Solomon and David Bates wished Hannibal well, it was clear that they thought he would be running into danger, even the possibility of being enslaved again, in a land where might made right. He wondered how they would respond when he asked to take Evalina with him, and he hoped that she might make them see it in a better light before he came to ask for her.

Early the next morning, he was on the road again. He had not even had a chance to speak to his love alone, to tell her in words what was in his heart. All he could do was wink expressively at her when her menfolk were not looking.

chapter fifteen

OFF AGAIN

Hannibal had no way of letting Gus know where he was, so he travelled by the long road from Windsor, coming across the Horton Mountains, and, from the high ground, seeing again the most beautiful district in Nova Scotia. It was another long day and he was ready for a good rest when he got home.

Within two days, the rector had sent out the word and the African people of Horton and Cornwallis gathered to hear Hannibal's report. Again the rector presided and was very firm in keeping the meeting in order; that was not an easy task, because a lot of those who turned up, especially the younger men, were in a mood to ridicule the endeavour. They were out for a good time rather than to have a serious discussion. It seemed likely that some drinking had taken place before the meeting began, and high spirits were a result.

After a few opening remarks, the rector turned the floor over to Hannibal, who told them that he had met John Clarkson and talked to him and that he trusted him to be as sincere a friend to the African people as there ever was. With a straight man like him, he said, there was no need to fear double-dealing. "He is a sincere Christian gentleman, an honourable man, and a virtuous one.

"But," he thought it wise to add," he is not a fool and he is not soft. He has been a naval officer since he was a boy, and he knows what it is to give orders and have them carried out. He does not want men for this voyage who are lazy or dishonest. All the settlers will have to be honest, trustworthy, and hardworking."

Some jeers broke out in the room and one voice in the crowd called out amidst laughter, "No one around here can make me work harder than I want to work and I'm doing all right. Once I get to Africa, I'll be able to pick bananas and oranges off the trees and not work at all, not till I'm good and ready anyway. I don't take orders from any man here and I won't do it there."

He made Hannibal so angry that he lost his temper. He clenched his fists and shouted, "You'll do as Mr. Clarkson tells you, or I'll know the reason why!"

Fortunately, perhaps, several big fellows thought that was funny and began to laugh. The laughter spread and the noise ceased, and the rector got control of the meeting again. He spoke a few words of warning to the unruly ones, then invited Hannibal to explain what he had learned about the Sierra Leone Company. So he told them how a flourishing colony could be planted on the coast of Africa if they were prepared to work hard there. Once again, some men were not in favour of taking part in the venture, for various reasons, but especially because they did not trust the intentions of white men far away in England. That country, after all, was the home of the slavetraders and their ships. Some even said they doubted that Clarkson was the honest and good man Hannibal made him out to be.

"Let me tell you the story of what happened to me in Halifax," he told them. "Then maybe you'll understand why I respect and trust Mr. Clarkson."

The room was quiet at last as he told about meeting Randy and how treacherously he had behaved. The rough men facing Hannibal seemed to be feeling what he had felt when he found the door locked and the window useless for making his escape. They got excited when he told them what he had done to get word to Clarkson, and joyous when he described the tussle between Clarkson's men and Captain Smith. The benches were rocking as they swayed in unison. "Hallelujah," shouted Tom the Blacksmith, and they began clapping hands softly. The meeting was turning into a thanksgiving service. Tom began to sing lines of praise to God for saving their young friend in the valley of the shadow of death and led the meeting in a rousing chorus in between each couple of them. "Hannibal Hoops, Hannibal Hoops, we thank you God for Hannibal Hoops," was one line that was sung over and over again.

The boy's eyes were wet with tears and the rector, too, was moved, though he probably did not like the undisciplined singing and praising. He did not approve of New Lights and Methodists who made their own paths to God and ignored the ancient and beautiful service of worship in the prayer books of the Church of England. However, he made no effort to control the outpouring of praise and rhythm.

In a few minutes, the meeting subsided into silence and the men gave good attention to their envoy as he completed his report of what the Sierra Leone Company offered to intending settlers, and what would-be settlers had to do to be accepted. When he had finished, they clapped their hands for a minute or two, until the rector held up his hands to get their attention. In good humour, it was agreed that would-be settlers would get their certificates and send them off to Mr. Clarkson, getting themselves packed and ready to leave for Halifax at a day's notice.

Hannibal had some urgent personal affairs of his own to attend to, and for his next trip to Five Mile Plains, he borrowed a neighbour's fine young horse. For the third time in a fortnight, he arrived at Solomon Bates's home. He found Evalina alone again and warmly embraced her as his promised wife.

"I want to talk to your father," he said. "We must start to make our plans and we must have everything in the open. Have you given him any hints of our understanding?" She had not said anything to her father, but had talked to her brother, and he had said that he approved of Hannibal as the kind of man to be his brother-in-law. At the moment, the two men were out chopping trees in the woods, but they would certainly be home at their usual time.

Hannibal put the horse under shelter and settled him for the night, then sat in the kitchen and admired his Evalina as she set about preparing the evening meal. Before long, her father and brother were coming through the door and Hannibal could see that Solomon Bates was surprised to see him again so soon. He thought everything had better be explained right then. He went over to Evalina and, taking her by the hand, faced her father and told him that he wanted to marry her and take her with him to Sierra Leone.

"Well, this is a surprise! What do you have to say, Evalina?" he asked.

"It's true, Pa. I'm sorry to have to leave you, but I am going to be Hannibal's wife, and where he goes will I go also."

"You are so determined to leave Nova Scotia, are you?" he asked the young man. "Do you not think it is a cruel thing to take a man's only daughter away across the ocean where he'll never see her again?"

"I'm sorry," Hannibal said. "But she wants to go to Africa as much as I do. We will make a life for ourselves there that we will never have here. When we get settled, perhaps you will come and live with us there."

In fact, years later, Solomon Bates, Hannibal's father-in-law, did go and spend his last days in Freetown with his family. But at the time he was invited ,even Hannibal did not believe it could ever really happen.

Solomon gave up the battle with a good grace, and shook Hannibal's hand, as did his son. "My loss is your gain," he said, "and since I had to lose her to some young man some day, I am glad the young man is Hannibal Hoops. May she be as good a wife to you as she has been a daughter to me. We shall miss her sadly, eh, son?" He sat heavily in his chair and added, "I wish you were not going so far away. Remember, if Africa does not suit you when you get there, you will always be welcomed back by the friends in Nova Scotia who love you."

That evening, the young couple made plans for their wedding. They would be married before they sailed, they were sure of that, but left the date open. They thought it should take place in Halifax, among their future fellow countrymen, when they were gathered together. In the meantime, Evalina would get her hope chest ready and collect the supplies she would need, while Hannibal packed up in Horton. He assured his intended that he would come over to see her as often as he could.

The next day, he rode back to Horton and got busy settling things for his departure. The farm was a responsibility. He wanted to leave it in good order for Master Clifford to dispose of. Perhaps it would be best to sell off the livestock, though it was not the best time of year. In fact, the market was poorer than usual because other intending settlers were selling off their stock and other property, and there were many bargains to be had. His problem was solved when Gus said he would stay on alone, at least until the warm weather, and look after everything just the way Hannibal had. Squire Lockhart seemed to think Gus would do all right, and he and the farmers who lived on either side said they would keep an eye on things and pull Gus up if things began to go wrong. The rector, who of course had known Clifford well, promised to take over the burden of correspondence with Carolina until Clifford had sold the farm or made some other disposal of it.

It was light-heartedly suggested by the Squire that Gus might marry and settle down on the farm as a tenant. Later it actually did turn out that way, as Hannibal was to hear, for Gus stayed on the farm, well-known in the area of the bluff for his jokes and merry nature, and married a hardworking young woman well-known and respected as the years passed for all the work she accomplished.

Hannibal packed boxes with the things he thought useful or necessary in Africa, and every week made a trip to Five Mile Plains to sit with Evalina and to share his thoughts with her as she with him. Usually he rode over on Sunday, and together they attended services to hear the Word of God and to sing His praises. As the days and weeks passed, winter set in with snow and cold, and it was sometimes a slow and difficult business, even with a borrowed horse, to cover the miles between their houses.

Hannibal had written to Clifford, through the good offices of Squire Lockhart, when he had first become interested in the Sierra Leone offer, and again when he had been to see Mr. Clarkson. In due course, a letter came back the same way by a small vessel coming up from Boston. Hannibal was relieved, because the winter weather was discouraging to boats coming into the Minas Basin, and the letter might easily have waited in some merchant's office until spring.

The letter read:

> Dear Hannibal Hoops:
>
> I am pleased for you that your dream of going to live in Africa is fair to be coming true, but sorry also that you are not staying on the farm. It would have been yours, as I more than once have told you, if you had chosen to stay there. Since you have determined on a different course of action, I am instructing Squire Lockhart to give you fifty pounds (Halifax currency) instead.
>
> You know that I will never forget how you saved my life that day near King's Mountain, so don't hesitate to write if I can be of service to you in your new home. I hope you will be as happy there as we seem to be here. Conditions in South Carolina are much more satisfactory than they were in '83.
>
> You have probably heard that a constitution has been worked out for a union of all the old colonies (now to be called 'states') and law, order, and prosperity are in a better condition than for years past. I am happy to be here, not only because my parents need me, but because there is work for me here in politics and government, to bind up the wounds of the past, and to build a future on solid principles.
>
> My wife and I pray that you, too, may find happiness and a useful purpose in your new home.
>
> your faithful friend
> C. COURTNEY

Hannibal treasured this letter and soon had a safe place to keep it. The local congregation of New Lights presented him with a very nicely bound Bible. He felt that the hours spent worshipping with these brothers and sisters had truly deepened and strengthened his own faith and understanding. They must have felt affection and respect for him, too, for they gathered around and laid hands on him, and dedicated him and the Bible to God's work in Africa. That Bible, carefully wrapped in a leather pouch, accompanied him to Africa and all the years afterwards, and in the Bible, inside the front cover, the letter from Clifford was safely kept.

While tending to his personal affairs, Hannibal also had to act as John Clarkson's local representative. He went around among the Free Blacks in all the Horton township, and the adjoining one of Cornwallis, to "stiffen their backbones" in the matter of coming away, for some who had been anxious to go had second thoughts and were backing out of their commitment. There were many, of course, who had never wanted to go, and others who had no chance of earning a certificate of good character. Those he did not bother with.

But there were those who were scared by their neighbours into thinking they were better off where they were. "You write when you get there, and tell us what it's like," they said. "If you write and tell us it is good, then we will come." Others quoted the proverb, "Better the Devil we know than the one we don't," or were just plain reluctant to face the upheaval and dangers of the trip. "Listen, Hannibal," they said, "it's a long way across the ocean—and it's the worst time of year, too. It's too dangerous, not that I'm thinking of myself, but for the wife and our little ones."

There were frequent meetings among the Free Blacks, and Hannibal tried to be at them all, and he would try to get a chance to talk to them. Sometimes other young men and women joined him in painting rosy pictures of the future in Sierra Leone, but at other times he seemed to be the only voice in the discussion that was not expressing fears about treachery, the slave trade, black magic and evil spirits, witchcraft and war, famine, plague, snakes and cannibals, cannibals, cannibals! "You just write and let us know," they said.

It was in vain that he pointed out that such an opportunity would probably never come again. These people preferred to stay in the conditions they knew in Nova Scotia rather than gamble so fatefully with their own and their children's lives.

Years later, Hannibal had kinder thoughts about the timidity of those who refused to enlist with him. He ceased to blame them. If he had not believed so strongly that it was his predestined fate to return to the land of his ancestors, perhaps his own heart would have quailed at the risks, too. In a way, those people who chose to stay behind were facing the reality of making a settlement on the African coast more honestly than he was. Hannibal never regretted the choice he made for himself and Evalina, but many of his fellow settlers did regret leaving Nova Scotia in the years when they were all trying to build up something unique and precious at Freetown.

Nonetheless, though they had difficult times surviving in Sierra Leone, so did those who stayed behind. Hannibal later heard from John Clarkson, who kept in touch with his friends in Nova Scotia for a few years, that after the settlers departed, many of those African people left behind petitioned the government for help.

In fact, they asserted that they were loyal and contented Nova Scotians and faithful subjects of the King (unlike those who had departed for Sierra Leone), and had never demanded special treatment nor complained of their hard lot. They said they had seen their discontented and wilfully-deceived neighbours set out, at great expense to the government, for a foreign land, while they who remained in Nova Scotia lived in a poverty unalleviated by any kindness from that same generous fount of blessings and pensions.

Unfortunately, as the government of Nova Scotia made clear, no money had been granted for the welfare of those people of colour who chose to remain in the Province. The Government of Nova Scotia spent some six thousand pounds on sending out the African settlers to Sierra Leone—a much greater sum than had ever been anticipated—so the African people who remained in the Province were forced to be content "with the knowledge of their own virtue and disinterest." The government was here very cruel, for they knew perfectly well that these poor people were in fact very interested in having justice done to themselves.

Their fate was no longer a concern to Hannibal and his fellow adventurers. It was on December 15 that the squire received word from Mr. Hartshorne that all intending colonists should gather in Halifax as soon as possible. Some would travel there by boat—and some of the Horton people favoured that—but he had doubts. The winter seas were often treacherous in and around the Bay of Fundy, and many good Loyalists had perished when making sea voyages on those waters in previous years.

On his final day in Horton, Hannibal walked to the edge of the high cliff of the bluff for a last look at the Windsor River and Minas Basin. The river was all white and purple that day. The ice was heaped in white jagged masses along the foot of the purple cliffs, and wherever the high tides of the previous week had brought dark crystalline cakes of the stuff to the beach. Grounding them there, it had slunk back to the riverbed, leaving the ice floes high and dry. Powdered white with every fall of snow, dyed in dark hues underneath where the tidal water had stained them, they would remain in great chunks until the warm winds of spring swept from the south to melt them.

Yet the retreating tide had not rid itself of all its frozen cargo. Though the river was bordered by stretches of mud, gleaming a glossy purple in the rising sun, there were still masses of ice in it. The water that edged the mud was also a clear deep purple, very beautiful to look on. But out in the middle of the river, where the current flowed steadily up to Windsor on the flood tide and reversed itself down and out to Fundy on the ebb, moved squadrons and legions of ice cakes. They had been created by the high tides of early December, tides that flowed over the desolate sea marshes deep in drifts of snow and froze them where they lay, then levered up the buoyant masses in unwieldy slabs, dashed them up and down, broke them into manageable chunks, and bore them out to sea.

Out in the millrace beyond Cape Blomidon they had drifted, out in the dreaded Gut by Cape Split. There the furious currents pushing out formed whirlpools that wrestled and tussled with the mighty Atlantic flood pouring up from the Gulf of Maine through the narrowing jaws of the Bay of Fundy. Soaked, toughened, and splintered, the reformed ice was swept back in on the rising tide until the whole Minas Basin was choked with it at high tide. With the sun on it, it was a vast plain of pure white reflecting the sun at thousands of points.

Beautiful it was, but not a sight to tempt one to embark in a small boat for a sea voyage. Hannibal was glad he had persuaded Mr. Hartshorne's agents to arrange for them to go to Halifax by land.

So a couple of hours after his silent farewell to a familiar scene, Hannibal with his fellow emigrants gathered at the local tavern where a sledge awaited. The African people of the community were out in force to see them go, and so was a good assortment of everybody else. Squire Lockhart was there, handing out advice and good wishes. There was much laughter, hand-shaking, embracing and tears. Then a jingle of bells was heard as a cutter drawn by a single horse drove up. It brought Mr. Hartshorne's agent, who told them it was time to start for the post road at Bishop's Tavern, at the foot of the Horton Mountains, where the sledges from the adjoining townships would meet and take the long road in close formation.

Arrived at the meeting place, they found that altogether some ninety people—men, women and children—were travelling in ten different sledges, led by several smart cutters equipped with seats for the agents in charge. The settlers were comfortable in the sledges, rough bobsleds used normally for hauling logs from the forest but now lined with straw and with heavy rugs and fur robes for comfort and warmth. There had been no trouble in hiring them. It was a slack season for everyone and generous payment for their hire was guaranteed by the government.

Away they went, in a jingle of bells from every team of horses, up the slopes of the mountain and into the woods, through Falmouth, across the frozen river at Windsor Forks, and, bypassing Windsor, on to Five Mile Plains. They stayed there in shelter gladly provided by the inhabitants. Hannibal was reunited with Evalina, and the next day she and her hope chest and another ten people came on with the caravan. The white road, smooth under the runners with hard-packed snow, ran before them up the Ardoise Hill and through the inhospitable wilderness of bog and bush that stretched beyond. There the evening came down and the moon rose and the adults sang their children to sleep with beloved songs and hymns.

At Sackville, they found the quarters that had been arranged, and very comfortably slept on fragrant hay. The next morning, they travelled in the light of day into the town of Halifax, where Mr. Clarkson met them and led the party to a barracks that had been specially prepared for them—and for a thousand other emigrants eager to be off to Africa.

chapter sixteen
GOODBYE TO NOVA SCOTIA

On Christmas Day in Halifax, Hannibal was married to Evalina as the young couple had planned, with their new countrymen around them and with saintly old David George present to add his blessing to their union. Thomas Peters, the prime mover of their migration, was there, as was John Clarkson. They took advantage of the humble marriage feast to make speeches, not just wishing the bride and bridegroom much happiness, but assuring the intending colonists that they had chosen wisely in leaving Nova Scotia, and that a land of milk and honey awaited all of them beyond the seas. Their sentiments were sincere, but coloured by a lot of wishful thinking.

Anyway, it was no time for sadness or bad omens. Mr. Clarkson had provided the whole body of settlers with fresh beef for a truly splendid Christmas dinner and wedding feast; there was much laughter and singing, dancing and feasting, among the more boisterous emigrants. Though the older people were quieter, they were not less joyful. For many, it was a farewell to the hard times of the past ten years or more and a celebration of the good times that lay ahead. The weather had never been more cheerless than in Halifax in the last month of that year, 1791, and it was good that they had the anticipation of warmer and better days to keep their spirits up.

Halifax at the end of the year was a cold and gloomy town. The wind blew off the Atlantic for days at a time, scourging the city with a cold moist breath off the icy northern seas. Sometimes clammy sea fogs rolled in and those outside felt the freezing moisture slowly absorbed by their clothes until they were actually soaked to the skin; at least to those among them who had been fishermen, that was nothing new. Still, there were other days when the sky was clear and the wind died away and the water of the harbour was smooth in a limpid glassy state, with columns of steam rising from it. It was pleasant, but cold, and patches of ice formed among the rocks and on the shore.

The New Year was welcomed with a party that lasted all night, and at dawn a group of the men and boys came to Mr. Clarkson's door and greeted him with a volley from their shotguns. A day or two later, they went on board the ships that had been gathering in the harbour. Once they were all aboard, Mr. Clarkson was rowed around in a small boat to visit all fourteen of them, coming up on deck in each and giving out the certificates he and Mr. Hartshorne had signed, giving the settlers their certificates of land entitlement in the new colony.

Some three weeks after Hannibal had become a married man, the voyage to Sierra Leone began in earnest. The fifteen transport vessels hired by the Governor's agent were underway down the harbour, past little George's Island and big McNab's Island, and then out into the open ocean. Hannibal and Evalina sailed in a craft with a well-omened name, the *Felicity*. They stood at her bow as she sailed out, gazing for a time at the flat horizon stretched out like a rod of dull iron against the sky. Then, going back to the stern, they watched awhile as the snow-covered and granite-grey shores of Nova Scotia on the horizon gradually sank down until at last they seemed no more than a range of distant waves. At some point, they looked and could distinguish no sign of them at all. Only the grey-green winter sea, broken ceaselessly by turbulent white-capped billows, stretched unbounded on every side.

For a few hours, all the ships in the little fleet kept a rough formation, but as the day wore on, some fell behind and others went ahead. After only two days, they were scattered out of sight of each other, and about that time they ran into the first of a series of terrible gales that tested the seamanship of the captains of the fleet. The gale laid the *Felicity* over on her side and rocked her back and forth without ceasing. Evalina took to her hammock on the second morning at sea, but Hannibal was not so affected and came on deck frequently for fresh air. He was a good sailor, but even he had some queasy days. From the deck, he saw only empty seas all around, and uttered silent prayers for his friends on the other vessels.

The weather was cold and bitter for a few days, worse than at Halifax, but then they moved into deep water and, as the sailors explained, were sailing through the Gulf Stream. It was amazing how warm it became, and then it was quite pleasant to stand around on the deck. They had calm stretches, too, when Evalina felt well enough to come up and take the air. They staked their claim to a sheltered spot on deck, and spent long hours there together. After all, it was their honeymoon.

Then, as their vessel struggled across the ocean, ever eastward, the winds freshened again and brought new bouts of sea-sickness to most of the passengers. As for the sun, it was hardly ever able to break through the clouds.

Hannibal was worried about the well-being of Mr. Clarkson. Before they sailed from Halifax, he had shaken hands with him when he insisted on gathering the emigrants together for a short prayer service. Clarkson had appeared by his posture and movements to be desperately tired, if not ill, yet he drew on his resources of spiritual strength to ask Almighty God's protection on the voyage in a voice they were all able to hear and understand. His family of colonists clearly saw his weakness and hoped that the voyage would restore his health, but they had not bargained on such a succession of storms. As Hannibal breathed his own prayers at the bulwarks, while the sea rose and dipped before him, he prayed especially that the saintly leader might arrive safely on the other side, as well as all the other passengers in the hospital ship with him.

His prayers were not unnecessary, as he later discovered, for during the voyage Mr. Clarkson was as much in need of medical care as anyone could be. He spent most of the time between Halifax and the African coast in a state of unconsciousness and delirium. At one point, while in this condition, he was thrown from his berth by the heaving of the ship and rolled backward and forward across the floor, half-drowned in the water bursting over him through a broken skylight. Fortunately, the captain of the ship happened to come in to see him at this point, and saved his life in the nick of time. So this good and great man was preserved to lead the infant colony through its first crucial years!

Gradually at first, and then more speedily, the passengers on the *Felicity* felt the rays of the sun becoming stronger and hotter, and knew their voyage must be coming to an end. Although it was the month of February, it was as hot as the hottest July days, the "dog days" in Nova Scotia.

The nights aboard the *Felicity* were moist and breathless, and many from below sneaked up on deck to sleep where there was a chance of breeze. Hannibal could not help but think of how his mother and the others being carried from Africa and across the Atlantic Ocean must have suffered at this part of the passage, crowded below deck as they were. The night finally came when they had little inclination to sleep, for the captain said to them, "When you wake up, you will see land ahead, and that land will be Sierra Leone."

His calculations were exact. By the first light of dawn, they were crowding the bow and bulwarks, and as the light strengthened they could make out rounded blue hills just above the horizon. Higher and higher they loomed into the sky as they came closer, seemingly almost overhead as they sailed into the magnificent estuary of the Sierra Leone River. Hannibal put his arm around his Evalina as they gazed on the tawny flanks of what the ancients called the Lion Mountains. They traced the lines of rich green verdure that climbed those flanks and at the crests that flowed like a lion's mane against the pure shining blue of the sky.

Something about the scene kindled old memories of words spoken long ago, and Hannibal knew this scene was what his dear mother had last seen as she was taken away from her home.

"Evalina," he said, "this is what my mother looked on when the slavers carried her away from Africa. This is the spot they carried her from. And in her vision—her vision of me arriving in Africa, the vision she had just before she breathed her last breath—it was this moment she saw: me looking up at the mountains of Sierra Leone, me returning home, the wheel turned full circle." He took Evalina's hand and went on, "She didn't see you then, my love, but I think she does now. It is true that she didn't know much about the True God, and that she never felt the love of Jesus. She was never baptized, even. But she was a good woman through and through, and I think God took her up to be with Him. I think she sees us both here and that she blesses us."

"I hope she does, my dear," replied Evalina. "She must have been a wonderful mother. We will not forget to honour her memory here, in her own land."

"Her land, and my father's land, Evalina, the land of my father's fathers. We must look for the Loko people of this land, and among them I will find my kinfolk. I should be able to greet them; my mother used to speak to me in the Loko language and I think I will soon remember it when I have found them. Oh, don't look so worried! I've no intention of going to live among them; I want only to visit. No, here on the shore we shall live, in our own 'Free Town,' under the shelter of these beautiful mountains."

By this time, the vessel had swung in close to the shore and dropped her anchor. Nearby were other ships, recognizable as part of the flotilla from Halifax, while further along were larger and unfamiliar ships that had evidently come straight from England. The settlers were wildly excited, and spontaneously began singing hymns and in the intervals cheered and shouted their joy. Now and again on one ship or another muskets fired a salute to the mountains and the echoes seemed to be a reply. The immigrants, as they now were, felt in high spirits and were anxious to get to shore, where they saw the white tents of the officials. Nova Scotia was part of their past. The Sierra Leone Company was now taking responsibility for settling them on the land, and the settlers and the Company together were going to build up a community that would be a revelation to the slave-owning countries of Europe and America, and a blessing to Africa.

Hannibal looked at Evalina and felt that they and their fellow settlers were in the position of the Israelites who had fled Egypt and passed through the waters of the Red Sea unscathed. But for the Black Loyalists, the Exodus was concluded; now they were turning back the pages to make a new beginning. They were back to the beginning of Genesis. Hannibal was bursting with joy and expectation and tried to express it fittingly to his bride.

"This is our land, Evalina, from this time forth. The Lord has brought us here to make our abiding place for now and forever. Here we shall rear our children in freedom. They will grow up as free men and women, to whom the slavery we have known will be only a story and a nightmare. We shall tame this land and civilize it and make it ours. They will never be able to take it away from us, never, never, never!"

acknowledgements

In the writing of this book I need to thank those who inspired and encouraged me in many ways. First of all, those historians whose research and writing recreated the plantation society of South Carolina and the effects of the American Revolution on the African-derived slave population in the southern colonies. Also those other historians who have written about the coming of the Loyalists to Nova Scotia, the rise and fall of their city of Shelburne, and of John Clarkson's mission to lead some of those former slaves back to Africa. Many things went into the mix to tell this story, which is fiction-based on solid history.

In 1957, I went to teach in the interior of Sierra Leone. Before I left my home in Canada, I read about the country, then a British possession, and was particularly interested in reading about the importance in its history of the migration of former slaves from Nova Scotia to found the city of Freetown.

During my four years of teaching teenaged African boys in a rural setting, I came to understand something of their different culture and their concern that in some parts of the world it was regarded as inferior and uncivilized. "What makes civilization?" they would sometimes ask me. "Are we not civilized?" Hannibal in this story is a composite of some of these boys.

I often visited Freetown and enjoyed brushing against its cosmopolitan multi-ethnic population. I met families proud to call themselves "Nova Scotian," as well as a variety of people of other origins who formed part of the Krio (Creole) population of the city, along with the many people from the interior or even adjoining countries who were being steadily assimilated to Krio ways and values.

I started to write this story a year after I arrived in Sierra Leone, and in the years since then I put it down and picked it up again many times. I was tempted to give up on it at intervals. But I always felt that my story was worth putting out to an audience, and now it will happen.

I am grateful to those who helped me attain my goal. First of all my wife, Edith, for typing and editing the original manuscript. My late mother, Jean, for reading the manuscript and encouraging me to go on with it. My cousin Mary-Sue Haliburton, for taking the computer version, which was in trouble, editing it, and fixing errors on the disk. The late Dr. Phyllis Blakeley of the Public Archives of Nova Scotia, for encouraging me after reading an early draft (and sharing it with her writing group), and beyond them a number of friends (including former Sierra Leonean pupils) who have read the manuscript and made suggestions. I especially thank Professor Edward J. Cashin of the Center for the Study of Georgia History, Augusta State University, in Georgia, USA, who read my manuscript and urged me to publish it; Rev. Alan Reynolds of Vancouver, who put me in touch with Word Alive Press; and Professor Richard Davies of the English department of Acadia University, who convinced me to make a substantial revision of my manuscript. I am also grateful to Caroline Schmidt, publishing consultant of Word Alive Press, and my editor Evan Braun.

The history of events forming the background of my work has been well-established in recent years. In 1962, as I was leaving Sierra Leone to undertake graduate study in London, Christopher Fyfe's massive tome *A History of Sierra Leone* was published in England. For the first time, the grand scope of the founding and development of the country in the eighteenth century could be seen.

In the past few decades, the historical background of this story has been dealt with by several writers, and their works include my friend Ellen Gibson Wilson's *The Loyal Blacks* (1976) and *John Clarkson and the African Adventure* (1980), and James W. St.G. Walker's *The Black Loyalists: The Search for a Promised Land in Nova Scotia and Sierra Leone 1783-1870* (1976). Most recently, Simon Schama has presented the whole story on television and his book, *Rough Crossings* (2005).

In fiction, it was treated in 1969 by Martin Ballard as *Benjie's Portion,* published in the Longman Young Book series. It has been treated most recently by Lawrence Hill with his very successful *The Book of Negroes* (2007), intended for adult readership. The present work owes nothing to these writers, but is based entirely on the research and emotions of

GORDON M. HALIBURTON
Wolfville, Nova Scotia
November 2009

about the author

Gordon M. Haliburton was born in Nova Scotia and trained as a teacher before going to work in Sierra Leone in 1957. He taught in a government secondary school for boys at Magburaka in the Northern Province. He also represented the London Missionary Society as an Associate.

Since serving there, he has undertaken further studies and taught African History for many years in Southern Africa. While there he co-authored a history textbook for Junior High School students. As well he wrote and published academic works.

Since retiring to Wolfville in Nova Scotia, he has researched and published in the field of local and family history.